Also by Sarah Singleton

CENTURY

Winner of the Booktrust Teenage Prize
Winner of the Children of the Night Award
Highly commended for the Branford Boase First Novel Award
Short-listed for the Birmingham Book Award

HERETIC

SACRIFICE

Long-listed for the Carnegie Medal

SIMON AND SCHUSTER

Acknowledgements

Lines from 'I Met at Eve' and 'Tartary' from *Selected Poems* by
Walter de la Mare (Faber and Faber, 1973) reprinted by kind
permission of the Literary Trustees of Walter de la Mare and
the Society of Authors as their representatives.

SIMON AND SCHUSTER

First published in Great Britain in 2008 by Simon & Schuster UK Ltd
A CBS COMPANY

1 3 5 7 9 10 8 6 4 2

Simon & Schuster UK Ltd
Africa House
64-78 Kingsway
London WC2B 6AH

A CIP catalogue record for this book
is available from the British Library

ISBN: 978-1-41692-591-0

This book is a work of fiction. Names, characters, places and
incidents are either a product of the author's imagination or are
used fictitiously. Any resemblance to actual people living or
dead, events or locales is entirely coincidental.

Typeset in Garamond by M Rules
Printed and bound in Great Britain by
Cox and Wyman, Reading, Berkshire

www.simonsays.co.uk

For my god-daughter Eleanor Ford-Elliott

With thanks to Sheila Wickham
and Rachel Charlton-Fabian,
and to Fuchsia for advice.

One

I wasted hours staring into the river. It was a superheated July. Brittle yellow grasses and vicious, black nettles thatched the river banks. The water was so low that in places you could cross on stepping stones. In other parts, the water was deep enough for swimming, where the bed plunged down into unplumbed stony basins. I never swam though – too scared of broken glass and weeds. A man in the local newspaper caught Weil's disease fishing in the shallows where the rats peed. He spent two weeks in a coma, had hallucinations that his body was riddled with worms and lost the sight in one eye. Not worth it, he said in the paper. A couple of hours' fun for a lifetime's suffering. So I didn't swim. Instead I sat on the footbridge near Mortimore's Wood, half a mile out of town, and gazed at the river where bright green weeds flowed like a nymph's hair, and the water varnished stones on the bed. I dreamed of immersion. I imagined what it would be like to lie underneath the clear, cold water, face-up like Ophelia in the painting, till the river drew out every last ounce of warmth from my overheated, sunburned body and I was dissolved and obliterated, entirely at one with the flowing water.

The summer holidays had just begun. I spent day after day on the bridge, just sitting on my own. Staring, thinking, sluggish with heat, stifled by aimless desire. The endless wait.

Further upstream, someone jumped into the water. Two feet kicked noisily, and ripples slapped against the dry mud banks. A pile of clothes and a pair of sandals waited on the bank where the swimmer had undressed. Then she surfaced, and swam in a circle, a girl with dark red hair and a madly freckled face, about fourteen – my age – wearing just her pants and a crop top. She spat out a jet of muddy, possibly Weil's-contaminated water. I stared at her sideways, partly covering my eyes. The sun struck the back of my head like a hammer. Had she seen me? Surely yes. I was sitting on the edge of the bridge, my chest pressed against the railings, my legs dangling high above the water. She glanced my way, still swimming in circles, panting a little. Then she trod water and shaded her eyes to look up at me.

'Why don't you swim?' she called out. 'Aren't you hot?'

I shrugged. 'No thanks.'

'It's lovely. Not too cold when you get used to it.'

'It can be dangerous,' I said, wary of implying she was stupid to try it.

'So's travelling in a car,' she answered, wiping her wet face with the palm of her hand. 'I bet you do that.'

I didn't move.

'Come on.' She grinned. 'You must be boiling.'

I shook my head, holding the railings tight in case my body headed down to the river without my say-so. The girl tossed back her wet hair and swam upstream into a pool of shade where dusty trees arched over the water. Everything was quiet for a few minutes. Distantly I could hear cars on the road. Three draggled plastic bags hung from a thorn tree by the water, impaled by earlier floods. Beneath my feet, way down, three small, brown trout nosed in the river.

Then she was back, hauling her way through the water with powerful strokes to the bank. She scrambled out of the river. Dry dirt clung to her wet feet and legs. Then she stood, breathing heavily, wringing water from her hair. She turned her face to me, white beneath the freckles, and grinned.

'You don't know what you're missing,' she called. 'You've got to make the most of it.' This with a swing of her arm in an arc that took in the blistering sun, the flawless sky, the summer all around us. She was tall and heavy-boned, but very slim. As she moved, you could see the skeleton just beneath her wet skin, the sculpted shoulder bones, the articulation of elbows and knees, the case of ribs on the flexible pole of her spine. She picked up her sandals and strode along the grassy path by the river and up to the bridge, and then she was beside me, close up, dripping water from her hair onto my back.

'I've seen you before,' she said, staring into my face. 'Around here.'

She smelled of the river. Water still beaded her neck and shoulders, soaking through her T-shirt from the wet crop top. I didn't know what to say.

'I'm Dowdie,' she said. I blinked and said my habitual 'What?' giving myself a moment to think.

'I'm Dowdie,' she repeated.

'Dowdy?' I echoed.

'You know – it's my name.'

'Dowdy's your name?' I repeated stupidly. I had to stop talking like an idiot, or the girl would go away. And oddly, I realised I didn't want her to go.

'Actually, the name on my birth certificate's Dorothy. But everyone's called me Dowdie for ever. Which is just as well,' she mused, "cos Dorothy's a crap name. I don't know what my mother was thinking.'

I didn't answer, not wanting to say the wrong thing. Did she want me to agree that Dorothy was a bad name? Or that her mother was stupid? But Dowdie was still staring at me, waiting for a response.

'I'm Amber,' I said. 'I haven't seen you before. Where do you go to school?'

She wrinkled her nose and shook her head, pushing back the wet hair from her forehead.

'Don't go to school. None of us do.' Dowdie stared into my face, searching for my reaction. 'You go to Harfield. I've seen you in your *uniform*.'

It was hard working out what she wanted from me. My modus operandi, of late, had involved calculating what people wanted to hear and then saying it. That was not so easy, this first meeting with Dowdie. But I was flattered. Unseen, she had identified me amongst the crowd. Twin feelings of pride and paranoia vied. Had she picked me out because I was different? If so, was this good different, or bad different?

'Yes. Summer holidays now though. Why don't you go to school?' I said.

She scrutinised me again. She had a way of looking, quite blatant, as if she wanted to see inside your head. Uncomfortable under such investigation, I looked away, to my solace, the river.

'Lots of reasons.' She sighed, as though she were stating the obvious. 'Schools breed conformity. They socialise children in a particular way – make them into cooperative team players with limited capacity to think for themselves.'

I didn't like school, but oddly her summary kindled an instinctive desire to defend it.

'It's not exactly like that.'

'No? How not?'

Unlike me, she didn't try and please, not at all. Dowdie said exactly what she thought.

'It doesn't always socialise you – make you a team player.' Her directness had upset me. I struggled to keep my voice even and stumbled over my words. 'Sometimes it has the opposite effect. It makes you realise how different you are to everyone else. And how alone.'

Dowdie twisted her head, to peer into my face. Her eyes were only centimetres from mine. I could see the delicate pores on the end of her rather beaky nose.

'I know that,' she said, offhand, stating the obvious again. 'You're not like the others. That's why I noticed you. I've seen you walking along the road with the rest of the herd and I've seen you walking apart from them, and the shadow over your face like you were walking into the gates of hell. I know that, Amber. I know lots and lots of things.'

She stretched up her strong, boyish arms and grabbed the sun-heated hand rail on the bridge, pulling herself up to her feet.

'Come on. Let's go. Where do you live? Are your parents home?' We'd only met minutes before but she spoke as though we were friends already.

I jumped up, ready to follow. 'They're at work. We can go there if you like. But it's not that great.' Already my mind was galloping ahead. We lived in a small, very new house on the Napier South estate. There was nothing remarkable about it, and Dowdie herself seemed so remarkable I didn't want her to see it. But Dowdie was not to be put off and I didn't have the strength of mind – or the will – to refuse her.

We talked all the way. Or rather, I asked her questions and

Dowdie answered at length. She told me she lived in the Community. This threw me at first. Where we used to live, in the house opposite, were four men with learning difficulties. They lived, as we were told, in the community. They had support workers who made sure they were coping. One of those men, with a big black beard and a vast belly, used to ask me very direct questions and in a flash I wondered if Dowdie, too—

'The Community,' she snapped, as though she'd read my thoughts. 'It's a spiritual community. Twenty of us. There's a terrace of three cottages made into one and a big, shared garden where we grow lots of vegetables and fruit. We're not part of all this.' Another sweep of her arm, indicating the busy road and approaching town with its shops, factories, pizza outlets, offices, car parks, retail barns. I think I loved her from that moment, because I knew what she meant without her saying it, and her face was animated and she spoke with a freedom and passion I had never seen in anyone before.

'What's it like – the Community,' I ventured, burning with curiosity. We crossed the busy road and headed along the pavement by the youth centre, and under the railway arches. Outside the cinema half a dozen people were queuing.

'I've lived there with my mum for the last ten years – since I was a little girl,' she said. 'Everything's held in common. We live simply, you see. No television, no computers, no phones.'

'So have people got jobs, or what?'

'Some have ordinary jobs. And there's a workshop at the Community where a couple of the men run a joinery business. And Green Shoots – the healthfood shop at the top of the High Street? The Community owns that. My mum works there.'

I knew Green Shoots. My own mum went there sometimes. It sold the usual selection of dried beans and organic muesli, health supplements, Bach flower remedies and suchlike. A noticeboard near the door carried advertisements for Reiki healing and meditation classes. Perhaps I had seen Dowdie's mum, then, working at the till.

'So, is it a Christian community?' I spoke tentatively, wary it might well be the wrong thing to say. So it proved.

'No! Christianity is another system of brainwashing and patriarchal control!' This with a toss of her head and a glint in her eyes.

'Jesus was a remarkable man,' she said. 'But the Christian church has precious little to do with his suggestion that we should live simply and love one another. That is what we try and do in the Community. To live truly and deeply as human beings, to be conscious of our relationship with one another and the universe.'

Dowdie, in her imaginary pulpit. None of the girls at school spoke like this. They were all wrapped up in closer concerns – trips to New Look, mobile phones, music magazines, Bebo accounts.

'It sounds . . . really cool,' I said, struggling for an appropriate response.

'Cool!' Dowdie snorted with laughter. 'Yes,' she conceded. 'Yes, it is cool. When I look at all this, I appreciate just how cool it is. If I had to live here – to be part of it – that would kill me.' The last sentiment she expressed in a clear, low voice, and with complete seriousness.

It felt like another criticism. After all, however unhappily, I lived 'here' and it hadn't killed me. Was I less sensitive than she was, then, that I survived it? Was Dowdie made of a more fragile and precious material?

We were drawing near the Napier South estate, a toy town of identikit houses, cul-de-sacs, open spaces where young, low maintenance saplings were tied by rubber bands to wooden stakes.

I had never much liked it, preferring our old Victorian terrace, but my parents were keen to take another step up the property ladder. True enough, the new house was warmer, lighter and less plagued by erratic electrics and damp. I no longer had to share a bedroom with my six-year-old brother either.

'This is it.' Number fourteen, Field View. I unlocked the door. Both parents were at work. My brother was safely spending the day at a holiday playscheme at the leisure centre. I stepped inside, sensing Dowdie's quick scrutiny of the magnolia and peach walls and the prints from Ikea. Of course I love my parents. They are generous, kind and completely committed to my brother and me. My dad works for a computer installation company, and my mum has a part-time job as deputy manager of a jewellery shop. Once a year we go on two weeks' holiday to Majorca where we take it in turns to decide what to do each day. I have nothing to complain about, parentwise. They're not cool, though. Not like Dowdie's mum, living in her Community, or one girl in my tutor group whose parents take her to festivals all summer long, even if she misses school. You know those endless makeover/holiday swap/trading places programmes on the television all the time? They always pick two diverse families, just to show a contrast and to get the sparks flying. I was watching one, where a smart woman from a big house on a development like Napier South lived for a fortnight with a huge, chaotic family on a social housing estate somewhere in the North East. And I realised that while the middle-class family stuck to the rules and did all the right things – ate their five portions of fruit and veg, spent quality time with their kids, fussed about their education – what they forgot to do was enjoy themselves. I think my parents are like that. They're so busy doing their jobs and cleaning the car and maintaining the house they've forgotten to have any fun. Even our family outings are in earnest – cycling together to get our quota of exercise.

'We'll go to my room,' I said, before Dowdie could examine the decor more closely. I galloped up the stairs, Dowdie close behind me. 'This is it,' I said. 'This is my place.'

When we moved to Field View (there is no field view, of course) a year ago, my kindly parents agreed I could decorate my room as I wished, recognising my need for self-expression and my disappointment in moving from the old house, with its aged apple tree and murky stained-glass fanlight. So I painted it black.

In pride of place on the inky walls was a poster of an antique landscape, towering cliffs where a city castle perched beneath a moon curved like a scimitar. Swags of torn lace hung in artfully arranged scallops beneath the ceiling. In a large alcove beside the built-in wardrobe, my dad had installed numerous shelves now chock-a-block with my book collection, which spilled over into boxes on the floor. On another shelf, above my bed, were three ornate jewelled perfume bottles my uncle had bought for me in Prague, a pair of black iron candlesticks looped with crystal necklaces and my CDs of Placebo, Bach, My Chemical Romance and Fall Out Boy. There were other pictures too, stills of Edward Scissorhands and old prints of castles, sinister fairy maidens and knights on horses, sealed in clip-frames.

I loved my room. In the midst of Dowdie's 'all this' it was my sanctuary. It was my place – just as I wanted it. Here I wove my own protective spells with books and music and poems, my web of dreams.

But what would Dowdie think? I felt a plunging panic for a moment, bringing her here. Perhaps it wasn't magical, but crass and predictable? The protective spell faltered. Sad teen's naff black room in unsuitable suburban house.

'It's very goth,' she said. Then, glancing at me: 'But that's not a surprise.'

What did she see? A shortish girl with mouse-brown hair wearing a shapeless black T-shirt and jeans. Nothing remarkable. Neither pretty nor ugly, neither fat nor thin. Not even very goth, truth be told – not on the outside at least. Merely camouflaged; receding into the background, not wanting to be noticed. If Dowdie thought my bedroom was tacky, she was sensitive enough not to say so. Perhaps she sensed the overlay of dream and desire I had painted along with the matt emulsion.

She moved across to the bookshelf. 'You read a lot,' she observed. Yes, I did read a lot. It was a path to other worlds, an escape.

'I want to be a writer.' This blurted out, eager to impress. 'I've written lots of stories. I'm halfway through a novel.'

Dowdie nodded, unsurprised, as though this revelation was merely a confirmation of what she already knew.

'Perhaps I could read it one day.'

'If you like. Yes, of course.'

She picked up a book or two, and then browsed through my CDs.

'I don't listen to much music,' she said. 'But I like it. I don't know these bands – perhaps you can educate me.'

She sat down on my bed, a CD in her hand. 'We're going to be great friends, Amber,' she said. 'I know it.'

I sat down beside her. 'How do you know it?'

'I told you, I know things. This will be an astonishing summer.'

'How do you know things?' She was so certain, and I sounded like a three year old. She took a deep breath, as though she might, after all, be nervous. Then she said:

'Have you heard of Amethyst children?'

'No.'

'James – James Renault – he's the elder at the Community.'

'The leader? He's in charge?'

'Not leader exactly – but kind of. Years ago, a spirit spoke through him and predicted that all over the world special children would be born – children with gifts and abilities not seen before, who would lead humankind into the future. They would be the next evolutionary step.' Her freckled face was perfectly serious, her voice was grave.

'These are the Amethyst children?' I said.

Dowdie nodded.

'They have certain features in common. They find it hard to fit in. They can't conform and struggle in ordinary schools, often because they are very intelligent and the lessons are too – obvious. So they get into trouble. They have an unusual perspective on things – take a contrary view. Some are healers, others are seers.'

'And you think you are one of them?' I tried to keep my voice level, wanting to express neither scepticism nor credulity.

'I don't *think* I am – I know so,' she said, staring at me, daring me to contradict or laugh. I did neither.

'How do you know?'

She laughed then – at stupid Amber. 'How do I know? How do we know anything? I know it because it's the truth.'

'So what does it mean? What are your special gifts?'

She put down the CD and stared at her hands. 'It's not something I can explain, just like that,' she said.

For a moment, I couldn't make out who she was – what she was doing. She was two things at once – older than her age, an adult in disguise. Or else a kid playing pretend, trying to lure me into her imaginary game. The two images diverged and drew together again.

She took another quick breath, as though she had made a decision.

'I think you're an Amethyst child too,' she said. Perhaps she thought I would laugh at her because her face seemed cold and hard for a moment, some kind of fierce protective shield going up.

I blinked. 'What?'

'That's why I wanted to talk to you. I felt it – when I saw you walking to school. And then, at the river, when you were staring into the water all the time.'

'You were spying on me?'

Dowdie brushed away the question. 'What d'you think?' she said.

My thoughts dissolved in a welter of contradictory emotions. Anxiety and doubt, and a gleaming golden thread of pride. Was she flattering me – or trying to trick me into something?

'I don't know,' I said in a hurry. 'I'm not special. I don't have any gifts. How can I be one of these children? I don't know anything about it.'

Dowdie shrugged, in control again. 'That's why I've come,' she said. 'To help you. We were meant to meet. I told James about you too, and he said I should talk to you – be a friend. And if you like, I'll take you to the Community. You can meet him yourself.'

About a year ago, on a school History trip to Glastonbury, we climbed the Tor. It was a brisk, chilly morning in March. The sky was a wide, cold blue and beneath us the Somerset levels spread into the distance. The Tor was steep, the anomalous peak woven with paths. Inside the tower at the top, two hippy types were sitting casually on the ground. A couple of the boys made insulting comments about dope smoking, but the young man and woman ignored them. They were slim and beautiful, with long, hennaed hair in wild dreadlocks and clear, pale skin. Each wore half a dozen necklaces, rings on their fingers, long boots, and layers of colourful clothing. The sight of them filled me with longing. It's hard to describe, the root of this curious pain. They looked like they had stepped from the pages of one of my books, and had an air of complete freedom and self-possession. They seemed like royalty.

Disinherited royalty perhaps, living in exile, but they were princes nevertheless. I ached to be them.

And now, sitting beside Dowdie in my little black room, the same feeling came over me. It was as though I'd glimpsed a foreign kingdom through a magic casement. The lost land I longed for.

Two

The police station – an anonymous glass and steel barn on a trading estate at the edge of the town. It isn't like I'd imagined – no red-brick building, no blue lamp outside, no constable standing guard. It could have been a DIY store, or an office-block filled with insurance salesmen. Parked cars fill the slip road, spilling out from the other warehouses and business units on the trading estate. But I can't see anyone. The pavements are empty.

I stare out of the window as Mum hits the indicator and the car turns on the mini roundabout. Plastic bottles and crisp packets litter the dead grass on the verges. I have a fleeting mental image of office workers mindlessly eating their lunch as they walk, and casting their refuse to the ground.

Mum glances at me as she turns the car into a bay marked for visitors. Half a dozen seagulls are tossed on the wind above the trading estate, but inside the car the gently heated air smells of synthetic lavender from the air freshener dangling beneath the mirror. Air freshener. As I breathe its chemical soup the irony nudges. Even now, you see, under such circumstances, I'm distracted. So many random thoughts. The mind never stops chewing.

It's hard to explain how I feel. As though a large, iron ball has lodged itself tight inside my ribcage and coldly presses against heart and lungs and belly. It is a steadfast, barren pain I cannot avoid however much I turn and twist.

Mum turns off the engine and gives a quick, anxious sigh. She unclips her seat belt and looks at me.

'Are you OK?' she says.

'Yes.' She's had to take an afternoon off work to bring me here. Had to make half a dozen hurried phone calls to switch shifts, to find cover. She's smartly dressed, in the little cream skirt and jacket combination she bought from Marks and Spencer, with a silky, rose-coloured blouse. Her face is very pale. Perhaps she too has been crying.

'Are you sure you're OK?' She puts her hand on my thigh, to reassure. She wants me to throw my arms around her as though I am a little girl again and she can solve my troubles with a cuddle. I read this in her face, her own pain at her inability to comfort me. But I haven't room for anybody else's pain.

'Yes,' I repeat. 'I'm OK.'

She gives another of her anxious sighs, then opens the car door and clicks across the road in her little stilettos to the police-station doors. It takes an effort to lift myself from the car seat. My body feels disjointed, as though my limbs are full of stones. I step into the reception area. A middle-aged woman, bursting out of a white blouse, stands behind a glass screen while on our side a very thin man with long, greasy hair assails her with complaints and excuses that seem to stem from a problem with his vehicle documents. The woman's face is blank. Probably she has heard it all before. He goes on and on, a convoluted story I lose track of straight away, as though the sheer quantity of words will eventually get him what he wants. Perhaps he thinks she will relent simply to shut him up.

Mum is fidgety and impatient, glancing at her watch. She wanders around the reception area, looking at posters and reading notices.

From time to time she smoothes the front of her jacket. I sit on one of three uncomfortable plastic chairs by the wall. A leaflet on the wall opposite admonishes me not to drink and drive. Another, with a picture of smiling people, advertises a support service for the victims of crime. The man drones on, and the minutes pass. For a while my mind drifts.

'Amber. Amber – it's us now.' Long-haired man has gone. Mum is standing by the glass screen now. She clears her throat.

'We've come to see Detective Inspector Ripley.'

The reception woman simply stares for a second or two.

'D'you have an appointment?' she says.

'Yes.' Mum is flustered now, tense and irritated. 'We were supposed to see him five minutes ago – but that man . . . well, we were here on time. We've been waiting fifteen minutes.'

'I'll ring him,' the woman says. She picks up the phone, but keeps her eyes firmly fixed on my mother, as though suspecting she will throw something at the screen. After a few seconds she replaces the receiver.

'He's not at his desk,' she says. 'Are you sure you have an appointment? He's been in meetings all day.'

She seems to find my mother's agitation deeply satisfying and for the first time I begin to sympathise with the long-haired man.

'Yes!' Mum says. 'Yes! Look, he phoned me up this morning, and I had to make all sorts of special arrangements for work. It's very important.'

For the first time, reception woman notices me.

'What's your name?' she says to my mum.

'Jane Renalden. Jane and Amber Renalden.'

Reception woman sighs deeply, picks up the phone again and announces on some kind of loudspeaker system that Detective Inspector Ripley has visitors in reception.

'Sit down,' she says. 'I expect he'll be with you in a few minutes.'

Mum does as she's told and takes the chair beside mine. We sit in silence. Various people come and go through a double door. None of them so much as register our presence. Finally, another ten minutes later, the door opens and a man in a very smart suit smiles at us.

'Mrs Renalden – Amber. I am so sorry to keep you waiting.' He tells us to sign in. Reception woman gives us plastic visitors' badges to wear, with our names scribbled on them.

The detective inspector is very courteous and helpful and tells us to call him Neil. He uses a security card to open the double doors again and ushers us inside. We follow him across a kind of indoor courtyard space, up a flight of stairs, along corridors and finally into a small office overlooking the car park. He pulls out chairs for us, comfortable padded office chairs with arms.

'Sit down, please. Can I get you a tea or coffee? What about you, Amber? Coffee? A Coke maybe?'

He sticks his head out of the door and calls to some minion to bring us refreshments. Then he plops down in his chair and treats us to a generous smile.

'Again, I'm sorry to keep you waiting,' he says. 'I've been in a meeting – relating to this . . . this incident.'

I take the time to look at him carefully, Detective Inspector Neil Ripley. He's in his early thirties, I would guess. Tall, strong, with a square, masculine face and bright blue eyes. His hair is dark blond, but his clean-shaved jaw is dark – as though rampant stubble is waiting to burst from his skin. I'd been expecting a man in a uniform but Detective Inspector Call-Me-Neil wears an expensive-looking tawny suit. When he unbuttons the jacket, it reveals a shimmering silk lining, a rich, exotic blue. His red tie is also silk and his cuffs fastened with gold links. Clearly he lavishes plenty of time, thought and money on his appearance.

I think he notices my scrutiny because he looks at me and asks me how I am.

'OK,' I say.

'I'm going to ask one of my staff to sit in on our chat, to take notes. Is that all right with you?'

'Sure,' I say. He also glances at Mum and she nods. While we're waiting for our drinks and the note-taking assistant, the detective inspector makes small talk with Mum. His manner is intimate and attentive. I can see my mother rather helplessly responding to him, to his good looks and charm. Is he trained to do this, I wonder, or does it come naturally?

A spindly young man with a spotty chin brings in a tray with our drinks and an older man follows on his heels with a tape recorder in one hand and a notebook in the other. He sets up the tape recorder and announces the date, time, and who is present in the room. Mum starts to panic. This has all become like a police drama on the telly – as though I'm a suspect in a cell.

'Is all this necessary?' she blunders. 'I mean, Amber hasn't done anything wrong. I thought you just wanted to talk with her? To get some background.' She stands up from her chair, as though she wants to make a break for freedom, but Call-Me-Neil reaches out to reassure her. He gently touches her arm.

'Please – sit down. There's nothing to worry about, Mrs Renalden. Please. This is just for our records.'

Mum is soothed, just. She flutters a little, then settles down again. The older man recedes to a corner of the room and the detective inspector takes a seat opposite my mother and me, giving us another flash of the blue silk lining. Then he clasps his hands together and smiles.

'Right. Where shall we start? First of all, Amber – how old are you?'

'Fifteen.'

'She had her birthday just last week,' Mum breaks in. The policeman nods at her politely but his attention is now fixed firmly on me.

'Fifteen,' he repeats. 'OK Amber, will you tell me when you first met James Renault?'

'At the end of July. The beginning of the summer holidays – just after I first met Dowdie.'

'Dowdie. That's Dorothy Johnson, right?'

'Yes. Dowdie lived with the Community. I met her first.'

'And she took you over there – to the Community?'

'Yes.'

'Can you remember the exact date of your first visit?'

'Not off the top of my head. But I could probably work it out, if I had my diary.'

'And did you meet James Renault that first time you went there?'

'Yes.'

Call-Me-Neil is quiet for a moment, as though turning things over in his mind. He unclasps and clasps his hands. He leans forward, propping his elbows on his thighs.

'What did you make of him?' he says. 'What were your first impressions, Amber? What kind of man was he?'

I am uncomfortably aware that everyone is waiting for me to speak – my mother, the detective inspector, the old man with his notebook, even the tape recorder. I don't like to be the centre of attention. I feel the blood heat my face and I twitch on the chair.

'It's hard to say.'

'Well try. You must have thought something about him, Amber. Anything.'

I sense my mother beside me, willing me to speak. What had I thought about him, that first time at the Community?

'He seemed OK.' I shrug. 'A nice bloke, you know? Very friendly. Very interested in everyone.'

He seizes on this.

'Friendly, yes? So when did you first talk to him, Amber? Can you remember what he said to you?' I notice how often the detective inspector uses my name. Perhaps this is a technique to gain my trust.

'I went over and stayed the night, Neil,' I say. 'In the evening, the Community had this kind of gathering thing. They all ate together and James gave a talk. Afterwards, when everyone was just hanging out and talking, he came over and spoke to me.'

'He gave a talk? Can you remember what it was about?'

I give a cold smile. The metal sphere trapped in my ribcage expands and contracts painfully.

'The Amethyst children and evolution,' I say. 'Connection. Revelation. Apocalypse.'

The charged words hang in the air, as though I have written them there. But the police officer brushes them away with a wave of his hand.

'Can you be more specific Amber? What exactly did he say? Do you know what he meant by that?'

Inside me, the question stirs like a forest of leaves. I close my eyes. What had James Renault intended, truly? What had he believed?

Three

That first afternoon, Dowdie stayed until my mother came home from work. She'd collected Justin from the playscheme on her way – I could hear him, tired and temperamental, arguing about what he wanted to eat.

'I'd better go,' Dowdie said. We'd been lying side by side on my bed, listening to Placebo, which she liked. She swung round her long, narrow legs and pushed the hair from her eyes. It was still ratty, from her swim in the river.

'D'you want to— are you doing anything tomorrow?' I said.

'I'll meet you by the river, shall I? On the bridge.'

We went downstairs. Mum called out a greeting from the kitchen at the end of the hall. When she saw Dowdie she stepped out, nosy, keen to check out the stranger.

'Hi – I don't think we've met before,' she said.

'This is Dowdie, Mum,' I said.

'One of your school friends?'

But Dowdie stepped forward. She held her hand out. 'We only met today,' she said. 'Down by the river.' She spoke confidently – adult to adult. Nonplussed, my mother took the outstretched hand and shook it.

'Nice to meet you,' she said, glancing at me and back to Dowdie. 'You're going now? Would you like to stay for something to eat?'

Dowdie shook her head. 'Thank you – but I have to be back.' She looked at me, over her shoulder, and winked. 'See you tomorrow,' she said.

Then she was gone. Mum closed the door, and for a moment we stood there, caught in the curious emotional eddies created by her presence and departure.

'Golly,' Mum said. 'Who's she? What a strange girl.'

'Why's she strange?' The remark irritated. Why did Mum have to react like that to anything that wasn't – strictly ordinary? But her comment was off-hand. Already she was heading back to the kitchen, where Justin was pulling packets out of the cupboard. I went back to my room, clumping up the stairs, and wondered how Dowdie would actually get back to the Community. It was out in one of the villages – at least three miles away. Presumably she'd walk. There were no regular buses as far as I knew, and she had no money on her, no mobile phone. She rose up, in my mind's eye, wending a solitary path through the fields and lanes, on secret tracks the rest of us had forgotten.

I lay back on my bed, put Placebo back on again, and dug out my journal from under my pillow. So much to write today – my mind was buzzing with it – but for once, I couldn't find the words to set it down. My journal was beautiful, with thick, creamy paper and a black leather-effect cover. A hundred pages were covered in my large, inelegant handwriting. Over these last empty days, staring into the river in the heat, I had written so much. I flicked through the pages. On one, in large capitals across the page, I had written: AMBER LACKS THE FLAIR AND ORIGINALITY OF THOUGHT TO BE AN OUTSTANDING STUDENT

OF ENGLISH. This was repeated on the three successive pages, in increasingly large letters. I had hoped, by writing it, to relieve the sentence of its sharp edge. So far this had not proved to be the case.

English is my favourite subject, you see. I'm a dunce at Maths, I hate Science, and I'm useless at Art. But I love writing. I want to be a writer – more than anything. And this year, Year 10, we'd had a new English teacher. He was a young man, Mr Stephenson, with olive skin, jet black hair and beautiful grey-green eyes. Very earnest and intense. I tried my best to impress him, tried desperately, but he refused to be impressed. He set up a poetry club and lots of the girls joined, though most of them had precious little interest in poetry. We met in the library on Thursday lunchtimes and each week everyone was invited to bring along work by a poet they particularly admired. When it was my turn, I took along the battered *Selected Poems* of Walter de la Mare, which I had bought three years before from an Oxfam shop. The girls, lounging like devoted hounds at Mr Stephenson's feet, watched me solemnly as I rose to my feet and recited two poems, largely from memory.

> *'I met at eve the Prince of Sleep,*
> *His was a still and lovely face . . .'*

> *'If I were Lord of Tartary,*
> *Myself, and me alone,*
> *My bed should be of ivory,*
> *Of beaten gold my throne;*
> *And in my court should peacocks flaunt,*
> *And in my forests tigers haunt,*
> *And in my pools great fishes slant*
> *Their fins athwart the sun . . .'*

I was self-conscious to start with, to be the object of so much attention. Then as the poems progressed I lost myself in the words, in Walter's unworldly embroidery of beauty and melancholy. When I stopped, and came back to myself, all the eyes were fixed on me still. No one moved or said a word. At last Mr Stephenson nodded kindly. He reached out his hand.

'Can I see the book?' he said. I handed it over, the dust jacket all sepia brown and torn at the edges. Mr Stephenson flicked through the pages.

'It's astonishing, isn't it,' he said. 'This man was writing in the twentieth century. He lived through both world wars. He's a contemporary of Wilfred Owen and TS Eliot.'

Around his feet, the girls shifted and stretched. Mr Stephenson, apparently forgetting about me and caught in the momentum of his argument, continued: 'I've not read any of his work before. Very strange – all these thous and thees and thys. Horribly self-conscious and anachronistic "poet" language, isn't it? Stilted rhythms, contrived rhymes. Men were dying in the trenches, nuclear bombs were dropped on Japan, and in some English backwater this chap was writing whimsical poems about snowdrops!'

'There are poems about the war,' I interrupted, my voice too loud. I struggled to stop the quiver in my voice. My face was hot, but my hands felt horribly cold. I felt, if I don't sit down I shall faint, but I couldn't make myself move. Mr Stephenson was taken aback.

'Are there?' he said.

'There's one called *Peace*.' Too quiet now. Mr Stephenson asked me to repeat myself. He turned to the poem and swiftly read it aloud. The obedient hounds turned their adoring faces towards him. Then:

'What do you think girls? Does de la Mare redeem himself?'

'Sentimental,' said a Year-11 girl, wrinkling her nose. 'Weak and trite. Embarrassing patriotic poesy.'

Mr Stephenson glanced at me. 'That's a little harsh,' he said. 'But I'm afraid I'd have to agree.'

My hands were shaking. Of course this didn't feel like a critique of Walter, but an assault on me for making such a terrible choice. How useless I was – how stupid – to like him. Perhaps Mr Stephenson finally sensed how much this was affecting me, because he said, more gently: 'Why don't you sit down, Amber? And tell us, why do you like his work?'

I took a deep breath. 'I don't, really,' I said. 'I just picked the book up. I think it's my mum's. I think you're absolutely right. Everything you've said.' And the saddest thing was, I did think he was right. How could I argue with anything Mr Stephenson had said? Walter de la Mare just wasn't cool. It was the ongoing question. How do you know what is cool? So many of the other girls seemed to know by instinct. They brought in poems by Carol Ann Duffy and Benjamin Zephaniah, Seamus Heaney, Sylvia Plath and Ted Hughes. These were all cool. Mr Stephenson liked them all – and so did I. But it went beyond poets. There were all the usual gangs at school – grebos, emos, chavs, beaners – but I didn't fit in with any of them. I wasn't clever enough to be a beaner, nor confident and elegant enough to be an emo. Clothes, music, language – the others had a particular flair for liking the right thing. But how do you know what the right thing is? My parents offered no clues themselves – they couldn't guide me. They had no Heaney or Hughes on their shelves (my mum likes big romances, my dad, books about soldiering in World War II). They listen to Dire Straits and Mariah Carey. They aren't cool at all.

So, and I know I am coming to this the long way round, that is why I wasn't overly surprised by Mr Stephenson's analysis of my performance in his English lessons – even though I was upset. Lacking flair and originality of thought – it was a horrible remark. It was much worse than saying someone was lazy, or careless or untidy and disrespectful. It was so much more personal. How could I be a writer without flair and originality? Deep down, I hated his report because secretly I feared he was right.

I picked up my pen. I wrote: *Today I met a girl called Dowdie, while I was sitting on the bridge over the river.* Then I ran out of steam. How could I best describe her? Dowdie was beyond cool. She lived outside the kingdom. She was untouched by its laws and regulations.

Downstairs, I heard my father come in through the front door, home from work, and Mum called me down for tea. We had pasta with cheese sauce and salad. Justin was full of himself, boasting about the friends he had made at his playscheme, at the leisure centre. Until two years ago, I had also spent several summer holiday weeks at the activity-week sessions because my parents were at work and I was too young to be left on my own. It was worse than school – a programme of football, swimming, so-called arts and crafts, idiotic 'team games'. I begged and begged Mum to let me stay at home on my own, but she wouldn't hear of it, not until I was twelve. My brother though, six-year-old urchin with golden curls and the cute, chubby face, he loves it. Can't get enough – hates leaving at the end of the day even though he's dead tired and fractious after so much socialising, all those games and roller discos. Sometimes I look around the table, at Mum and Dad and cheeky little Justin, and I wonder, did they adopt me? Did they find me on the doorstep? Why don't I feel like I belong?

As the thought rose up, I remembered Dowdie telling me I was an Amethyst child. This peculiar Dowdie nugget I had tucked away at the back of my mind. Now I took it out, turned it over, mulled a little while. Could it be true? Is this the reason I never felt a part of anything?

'How was your day, Amber?' Dad said. 'What are you dreaming about? You were miles away.'

My dad turned forty last year. His hair's receding fast, and he's got a bit of a paunch from, he says, too many pub lunches when he's out and about installing computer systems all over the country. We used to be good friends when I was a kid. Lately, he'd been away a lot and somewhere along the line he started to get on my nerves. I think I got on his nerves too. Most of the time he only spoke to me to tell me off about something – to nag about homework usually.

'Yeah, fine,' I said.

'D'you do anything interesting?'

'Not much. Y'know. Stuff.'

'Relaxed with your mates, I expect. Lucky you. It's all right for some – the rest of us have to go out and earn a living. You enjoy it while you can, I say.' It was a joke, of sorts, but it caused me acute irritation. Enjoy it while I can? It was the horrible doom adults dangle gleefully over your head. You can't avoid it, they are saying. You'll soon be me, like it or not. You'll have a miserable job and a paunch and a million chores to do at the weekend.

'I've finished,' I said. 'Can I go?'

'*May* I, not can I. May I leave the table,' Dad said.

'May I leave the table,' I repeated. My modus operandi, remember? Say what people want to hear. Don't upset anyone. Lie low, and keep out of trouble.

Mum and Dad watched telly most of the evening, once they'd

washed up, tidied, got Justin to bed. With no particular time to be up in the morning, the bedtime rules were relaxed for me. I played games on the computer for a while, surfed the Internet, read the blogs of some writers I like. I'm a habitual lurker. Sometimes I wish I was brave enough to comment, to wave my virtual flag – hey, I'm here – this is me! But the Internet didn't hold my interest for long, so I went back to my room, turned on the music and tried once again to write about my meeting with Dowdie.

It was so hot that night I struggled to sleep, even with the window open and the covers thrown back. My legs itched. The heat crawled over me. From time to time I sank into the shallows of sleep. Confusing dreams unfolded in my head, stories that seemed to repeat themselves, paths I ran along in panic, doors that closed in my face, classrooms I couldn't find. Then the brief dark was over, and light stole through the gaps in my curtains into my black room. It was still very early – five, maybe. I climbed out of bed, stupefied by lack of sleep, went downstairs and made myself a strong cup of coffee. The house was silent. My parents wouldn't get up for another hour or more. Even now, it was hot. I had a cool shower but I was sweating again by the time I pulled on my black jeans and vest top. I was supposed to meet Dowdie at ten so there were still another four hours to pass. I tried to read, but for once couldn't lose myself in a story. So I lay in a tired trance upon my bed, strange electrical currents sizzling in my brain while my limbs were heavy as clay.

I heard my parents' alarm go off at 6.45pm, and the low murmurs and movements of my father getting dressed. Ten minutes later Mum went into the shower. Justin stomped across the hall, and pushed open my door.

'What are you doing in here? Who said you could come into

my room?' I snapped. Justin, cute and sleepy in his pyjamas, was only half awake. My irritation washed over him. He climbed onto my bed and cuddled up to me. A silvery film of sweat glistened on his face. I could feel his hot breath on my shoulder. It was hard to be cross with him for long.

'Will you come with me today, Amber?' he said. 'Please come with me. There's swimming. And cooking. I like it better when you're there. Please. Please come.'

I lay down beside him, so his face was centimetres from mine.

'No,' I said. 'Too old for the playscheme now. You'll be OK – you've got lots of friends.' His face clouded and then brightened as I spoke. Nothing impinged on him for long. His feelings seem to slide over the surface, like water on glass. Not like me. I'm a hoarder. I can nurse a bad feeling for ever. Yes, Mr Stephenson – for ever.

Mum was calling so Justin rolled over and clambered to his feet. He headed downstairs for his breakfast. There was half an hour of brisk activity – dressing, lunch-making, washing up – and then Mum called out goodbye, the front door closed and I had the place to myself again. I left for the river very early, at eight-thirty. It was a fairish walk, the roads clogged with rush-hour traffic, car windows open, drivers in shirt sleeves with shades on. Dust covered everything – the pavements, verges, the tatty hedgerows. It was as though the heat itself had distilled into dust, settling over the town. I could smell it, taste it on my lips. On the other side of the busy road, I saw a boy walking in the opposite direction. There were lots of people about – heading for work mostly – but the boy caught my eye. He looked a little older than me, tall and very thin. His clothes emphasised this thinness. Ink-black hair, brushed forward over his narrow face. Skinny black jeans, giving him stork legs, and a clingy black and white striped shirt. What was he doing out, at this unearthly, uncool hour? He must have felt the intensity of my stare because he lifted his head and looked directly across the stream of traffic – at me. We were too far apart for me to see his face well, but I looked away instantly in any case. I didn't want him to know I was staring. But I felt the impact of his glance and felt my heart beat anxiously. As soon as a safe distance had passed I looked back. He was striding up the hill with a peculiar, rapid, stilted pace. I'd never seen him before, never noticed him around. But I pushed this speculation out of my mind. I crossed the road at the roundabout, walked down a lane to the river. Then I headed along the riverbank, past the waterworks, a further twenty-minute walk to the bridge where I had first seen Dowdie.

I arrived three quarters of an hour early. Dowdie turned up forty minutes late. This was my first lesson. Dowdie was always late. I had started to think she wasn't coming at all. Even my habitual river staring had lost its appeal. I was numb with boredom by the time she turned up.

I saw her in the distance, following the path by the river from the opposite direction. She didn't walk purposefully, even now. She disappeared from view behind a billow of brambles, and when she reappeared she lifted her arm and waved to me, sitting on my habitual spot on the bridge. She was accompanied by a fat, white terrier which bounced along the lane ahead of her.

'Hey!' she called out. 'Amber! D'you wanna swim today?'

I shook my head. 'No, thanks. But you go ahead if you want.' She made no apology for her lateness and I was so glad to see her I didn't mention it either. Dowdie climbed onto the bridge. The little dog jumped up, thrust its nose in my face.

'Don't worry about him,' she said. 'He's very friendly – aren't you Max?'

I didn't seem to impress Max, because he gave me only a brief sniff before heading off to investigate the undergrowth along the riverbank.

'Why won't you swim?' Dowdie demanded. 'Worried you'll drown?'

'I just don't feel like it.'

Dowdie scrutinised me. She shrugged. 'Maybe later. You look tired.'

'I am tired. I hardly slept a wink. It's so hot.'

She sat down beside me. 'Does that happen often? Insomnia?'

In the bushes, Max sent a moorhen squawking into the water. Way down, beneath our feet, the eternal river flowed.

'Quite often, yes.'

She gave a satisfied little smile. 'It's one of the signs, you see. One of the signs of the Amethyst child.'

I felt a peculiar shiver of emotion – fear and excitement mingled.

'I worry a lot,' I blurted. 'That's often why I can't sleep. I worry.'

'About what?' Her face was calm and attentive.

'It's hard to explain. I mean – I worry about everything. Climate change, the environment, war, hunger, terrorism. I worry about being helpless. I worry that I am eating when other people are starving. I worry that I'm too weak and passive, that I don't make a difference because I'm too scared to.'

The words came out in a gush. I hadn't spoken to anyone about this before. Dowdie didn't say anything at first. She looked away from me and down to the river.

'I shall tell you what Amethyst children are like,' she said. 'And you tell me if this matches up. First of all, they feel out of place. They see the world in a different way to ordinary people and they are so acutely aware of the problems we face they want to be part of changing it. They are creative people, who have difficulty fitting in with anyone else and they have different aspirations. They don't like conforming and being told what to do, and they have psychic and spiritual powers, such as telepathy or channelling, a highly developed sense of intuition, visions and awareness of other worlds and dimensions.'

I looked at Dowdie. 'And you – you're like this? I mean – telepathy? Lots of the things you said – yes, I do feel like that. Feeling out of place. But I don't have visions, Dowdie. I can't read anyone's mind.' I was afraid she would be disappointed, but Dowdie gave me a grave smile.

'Trust me,' she said. 'You are an Amethyst child, Amber. I know it. And you know it too, if only you were brave enough to admit it to yourself. You're afraid, that's all. You've had to defend yourself for so long, you've put a shield up. And that's what I'm here for – to help you. To set you free.'

'But what can you do? Do you really have special powers?' I tried not to sound sceptical. I wanted to believe her and Dowdie's own certainty was – seductive. But a bitter, nagging voice in my head wouldn't shut up. This was a game, wasn't it? A slice of New Age hokum. Old hippie stuff, made up by parents who wanted to believe their kids were extra special. Dowdie looked at me, her head on one side, as though she could indeed read my thoughts.

'You'll see,' she said. 'Give me a chance.' She drew up her long legs and scrambled to her feet. 'Shall we go?'

We spent the entire day together, walking and talking. I shall never forget it. It seemed to me that with every step we took, we wandered deeper into a kind of enchantment, into a world I had known in a previous life, but had forgotten. The heat filled the air with a tremulous haze, leaching out the pale colour of the meadows by the river, newly mown and spread out like sheets to bake in the sun. I remembered my imagining the previous evening, of Dowdie walking lost paths, and this vision, at least, seemed to be true. I had lived in the area for eight years but I had never strayed too far from the well-known paths. Dowdie, however, knew every green lane, buried stile, byway and footpath. She had memorised the old names for the fields – arcane names that seemed imbued with meaning: Mordack's Close, Oak and Elm Piece, Shoulder of Mutton, Tinker's Close, Old Chapel Field.

She showed me a huge ditch overgrown by hedges so it formed a shady green tunnel in which we could walk. Golden light filtered through the dark, sun-soaked foliage. We sat upon the dry dirt floor, on haphazard pillows of dry, skeletal leaves from the previous autumn, while Max ran ahead, pursuing rabbits. The sun cast tiny molten jewels of light upon the ground through chinks in the leaves. This long, arboreal cave possessed the architectural calm of a cloister in a cathedral.

When I asked her how she knew so much, Dowdie laughed.

'My education,' she said. 'Surely the first thing an education should do is teach you about the land you live on. It was a project I set myself. I went to the Records Office and studied old maps, and then I spent days and days on my own, just walking and exploring. I made lots of notes and maps and drawings. I can remember it all.'

'Aren't you scared, walking on your own? Aren't you worried someone might attack you? Doesn't your mum want to know where you are?'

'Who's going to attack me? You worry too much. Do you actually know anyone who's been attacked? This is a very safe area. Don't you think perhaps people want you to be scared to control you?'

It's hard to put into words how magical that day was. Our new friendship created an alchemical spell that wove itself around us. We walked for hours, to places I had never seen before – a lost pond hidden under willow trees, black and still as jet, an old cottage with its roof collapsed and broken, engulfed by undergrowth in a wood, a stone path covered by moss, starting seemingly at random halfway over a field, and finishing, equally unexpectedly, in the next. We walked by ancient, bulbous oak trees with barbed wire grown into their hard skins. In the roots of one I found a ball of glass the size of my fist, worn smooth but opaque, like sea glass. Everything seemed to be more than it was – to have a meaning I had previously been blind to. Every crooked branch or assembly of stones was a message offering some greater understanding, if I had the wit, the openness to receive it.

Lunchtime passed and without anything to eat I was hungry for a while. But we kept on walking and the hunger passed. In the corner of a field Dowdie drank a little water from a spring that bubbled into a ditch. For a moment my old fears flared (dirt, bacteria, chemical run-off) but I was thirsty and put them aside, cupping up a hand full of clear, cold water that tasted of stone. Then we lay on our backs in the grass, in the vast hedge's cloak of shade, and lapsed into silence for a time. I could hear the distant violin-whine of insects and beneath me, the up-thrust of the dry Earth, cradling me, holding me up. The minutes drifted by. At last, (after how long?) Dowdie sat up and said it was time to move again.

We seemed to walk through time, as well as space, as though in our mutual frame of mind the barriers of the present no longer existed. Dowdie took me to the site of a Roman villa (we could see nothing – just, perhaps, a levelling of the ground in the corner of the field) and then to an abandoned orchard where she said pottery pieces dating back to the ancient Beaker people had been uncovered.

'Much older than the Romans,' she said. 'Older than the Celts. Four thousand years ago – can you imagine it? They were immigrants – expert archers and metal smiths. They were here – just here.'

And truly I could sense them, sitting in the sunshine. The narrow field was overgrown. A couple of aged apple trees sagged beneath the weight of their own branches. All around us, dense grass, peppered with docks, nettles, hemlock and the red stab of poppies. Silence and heat. Thousands of years ago the Beaker people had stood where I stood, and laughed and eaten and talked and fought. Perhaps in the soil and air particles of their physical bodies still lingered. The stones beneath my feet contained the echo of their voices. For a moment – just a moment – the Beaker people were not simply a fact in my head. I could *feel* them. Past and present meshed together, as though the past were not a room locked away, but a long tunnel. And I caught a glimpse, nothing more, of these short, strong people moving around us, and smelled their perfume of earth and wood smoke, and heard the disturbance of their voices. Then it was gone. A half second. Maybe no time at all. We were two girls sitting in an overgrown field. Dowdie glanced at me.

'Do you know what I mean?' she said.

Perhaps I had imagined it. I was tired and hungry from the walk, and strung out on nerves and excitement after my long conversations with Dowdie. But my hands were shaking and somehow our surroundings had altered. Nothing seemed quite solid any more, as though the reality I had always felt anchored inside had shown itself to be an illusion. Was this the truth then? Was reality mutable? Could we turn it around and play with it? I looked up at Dowdie. Her face seemed strange, like a mask I couldn't see through. What was she thinking?

'Where are you?' she said. The sunlight glinted oddly in her eyes, making her almost inhuman.

I pressed my hands together, squeezing my fingers tight. 'I don't know. To be honest, I was there, just for a moment. I thought I could see them, the Beaker people. I think I must have imagined it.'

Dowdie smiled. Then she scrabbled to her feet. 'Come on,' she said. 'It's time to go.'

Slowly we headed back to the town. Everything was different now, as I trailed the aftermath of my experience in the orchard behind me. My head buzzed with contradictions. The summer fields seemed unreal, and at the same time more beautiful and intense. The dog roses glowed a supernatural pink in the hedges. The stones on the riverbed coiled into patterns underneath their silver lid of water. Up in the sky, the chariot of the sun arched over the horizon, and down towards the rim of the Earth. And somewhere, not far away, people were driving home from work in factories and offices, ready for dinner and the anaesthetic of television before they shut the doors, locked the world out, and lay passive in their beds for a night of obliterating, dreamless sleep. I didn't want to go back. Instead I stayed out with Dowdie till ten o'clock at night, just sitting on the bridge across the river and watching the light and colour slowly seep from the sky. I talked a lot – about my family and school, about the books I read and the people I knew, and how lonely I was most of the time and how I'd never had a friend I could really talk to before. Dowdie listened, her face so calm and wise, soaking up everything I had to say. She didn't interrupt or comment or offer advice. When at last my mobile rang, and my mother's anxious, irritated voice asked where

I was and what time did I think this was, and could I come home right now, she sounded like a stranger. Who was she, this woman, intruding on my new world?

But I wasn't cross. I was too far away to be affected.

'I'll be back in twenty minutes,' I said, across the distance. 'Don't worry, Mum. I won't be long.'

Dowdie and I embraced, upon the bridge, while a few hundred metres away the streetlights fizzed and an intermittent stream of cars drove past on the ring road. Then I strode home, on my own, in a new night-time realm. Hardly anyone was out. Despite the late hour my body felt clean and hard and light, as though I could walk for ever.

Four

'Tell me something about Dorothy Johnson,' the detective inspector says.

'Dowdie,' I jump in. 'She's called Dowdie.'

'OK. Dowdie. What was she like? What did you most admire about her?'

'Her courage,' I say, without hesitation. 'She spoke her mind. She didn't mind upsetting people. She was incredibly brave.'

'She was brave? How was she brave? Give me an example.' Neil the policeman leans towards me, making eye contact, encouraging me, with his body language, to relax and trust him. It is all so obvious – so much like an old episode of Prime Suspect – that I am overcome by an urge to laugh.

'Well, often when we went out together, she brought her dog, Max. She had a little embroidered bag, with tiny mirror sequins sewn onto it, and if Max did a poo on the footpath she'd pick it up in a plastic bag, tie it up, and put it in her embroidered bag till we found a bin.'

Neil nods uneasily, clearly not sure where this is leading. I sit back on my chair.

'One day we were out together – walking to the Community. We'd crossed the narrow lane to the village, where the hedges are really tall, and saw a car was pulled up in the little lay-by there. Four men were sitting inside the car. Young men – about nineteen or twenty. They looked round and stared at us, and the one in the passenger seat got out. He was very pale, with piggy little eyes and a bruise on the side of his face. He was wearing this baggy white sportswear stuff. I didn't like the way he was staring at us, and I put my hand out to grab Dowdie and suggest we turn around and run away but Dowdie just walked on, towards him.

"'Hello girls," he said. "Enjoying your walk?"

'He had a horrible leer on his face. I'm sure he was on something. I was very afraid – we had no idea what he wanted, or what he might do. But Dowdie just kept walking, her head held very high. He stepped right in front of her, wouldn't let her past.

"'Have you got any money you could lend us, love?" he said. Inside the car the other three were staring and smirking. What if they got out too? What if they grabbed us? All these thoughts were running through my head. There was no one else nearby. And I didn't have my mobile phone. Images streamed through my head – kidnap and hurt and rape and bodies lying in the ditch covered in blood. This whole horrible episode probably only lasted two minutes but time stretched out so slowly – and all around us the hedges full of birds and flowers, and just down the road all the pretty cottages covered with roses. It was utterly weird and surreal.

"'We need money – for petrol," the man said. "Can you lend us some?"

"'I haven't got any money," Dowdie said. Her face was pale and proud. She tossed her head and tried to walk past him.

"'What's in the bag then?" He pointed at her bulging embroidered bag.

"'You want my bag?" she snapped. "You're going to steal my bag – you filthy, disgusting robber?"

'The man was taken aback. Inside the car his mates were all laughing. She was fierce as a wildcat and they thought she was funny. I was more afraid. Don't upset him. Don't make him angry, I prayed in my mind. He wasn't laughing. She was making a fool of him in front of the others. I could see a storm brewing in his face.

'"Give him the bag," I said. "It's not worth it. Give him the bag."

'The driver was revving the engine now, preparing to leave. Cool as a cucumber, keeping her eyes fixed on the robber's face, Dowdie took off the bag and handed it over. The man jumped back into the car and before he'd even slammed the door they'd pulled away with a screech of tyres. We could hear their hoots of laughter, even above the shriek of the engine.

'Then everything was quiet. For a moment we stood in silence. Everything was still. Then we looked at one another and instantly erupted into laughter. Hysterical laughter. We laughed till our bodies ached and we couldn't stand straight.

'"He's going to get such a surprise when he looks in that bag," Dowdie said, and we howled again, till the tears were running down our faces.

'"We'd better go," I said. "In case he comes back for more." And we laughed again, helplessly, till it actually hurt. I suppose it was shock and relief – but it was also very, very funny.'

I've been talking for ages, and now, abruptly, I stop. Neil Ripley, my mother, and even the man taking notes are all staring. All I can hear is the whirring of the tape recorder. Mum's face is shocked. Her mouth opens and closes.

'Good god, Amber. You never told me about this. You never said – you could've been hurt,' she says.

'You never thought to report this incident to the police?' Neil says.

'What? The theft of a large lump of dog poo? What would you have done?' I say.

Although Mum is still quaking in her seat, Neil's careful self-control falters for a moment. He relaxes and snorts with laughter. His jacket flashes its silk lining. The cufflinks blink.

'Serves them right, picking on two little girls,' he says. 'He got what he deserved. And she was a cool customer, Dowdie. You were sensible though — it's best not to antagonise people in a situation like that. Especially if you think they've been drinking or taking drugs.'

As he concludes this little piece of advice, call-me-Neil regains his detective inspector demeanour, sits up straight, and returns to his questions.

Five

The next morning, when everyone had gone out, Dowdie came to my house and dyed my hair a dramatic bleached blond. I'd bought the potent chemical brew weeks ago. The box had lain among my notebooks and pens in a drawer, waiting for me to raise the courage to use it. She wrapped my shoulders in plastic bags to protect my clothes, and squirted and combed the stinking liquid into my hair. It had the consistency of snot, and over an hour leached the colour from my mousy, nondescript locks while we sat in the living room, watching *Lawrence of Arabia*, my favourite film, on DVD. When I had showered the dye away, and used the sachet of conditioner, my hair was almost white and curiously soft, like the weed at the bottom of the river. A mermaid's hair.

'It's actually very long, your hair,' Dowdie said, combing it through. 'I hadn't noticed before but it's nearly down to your waist.'

Then: 'Won't your mum mind?'

I shook my head. 'I asked her before I bought it. She said it was OK, as long as I didn't get into trouble at school. According to the rules, we're allowed to dye our hair a "natural" colour.'

Dowdie sniffed. '*Natural?*

I stood up and looked in the mirror. A stranger stared back. The new colour had changed the shape of my face. I still wasn't pretty – but something was there that I hadn't seen before. Perhaps I had always hidden in my hair, obscured myself. Now I looked . . . revealed.

'See how blue your eyes are,' Dowdie said. We both stared, at the girl in the mirror with long white hair.

'I want you to come to the Community now,' Dowdie said. 'Stay the night. We've got a gathering – a party. Ring your mum and ask her.'

I felt a surge of excitement. I had been waiting for her to ask me – hadn't dared invite myself. Mum was busy and distracted at work when I rang and said yes without question. We cleared up the plastic bags and hair dye detritus from the bathroom and I packed up some clean clothes and a toothbrush. At the front door Dowdie said: 'Leave your phone here.'

'What?'

'We're not allowed mobile phones. They're a distraction. Leave it here – if you want to come.'

'But Mum always likes me to have it – so she can contact me.'

'She knows where to find you.'

'But I always take it,' I said, hearing a whine in my voice.

'Then break the addiction.' For a moment, at an impasse, we stared at one another. Dowdie was resolute. I took the phone from my pocket, turned it off, and dropped it on the kitchen table.

'OK,' she said. 'Now we can go.'

As we walked through the Napier South estate, I was acutely conscious of people staring at my hair. Kids I recognised from school, mostly. What surprised me, striding beside Dowdie, was that I enjoyed the attention.

It took an hour to walk to Dowdie's home, in a village about three miles out of town. It was very hot. I had dressed as cool as I could, in a vest top and my cut-off black combats, but within minutes we were sweltering. We stuck to the shady paths, hiding from the sun in long tunnels of leafy shadow.

The Community was out on the far edge of the village, a terrace of three large red-brick cottages set a field away from the other houses. Two men and a woman were working in the vegetable garden at the front when we opened the gate. One of them – a man with long hair in a ponytail – stood up straight, leaned on his hoe, and waved.

'Hi Chris,' Dowdie called out. I didn't know much about gardening, but the plot looked impressive, boiling over with lush growth. Not an inch of space was wasted. At the front of the house, in grow-bags, grew huge tomatoes and courgettes, soaking up the sun.

Dowdie led me across.

'Chris – this is Amber,' she said. 'Amber's an Amethyst child. I found her. I'm taking her to James.'

Chris stared at me, gently inclining his head. He held out his hand.

'Amber, I'm happy to meet you,' he said, utterly serious. His hand was warm and dry. He smelled of soil and sun, from his gardening. I smiled, not knowing what to say. The other two, on the other side of the vegetable bed, also looked up and smiled.

'Come on,' Dowdie said abruptly. 'Come on.' She led me towards the house and through the open front door. We stepped from the violent sunshine into the cool.

It was a beautiful place. Several rooms had been knocked into one large living space, with a red-tiled floor and a huge fireplace in the middle. Mismatched but comfortable-looking armchairs and sofas stood around the room, with bright embroidered patchwork cushions piled on them. At one end, books crammed a small bookcase. Several pale watercolour pictures hung on the wall. Otherwise, the room was plain and uncluttered.

'Hello? Is that you Dowdie? Who's your friend?' A young woman in her early twenties, with pale auburn hair in a long plait stepped through a doorway, rubbing flour from her hands.

'This is Amber,' Dowdie said.

'Of course – Amber.' The woman reached out her elegant, floury hand to shake mine. Again, that serious scrutiny, the respect. It made me a little uncomfortable. 'I've been looking forward to meeting you,' she said. I glanced at Dowdie. What had she told them?

'I'm Diane. Would you like some lunch? I've just boiled some eggs and there's bread fresh out of the oven.' We followed her into the kitchen, flagged, like the living room, with large, red tiles. A huge wooden table filled the middle of the room. Again, the hotchpotch of furniture – mismatched chairs, old-fashioned pine cupboards and shelves come from perhaps a dozen different places. Still, it looked achingly lovely to me. Acres of blue and white china covered a towering dresser, where a fat tabby cat dozed next to a basket of fruit. A bunch of yellow roses stood in a vase in the middle of the table.

Diane flipped her hand. 'Flies! So many of them.' Then, shaking her head, 'Climate change. It's upon us, isn't it?' She seemed pretty good-humoured about the impending catastrophe though. Dowdie sat by the table and Diane served up boiled eggs, weighty wholemeal bread still hot from the oven and a bowl of salad from the garden, emerald leaves, crunchy with bean sprouts, sweet with the reddest tomatoes I had ever seen. I've never been a salad fan but Diane's offering was like nothing I had tasted before. Clean and fresh and simple, as though I were dining in the

Garden of Eden. I was so happy, sitting with Dowdie and Diane while the sun poured through the window and the perfume of fresh bread and spicy roses hung in the air. I didn't say much. Diane and Dowdie chattered about what was going on with people at the Community and the meeting that evening. They didn't seem to expect me to contribute. What would it be like to live here, I wondered, in this beautiful place among these intense, serious people?

After we had eaten, Diane went to change, before heading off for a shift at the wholefood shop. Half a dozen men came in, from the workshop Dowdie said, along with Chris and the others from the garden, and had their lunch too. Dowdie introduced them all, though I didn't remember the names. And like gardening Chris and the beautiful Diane, these men, dusty and scented with wood, treated me with an intense and peculiar respect. They were various ages – a dreadlocked couple, and an older man with long, grey hair and a beard. Dowdie was comfortable and familiar with them all, and she had them erupting with laughter at some reference I didn't hear. But I felt awkward among so many unknown people and I was glad when she pulled me away, and we headed out of the kitchen, leaving the carpenters to their bread and eggs.

'Shall I show you around?' she said. 'Come on. I want you to see everything.'

'Where's James?' I said. 'Am I going to meet him?'

'He's out. He'll be back later.'

Already, without even meeting him, I was intrigued by the man at the centre of the tribe. The man who channelled spirits and received divine revelations.

'Come on.' Dowdie was impatient. I scuttled after her.

I loved the place. It seemed like a paradise in the golden July sunshine. On the other side of the large living area was an office, complete with computer and Internet connection, where an older woman with grey hair was filling in spreadsheets. It surprised me.

'Didn't you say there were no computers?' I asked. The PC, bulky photocopier and fax machine all seemed out of place. But Dowdie explained they were a necessary evil, to run the businesses and keep up the Community's accounts – and not for personal use. She showed me a smaller meeting room on the ground floor, this one lined with books, where we interrupted two young men engaged in a heated debate. Open volumes and papers lay scattered on the table.

'This is our study room,' she said, drawing the door closed on the discussion. 'That's where I do my schooling. They are all my teachers – all the other members. I learn from them all.'

Two staircases led upstairs, one at either end of the house. Ten higgledy-piggledy bedrooms with low doors, off a narrow corridor, then a spiral staircase to the attic and a further three small rooms beneath the sloping roof. Most people shared, two to a room, she said. But Dowdie was lucky – she had one to herself, though it was the tiniest room of all, tucked away at the end of the attic. And it *was* tiny – just big enough for a single bed, a little chest of drawers and a miniature desk. The window was very low, so I had to lie down on my belly to look out, over the back garden. A bunch of fiery orange nasturtiums flamed from a jar on the deep window-sill.

'Oh, I love your quilt.' I sat on the edge of the narrow bed. The pillow case was a soft, well-washed white and against it, the bedspread a blaze of gold, amber and brown patchwork.

'My mother made it,' Dowdie said. 'Isn't it glorious?'

'Absolutely glorious. You are so lucky.' My eyes filled with tears. I couldn't help it, just overcome with feeling. I turned away, embarrassed, stooped down and pretended to scrutinise the garden again, through the window.

'Would you like to see outside?' Dowdie said.

They had a huge plot – about five acres altogether, she told me. Informal lawn edged with wild-flower verges, occasional sheltered bowers with tables and chairs, and then through a hedge to a mighty fruit and vegetable garden (organic, of course). Then workshops in a long red-brick shed, an orchard and a paddock where half a dozen cows grazed. There were chickens too, fierce looking birds with lean bodies and gold-freckled feathers, in palatial accommodation with their own wired-off kingdom of scratched dirt and dusty bushes.

The rest of the world disappeared, that afternoon. It was indeed like the Garden of Eden, to me. I couldn't stop looking, taking it all in. Everything was strange and marvellous and beautiful – the towering raspberry canes and their cargo of smoky-sweet fruit, the potato plants growing rampant on their heaped-up mounds of soil, the ranks of jewel-bright tomatoes, the majestic chickens, and beyond the final fence, the vista of fields and trees, the faraway curve of the horizon. It was as though Dowdie lived in the world my favourite books described. Partly I think it was down to the curious chemistry generated by her company that everything seemed brighter than usual, every scene charged with significance and meaning.

We sat on metal chairs in a cave of climbing roses, and Dowdie grinned at me.

'You like it, don't you?' she said.

I nodded. 'How could I not? How could anyone not?' I remembered Dowdie's 'all this', her gesture at the tatty town and the traffic, the place where I lived. A mean little jealousy stabbed, and I said: 'Of course James must be very rich – to have bought all this.'

Dowdie shrugged. 'I've never thought about it,' she said. 'I'm not bothered about money. Money's not important.'

'But if my mum and dad wanted a place like this – they couldn't afford it.'

Dowdie laughed. 'But my mum hasn't got any money – and we live here. It's a community, Amber. Let it go, will you?'

So I let it go. Mostly. It still irked, a little grit I added to my afternoon to irritate myself. A nasty carping voice that reminded me this Eden hadn't sprung from wishing for it – that somewhere along the line, money and mortgages and all the nasty 'all this' world stuff couldn't be avoided, even by a man who channelled spirits. Like the serpent in the garden, a niggling inner voice that stopped me ... stopped me what? From committing myself, maybe. From believing it all, hook, line and sinker. Lack of courage, you see. My fatal lack of courage.

Evening drew on, and gradually the house filled with people, the residents at the Community returning from their various daily occupations. Half a dozen, men and women, were busy in the kitchen preparing the meal. It seemed to take a long time, but everyone was relaxed and good-humoured. Most of the others were hanging out in the garden, waiting, enjoying the sunshine. There were a couple of young kids, both blond-haired, blue-eyed little cherubs. Some of the people said hello and shook my hand. Everyone was friendly.

At last the meal was prepared, a feast laid out in a buffet on the kitchen table. We loaded our plates with roast chicken, new potatoes and salads and then ate out in the garden, all of us together, twenty perhaps, all sitting on the grass.

'Which one's James?' I said, tucking in. Dowdie, a slow eater, raised her head slowly from her plate.

'Over there,' she said. 'See, with the blue shirt on.'

'What – him? That one?'

Dowdie nodded. 'Yeah. That's James. I'll introduce you later. He wants to talk to you.'

'And your mum, Dowdie. Where's your mum?'

'She'll be back later. She's staying down in Glastonbury tonight, on a course.'

James Renault was sitting with two women on a bench, a plate of food balanced on his lap. He wasn't like I'd expected. What had I expected? This man was older than my father, balding, with shaved black hair and a strong, bony face. He was short and stocky, with square hands. I felt a flash of disappointment, seeing him. I had thought he would seem more – extraordinary. I think I had envisioned a beautiful man with long hair – a hippie Jesus. And this man – he looked like our postman. Perhaps he felt my scrutiny because James Renault suddenly looked up, directly at me. He stared at me for a moment, chomping his salad. Then he grinned and waved. The woman beside him said something and James looked away.

When the meal was over, and the plates taken back to the kitchen, everyone sat in a large, ragged circle on the ground. I watched James Renault – noticing how everyone wanted to talk to him, how physical he was – shaking a hand, patting a knee, putting his arm around a young man's shoulder. Nothing heavy – he was perfectly calm and relaxed – but I could see how they looked up to him. When at last he stood, in the centre of the circle, a hush descended upon us. James turned, smiling a welcome to us all, taking us into his confidence.

'We have a visitor,' he said. To my alarm, he turned and gestured to me.

'Everyone, this is Amber. She's Dowdie's friend. Amber – you're very welcome.'

Instantly everyone applauded and cheered. I went hot and cold with embarrassment, which James seemed to enjoy.

'We're pleased to have you here, Amber,' he said, now addressing me directly. It's a cliché, isn't it, to say that someone can make you feel you are the only person in the room. But that was the power James Renault had. I felt it, in that moment, in the garden, among the twenty people. His attention was complete and compelling, as though I mattered to him – that it was serious between us, and that without any further words, we had an understanding.

Then – it was over. He turned away, spreading his arms as though to embrace us all – his brothers and sisters, his children.

'Well,' he said. 'Well, what a golden day. What a day, what a glorious evening! Look around us, at the trees and flowers, and the sky arching over our heads. What gifts they are, all freely given to us, for us to enjoy.

'There is everything we need, and more, here and now. So what has happened to you today? Something good – tell us about it.'

Chris spoke up, the man I had met first, in the garden.

'I – I – I saw a dragonfly, by the stream,' he said. Chris seemed very nervous, speaking in front of the gathering. There was something curious about him that I hadn't noticed before, in the way that he spoke and moved. But everyone smiled and nodded, encouraging him, and Chris continued: 'Like a fairy knight, it was, its armour all shining, petrol blue and silver and glistening. And it hovered in front of my face. I kept perfectly still, and there it was, just in front of me, staring at me.

'"Good morning, Sir Knight," says I. And there it hovers, gently up and down on a movement of the air, its wings like spun sunlight. And I looked into its eyes, thinking how bright the day must be to a dragonfly after so long growing up in the muddy vaults at the bottom of the river.' He wasn't nervous any more, caught up in the moment of his story, conjuring up the image of his dragonfly.

'Then it ducks away, just like that, over the stream all dappled with sunlight, and it disappears into the shadows.'

The story concluded, and everyone cheered and clapped. It was late now, nearly nine-thirty and the sun was declining. A soft, wine-coloured light submerged the garden. Unconsciously everyone had moved in, making the circle tight. The atmosphere intensified.

'Chris had a nervous breakdown three years ago,' Dowdie whispered. Her hair tickled my face. 'He couldn't handle the modern world. This was before he came to the Community. When he went off the rails, he was sectioned – you know, locked up in a mental hospital where they filled him with drugs – closed him down. Then they let him out and James found him, living like a zombie, on the streets in Bristol. He brought him here. Now he doesn't need any shitty drugs. He can be himself.'

A woman was talking now about someone she had met in the healthfood shop who had expressed an interest in the Community. Another, the mother of the two blond girls I think, talked about their artwork while the girls beamed with pride.

'Are they Amethyst children too?' I asked.

'Yes of course,' Dowdie said. 'That's why their mum, Marie, moved here when her marriage broke up. So she could bring up the children in a safe place.'

Nodding and acknowledging their contribution, James Renault began to speak again.

'It is a beautiful night and an occasion for celebration because we're all gathered together,' James said. 'It is important, especially now, to seek out these moments – to treasure them – because we have many challenges ahead of us.

'You know, all of you, that we live in extraordinary times. We're standing on the brink. The age of war will soon be upon us. The age of destruction and the will for death. The age of waste and hunger.

'For thousands of years humanity lived in tune with the Earth, and with the spirits, taking what was needed and giving back in times of plenty. For thousands of years we lived in balance, in awareness and consciousness.

'Then, maybe ten thousand years ago, mankind set himself apart. He laid claim to the Earth, instead of acknowledging its claim on him. He broke the soil with his plough and mined it for minerals. He turned his back on the forests and set up cities full of filth, and gave authority to priests and soldiers and kings, who lived on the labour of those who allowed themselves to be slaves.

'And then he created the industrial machine, which has poisoned the air and fouled the seas, while the ever-growing, blind, selfish mass of mankind clamoured for more of the stupid, toxic little toys we have created to block our senses and stop ourselves acknowledging how perilous our situation is, how much we have lost and still have to lose.'

He paused for a moment, looking around the circle, drawing us into his confidence. We were rapt, all of us, carried by the passion and intensity of his voice.

'The end days are drawing near,' he said. 'All balance is being destroyed. The Gulf Stream is dying and climate change will spread deserts over the face of the Earth. In just fifty years the age of oil will be over and the industrial machine will cease. Its death throes will be agonising. Without oil, modern agriculture will fail.

In the coming decades we face endless war, disease and starvation – a terrible and unavoidable apocalypse.'

He waited again, as the scenes he had conjured up played out in our collective imagination. Darkness gathered, the gardens receding as visions of the end days flickered and danced among us, like flames.

'Are you afraid?' he said softly. 'Often I'm afraid, when I see what is already happening, and what lies ahead.

'But there is hope. Cling to that. I know there is hope. The old game is playing out, but it isn't the end. The spirit that speaks through me knows so much more than we do. The spirit has told me there are children among us who are part of a new wave of consciousness. They have chosen to incarnate in these difficult times because they will lead us into a new era. They are spiritual warriors, who have clear sight. They are with us now and it is up to us to find and nurture them. We have to take care of them. These children will face so many difficulties growing up in our machine age. They will be misunderstood, and many people will try to crush their spirit, to subvert them and make them fit in to the machine. But the children will prevail.'

Marie, the mother of the blond children put her arms around them. Somewhere in the darkness a woman sobbed. Nobody else moved. I remembered all the nights I had lain awake in bed, already afraid of the future James had mapped out. I knew it all. Fear had pooled in the dark recesses of my brain, in my nightmares, in the small hours on my own in bed, unable to sleep, to trust myself to sleep. No, James didn't need to sell me fear; I had a home brand of it, already stockpiled. But James had something else to offer.

Could it be true, that a spirit had spoken to him? Everyone here believed it, without a doubt. Could it be true that a new generation of children had a different view of the world, and the ability to change the course of mankind? The dull, sensible voice in my head sneered at the idea. Another light, bright voice edged forward and said – open your mind. What if he is right – and I am one of those children?

Six

'Now James Renault had a pet project,' Neil says. His voice is careful. 'He believed, or said he believed, that a new kind of human being had evolved – his Amethyst children.'

'Yes,' I say. 'He did believe it. Completely.'

'And you, Amber – did he think you were an Amethyst child?'

I nod.

'Did you believe it? Do you believe it now?'

'Yes, I did believe it. Now, I'm not so sure.'

'And what did it mean, to be an Amethyst child? That you were special?' His lip almost curls as he says it.

'All children are special,' I say. I am trite, to annoy him because he is annoying me. Amethyst child or not, some adults seem to me very clumsy and obvious. The detective inspector is one of them. Every now and then I begin to warm to him – then he does something stupid, like communicating to me how ridiculous he finds the whole Amethyst child project. He should be open-minded, shouldn't he? And sensitive to my feelings?

'OK,' he says. 'Listen – I've visited his website and I've read up on his theories. He claimed his ideas on human evolution came to him from a spirit entity, a higher being. You're a sensible, intelligent girl – why did you believe it?'

I consider him, this narrow-minded policeman who thinks he knows everything.

'Vast swathes of the human population believe in a higher being,' I say. My voice is level. 'Christians, Muslims, Jews. They believe in angels, who are messengers. Would you patronise them too? Tell them they were too sensible and intelligent to believe it? Why are James Renault's spirits any different?'

I am changing. My modus operandi – say what they want to hear – has started to crumble. It is too much hard work. I've let it go.

Mum wriggles on her seat. I sense she is agitated by my responses. She knew so little about those hot summer weeks with Dowdie and the Community. She was busy at work, and she had let me off the leash. I hadn't told her anything about my adventure – I'd consciously cut her out of it. I'd stepped into a different world, one she wasn't part of.

'James was compelling,' I offer, mostly for my mother's sake. 'You think he's a mad cult leader – but it wasn't like that. He was the most sane and reasonable man I have ever met. He had a kind of natural authority – without any obvious effort. People were drawn to him – especially people who didn't feel comfortable anywhere else – people who didn't fit in with . . .' I gesture vaguely.

'The real world?' Mum offers.

'The dominant world-view,' I respond. It was one of James' phrases. The dominant world-view. And I am telling the truth. James was the most remarkable person I had ever met. He saw things with such clarity. There was no pretence, no convenient wriggling out of uncomfortable truths. We wear blinkers, all the time, for our own comfort. The world is full of death and suffering – right now, in this very instant – but we turn away and focus on petty personal concerns. If we all cared – cared to the core – if we all put down our distractions and said together, this can't happen, we have to stop it now, what

*could we achieve? James asked me this question, once, in the garden
at the Community, as we stood outside the hen palace. We were alone,
and it was late and still very hot. I was conscious of my vest-top
sticking to my back. Ribbons of musky-sweet perfume drifted from the
rough coils of honeysuckle in the hedge.*

*'What could we achieve?' The question also hung upon the air, and
I didn't know how to answer. It wasn't a question my parents had ever
asked me, or perhaps asked themselves. I struggled for something to say
to James, for an appropriate reply.*

*'It's OK,' he said softly, touching my bare arm. 'How can you
answer? How can I? We just don't know.'*

*The chickens fed, we headed back to the house. The sunset was
astonishing, a gilded billow of low cloud and at its core, a furnace of
crimson and gold. In the darkening sky a solitary star blinked over the
horizon. There was no need for words – we glanced at each other,
with half a smile, sharing the rapture of the moment. I was
immeasurably glad.*

*This I try to explain, awkwardly and without grace. How can I
communicate exactly what I saw and felt?*

*Mum harrumphs. 'He appealed to your youthful idealism,' she says,
as though this were a bad thing – a criticism. But Neil holds up his
hand, to silence her.*

*'Do you think it would be that easy, to do away with war and
hunger? Just by us all wishing it?' he says. He seems sincere, for a
moment.*

*'If we wished it hard enough, maybe we could,' I say. 'If we wished
it enough to put down all the other things we have in our hands.'*

*Something seems to beetle about in Neil's brain. Then he shakes his
head and changes tack.*

'Tell me about Johnny,' he says. 'How did you meet him?'

Seven

I spent most of the next week at the Community. I think Mum and Dad were glad I wasn't hanging around at home the whole time – they were happy I had a friend to be with.

The morning after that first sleepover Dad came in his car to pick me up. I had said I would walk back but I think he wanted to check the place out. James was in the front garden, where Chris and several others were hoeing around the plants, when Dad pulled up. James shook Dad's hand, and they chatted, man to man, while inside I gathered my few belongings. Dowdie was coming with me, back to my house, so we could spend another day together.

I don't know what they were talking about, James and my dad, but I could see they were getting on well. Soon they were laughing, a loud, male laugh.

Dowdie and I jumped in the back of the car but it took some minutes for Dad to tear himself away from his new friend. Finally, as he turned away, James saw me staring at him – and winked.

'What a place!' Dad said, as we drove back to the town. 'Fancy living out here. Must be worth a fortune. Nice guy though. He's your dad?' This to Dowdie. To my immense surprise, she said: 'Yes. Yes, he is.'

'And there's a whole bunch of you living there,' he said.'

'That's right,' Dowdie said. 'Twenty at the moment. It changes. People come and go.'

Dad was in a good mood. He put a Dire Straits CD in the car stereo, turned the volume up and wound his window down. He dropped us outside our house, and then headed off to work. Mum and Justin were already long gone.

'I didn't know James was your dad,' I said. 'You never told me.'

'You never asked. Anyway, it doesn't make any difference to anything. He and Mum aren't together – haven't been for years.'

'And you don't call him Dad,' I said, gently. I was still a little intimidated by Dowdie. I was afraid of upsetting her – making her angry.

'No. He can't treat me differently from the others,' she said. 'He can't have favourites. It's part of his mission.'

Even his own daughter? I didn't say anything more though. I could sense she didn't want to talk about it, shaking her head, raising invisible hackles. I met her mum, Eliza, on my second visit. She was spectacular – tall and gaunt with a dry, tanned and rather lined complexion and a mane of red and brown dreadlocks tied in a mighty ponytail. She wore no make-up and simple, hippyish clothes. She and Dowdie spoke to each other like friends, like any other two adults living in the Community. I admired it, to start with, this cool, amicable distance between them. No heated mother-daughter intimacy, no stifling weight of expectation.

Anyway, once Dad had reported back to Mum they were perfectly content to let me spend as much time at the Community as I wanted. Presumably it was better than loafing at home with just the telly and computer for company.

At the weekend I spent Saturday shopping with Mum but disappeared off with Dowdie the following day. On Sunday night, we appeased my parents by staying for dinner and that night Dowdie slept at our house. We had become inseparable.

The second week, as August dawned, a thunderstorm broke over the town, and we had two hours of torrential rain. The parched drains, choked with rubbish, quickly flooded and water covered the roads. By the morning the water had gone and the sky was a flat, beaten blue. It was as hot as ever. I became a member of the Community, near enough. Every few nights I went home but in spirit, I had signed up without reservations. I got to know the other residents better. I helped them tend the gardens and the animals. I joined the communal meals, listened to James. Most of the time though, I just hung out with Dowdie. We walked for miles, read books, talked, talked and talked. A metamorphosis was taking place – for both of us. As though in the heated forge of our friendship, two new beings were created. At the outset, Dowdie was the leader – she talked the most, made many of our decisions – but I realised this experience was just as new for her. She had never had a friend before. Growing up in the Community, home-schooled, she had always been surrounded by adults. Perhaps this explained her peculiarly grown-up and serious manner. She had no experience of twenty-first-century-girl world at all. To anyone else my age, she would seem a little – freakish? Passionate and proud, she wouldn't fit in easily. She had never had a friend to mess around with, to make her laugh. And we laughed a lot. The more we were together, the more we laughed, till we drove everyone else – at home and at the Community – mad with the sound of it.

Then, at the end of the second week, Dowdie's mum announced out of the blue that she was taking her daughter to

Glastonbury for a couple of days. Dowdie protested (familial strife after all) but to no avail. I walked home on my own that day, utterly bereft.

I didn't know what to do with myself. The two days stretched out like a desert in front of me. I suppose I could have gone to the Community on my own – I was always welcome – but it wouldn't be the same without Dowdie. Bored and miserable, I returned to my old pursuits, hiding away in my black bedroom with my music and books.

I stayed inside all the first day, read till my head ached, and went to bed early. The following day, a Friday, I returned to my familiar old haunt, the bridge over the river by Mortimore's Wood. Beneath me, the water flowed, as always, temptingly cool in the burning heat. The soft weed undulated. One hour merged into another.

'You'll get sunburnt.' Converse-wearing feet at the end of two long, thin black legs poked through the railings. A tall boy plopped down beside me, his legs dangling over the river, beside mine. Choppy black hair, pale, narrow face – I'd seen him before, early in the morning, on my way to meet Dowdie. My thoughts tumbled over each other in a horrible shock. I was embarrassed, excited, mortified all at once. Who was he? What was he doing? I looked around, for his mates, for people laughing. He was listening to music through an iPod, but now he stuck it in his pocket.

'I like your hair,' he said. 'You've changed it, haven't you. It looks gorgeous. In fact,' he scrutinised me, 'you look quite different.'

No one, certainly no one other than my parents, had ever told me any part of me was gorgeous before. He said it easily, a cool matter of fact. My stomach turned over. I thought I might be sick.

My brain seized up. But the boy carried on talking, as though he hadn't noticed my failure to respond.

'Where's your friend today? I've seen the two of you about the place.'

'She's gone to Glastonbury,' I blurted. 'With her mum.'

'Johnny,' he said. 'The name's Johnny.'

'Amber.'

We sat in silence for a moment. I realised he had – a posh accent.

'Where d'you go to school?'

'Oh.' He frowned. 'You won't know it. I go to a private school in Yorkshire.'

'What, a boarding school?'

'Yeah.' He laughed, dismissive. 'Long way to go to school every day.'

I glanced at him, trying to look without being too obvious. He had a long, elegant, entrancing face. A line drifted into my mind . . . *I met at eve the Prince of Sleep, His was a still and lovely face* . . . Johnny, oblivious, reached into his pocket and drew out a packet of Polos. Only three remained. He offered me one, put the other two in his mouth, and threw the scrap of paper and foil out from the bridge and into the river with a violent sweep of his arm.

'No!' I cried out, unthinking. Too late, his rubbish was out of reach, drifting down to the water. It came to rest on the surface of the river, and floated downstream for a moment or two before sinking into the water.

'Why did you do that? You mustn't throw rubbish in the river!'

'Why not?' he said. 'The world's full of rubbish. What does it matter, one bit more?'

'It does matter! The river's beautiful.'

Johnny leaned back on his elbow, a lazy smile on his face. 'So what should I do? Put it in a bin, so someone else can stuff it in a big hole we've dug in the ground and bury it? The rubbish will still be there – it's just that you won't see it,' he said. 'The world's a garbage heap. Might as well be honest about it.'

I just stared at him, helpless.

'I've upset you now,' he said. 'Well, I'm sorry about that. You'll just have to get used to me.' He rubbed his hair with the palm of his hand.

'It's too bloody hot,' he said. 'D'you want to come to my place?'

My stomach lurched again. 'What?'

'My place – d'you want to come? Or will you sit here all day?'

Confusion again, words jammed in my throat. Was he serious? Did he really want me to go with him? Was it safe? Should I trust him? Maybe it was some kind of horrible trick. These thoughts climbed one on top of another, but my voice seemed to make a decision on its own.

'OK,' I said.

Johnny walked fast and I scuttled to keep up. He led us back into town, through a narrow gateway in a high wall to a huge old house, between the river and the town centre. I had probably walked past it a thousand times, and never noticed it before. The house was largely obscured by half a dozen ancient pine trees. Once inside the gloomy garden, the sound of the endless traffic was muted.

Johnny smiled to see me standing in awe before the towering pile of Victorian gothic, with its dark, stained-glass windows and a turret. 'It's quite a place,' he said. We scrunched across weedy gravel to the back door, which wasn't locked. Johnny just opened the door and I stepped into a vast kitchen. It was dark inside, full of green light as though underwater. The house was silent.

'Your parents at work?' I said. Huge cupboards, ranks of copper pans, a stove the size of a small car – but all rather shabby and neglected. Red wine rings dappled the old oak kitchen table. Dishes crammed the porcelain sink.

'They're on holiday, in Greece,' he said. 'Gone to Ithaca for three weeks.'

'What – you're on your own? Why didn't you go?'

'They didn't want me to go. And frankly, I didn't want to go either.' His voice was perfectly level. His tone suggested – distaste?

'How old are you?' I blurted.

'Sixteen. As of last week. Anyway, I'm not entirely on my own. The housekeeper comes in every day, believe it or not. She's supposed to be keeping an eye on me – in theory.'

'But – aren't you lonely? Isn't it scary being on your own?'

'I'm always on my own,' he said, simply.

'Even at school?'

'Even then.' Johnny went to a cupboard, took out two mugs and a cafetiere. 'At school everyone calls me an emo fag,' he said. 'But I don't care. Stuff them, I say. D'you want coffee Amber? It's good. Might as well use it. Unless you'd like some wine. They've got bloody good wine too, *les parents*. Make the most of it, while they're away.'

He was so very cool and calm, putting the kettle on, spooning out quantities of his parents' inestimable ground coffee. When the water had boiled, he filled the cafetiere and put it on a tray with the mugs and milk, and a packet of cakes from Waitrose. Then he picked up the tray and made for the door.

'Come on,' he said. 'We'll go to my room.' He vanished into the corridor, so I had no choice but to follow. (Of course I had a choice; I could just leave the house – but why would I want to do that?)

I couldn't work him out. If a sixteen-year-old boy asks a girl to his room, doesn't that suggest something? And yet Johnny didn't give the impression he had any ulterior agenda; he sounded – perfectly innocent.

The house matched the kitchen – oversized antique furniture, oil paintings, framed black and white photographs of characters who might have stepped from the films of the 1940s. And over everything, a dustiness, a slight air of neglect. The carpet on the stairs needed replacing. Over the landing, a window of wine and emerald coloured stained-glass yielded an eerie light.

'This way,' Johnny said. Strangely, his own room was locked. He put the tray down on the floor to fish in his back pocket for a key to open it.

Johnny's room wasn't dusty. It was huge and white, with a high ceiling and a fireplace. A new carpet of black cord on the floor, and pride of place in the bay window, acres of desk and a giant computer screen. Beside it, the slick, matt-black computer equipment – a stack, printer, flat-bed scanner, cameras and lenses.

I looked around. A double bed, a sofa and comfy chair, also black, and half a dozen pictures on the wall. Framed photos, mostly. One – half a cow in a tank of formaldehyde.

'Damien Hirst,' I said. 'You like his work.'

'Yes,' he said, pouring the coffee. 'I don't imagine you like it. What do you go for? The impressionists?'

The impressionists, apparently, were not cool.

'I don't know much about art,' I said. 'But I don't like Damien Hirst. In fact, I hate his work.'

'Why?'

'He has no respect for life – for the animal's spirit. He just uses it – treats it like a *thing*. No dignity. In fact it makes me sick.'

I don't know what made me so bold, talking to Johnny. I didn't know him at all and I was shaking in my boots, to be alone in a room with someone like him. Perhaps in some perverse way, it was nerves that prompted the outburst. Still, I shut up, in a panic. Had I upset him? Would he not like me any more? I turned to face him.

'Do you think perhaps that is what his work is about?' he said. 'Maybe it says something about how we regard animals. Do you think a chicken in a battery farm is any less *a thing* than a cow in a plastic box? Only when you're tucking into your chicken bucket or pulling on your leather boots you're not confronted with the fact.'

'Even if I believed that,' I said, 'why would I want it on my wall?'

'Then don't put it on your wall,' he said, shrugging. 'How d'you take your coffee?'

I didn't relax for a moment, stricken with nerves, acute with excitement. I felt like a kid at a glamorous grown-ups' party. In my head I was already telling Dowdie about the adventure – the strange, beautiful sixteen-year-old boy who had approached me, out of the blue, and invited me to his house.

Johnny's only interest was art, he said – specifically photographic art. He turned on the computer, logged on to the Deviant Art website, and showed me his gallery. His work was stunning. Scary, yes. Something disturbing, something – perhaps appropriately – deviant. Once he'd loaded the gallery, he gestured for me to sit in the big office chair at the desk and passed me the mouse.

'Have a look around,' he said. 'See what you think.'

The first picture, his latest work, was a grainy sepia image of rooks, like bits of burnt black paper, circling over the curled skeleton of a baby. The tiny bone hand gripped a bright, white daisy, the one spot of clear, luminous colour in the stew of murky images. It was beautiful, oddly. Some quality of the picture stirred a peculiar kind of sadness.

'They're photo manipulations,' he said. 'I take all sorts of images, use stock pictures from the Internet, textures and drawings I scan in, and weave them all together.'

I wondered, had he shown these to anyone before? Of course, he had his fans on the Deviant Art website – other deviant artists with contrived nicknames who left admiring comments about his work. But a real, flesh and blood, present person? I wanted to ask, but didn't dare.

The next picture was just as striking. The same web of sepia shadows, a sky marked with an arcane Latin script, louring over a broken city where a little boy walked with a pale golden violin in his hand. The boy's face was smeared, but he had a mouth like a red rosebud. Like the first picture, it made me shiver, pierced me with sadness so my eyes filled with tears. How had he done it, folded so much feeling into his clever web of images? Of course I'd seen photo manipulations before. Several of the eye-lined, arty types at school did it too. Some had pages on Deviant Art. But much of it was clumsy or trying to be too clever. They were – what? First efforts maybe. Johnny had moved into a different realm.

I browsed through the gallery. He had over a hundred pictures posted, and they were all amazing. I clicked on one after another, filling the supersize screen with his sad, beautiful pictures. I sensed he was waiting for me to respond, but I didn't know what to say. So I carried on looking.

'They're fabulous,' I said. It was a lame assessment. Johnny loomed over me, restless and fidgeting. I sensed he yearned for a more sensitive appreciation.

'I've never seen anything like this,' I plunged on. 'They're the best I've seen. They're stunning.'

'It's OK,' he interrupted, with a strange grin. 'Don't go on. I know you like them – I know you *got* them. I could see it in your face. You had tears in your eyes.'

The rest of the afternoon Johnny, the computer and I spent together, checking out pictures, by Johnny and his favourite photographers and artists. He was animated, talking about them, explaining what he liked and didn't like. His long, thin body was always on the move, burning with energy.

'This stuff,' I said, gesturing at the computer and all his equipment. 'It must have cost a fortune.'

'Yes,' Johnny said. 'As you will have guessed, Mummy and Daddy have plenty of money. Not much of anything else, unfortunately. But they give me the cash to get what I want. It keeps me out of trouble.'

He gave me no clue about his feelings for his parents, except for a slight steely light in his eyes. When he talked about them, his voice was perfectly calm and under control. Was he really glad they'd gone to Greece without him?

'So you must have done your GCSEs then. How'd it go?' Somehow, the presence of the computer, like some discreet intermediary, made it easier to talk to Johnny. When I asked this question, I was still staring at the screen. I didn't have to look at him. 'I expect you'll get a string of A stars, if you go to a posh boarding school.'

'No. I messed them up,' he said.

'Everyone says that.' I was teasing and sceptical, sensing that Johnny was perhaps unusually clever. But he didn't answer, just shook his head and brushed my comment away.

I was expected home at six o'clock, and reluctantly I told him

I'd have to go. I didn't want to leave – afraid this enchanted afternoon was a one-off, that I might not see him again. Perhaps I had not lived up to his expectation – not thought of good things to say, not displayed enough precocious talent to maintain his interest.

He guided me downstairs to the kitchen and the back door. When we parted he held out his hand, which I shook, gravely. His skin was cool and dry. Fine, black hairs grew on the back of his hand; his fingers were very long, the nails scrupulously clean.

'It's been a pleasure meeting you, Amber,' he said. 'D'you want to come around again tomorrow? Are you busy?'

Thoughts, like cogs, ground against each other inside my mind. Tomorrow I was seeing Dowdie again. Dad was dropping me off at the Community in the morning. I couldn't let Dowdie down, and anyway, I was dying to see her.

'I've— I'm busy tomorrow,' I said in a rush. 'I'm meeting up with my friend. We made an arrangement. I'm really sorry – I'd love to otherwise.'

'OK.' Johnny shrugged. 'No worries. Another time then. Here – I'll give you my mobile number. Give me a call.'

Eight

'I understand there were experiments,' Neil says. We've been talking for two hours now. I am getting tired, and Mum is fretting on her seat, looking at her watch. Neil doesn't look tired and I sense he is just getting into his stride. Of course, we have only scratched the surface. There is so much more to tell. Neil is like a lion – no, not a lion, a jackal perhaps, one of those scavenging dogs. He prowls around his prey, taking his time, content to wait, and wait, and wait, for the right opportunity, for the moment of weakness, when he will move in and make the kill.

'Look,' Mum interrupts. Her voice is shrill. She doesn't want to offend the handsome police officer, the authority figure, but her maternal instincts are strong. 'It's getting on for five. Could we finish soon? I've got to get home. My husband will be back from work soon, and there's my son to pick up.'

Neil nods. 'I'm so sorry,' he says, all polite concern. 'I hadn't realised the time. Look – I'll call for another cup of tea. Please – feel free to call your husband. We won't be much longer.'

Mum is irritated and makes a peculiar squawking sound. But what can she do? She's not the sort to cause a fuss. Neil calls for refreshments, offers her the phone, and then turns back to me.

'Right,' he says. 'Where were we? Experiments, yes?'

'I don't know what you mean,' I say, shaking my head. 'What sort of experiments?'

'You know – a special education for you Amethyst children – attempts to bring out your latent skills.'

'Ah, yes,' I say. 'They weren't experiments – they were lessons.' In response to Neil, I am adopting a rather stylised way of talking, like a role play – a discreet little drama. Is he like this at home, I wonder? Does he talk to Mrs Neil as though they're living in a serious cop drama?

'Then tell me about these lessons,' Neil says. 'What did they involve?'

I look at my knees, and smile. How ridiculous this will sound.

'Well, James thought we might have telepathic abilities. He wanted us to focus on extrasensory perception. One afternoon at the Community, out in the garden, he blindfolded Dowdie and me. He said: "I want you to follow me and find me. You mustn't look. I want you to focus on your inner vision, to open your mind." So Dowdie and I had to count to ten, and then we had to find him, with our eyes covered.'

I look at Neil, daring him to smirk. His face remains serious, but I hear my mother snort.

'How did it work out?' he asks.

I cast my mind back, to the stifling heat of that summer afternoon. I feel the slick of sweat on my skin, the dry grass under my bare feet. At first, Dowdie and I were stricken with giggles. Then Dowdie composed herself – instructed me this had to be taken seriously.

'It was strange,' I say. 'At first, I was just stumbling around and afraid I'd step on something, or walk into a fence. I lost track of

Dowdie quickly – couldn't work out where she was. Then, because I couldn't see, all my other senses were heightened – the skin on the soles of my feet and on my face. I could smell everything – and yes, I could "see" James. His presence. He was standing near the gate into the paddock. I held out my hands in front of me and put them on his chest.

'Very softly, James said: "Well done, Amber. I knew you could do it. There's nothing you can't do, if you have enough faith." I could feel the rhythm of his heart, beating in his chest like a signalling drum in a jungle. I believed in his power, then. I could feel it pass into me, like a tide.

"'Do you believe in me now, Amber?" he said. "I know you've been polite up to now – that you've listened without entirely committing yourself. But it's time to trust yourself – to make a commitment to me. Are you ready to do that?"

'My eyes were still blindfolded. I don't know where Dowdie was – I guess she was still stumbling around the garden. I could smell the heated, overblown vegetation and James's warm, clean body. I was afraid for a moment – vulnerable, because I couldn't see. Then the worry drained away – I just kind of let it go – and all of a sudden I was light and free.

"'I do believe in you," I said. "I do. I really do."

'James put his hand over mine. Then he removed the blindfold. "Then there's no going back," he said.'

For a moment I have lost myself in the recounting of this little narrative. Now I return to the nondescript police station room. Neil is staring at me intently. My mother, also, has her eyes fastened on my face and she is very pale. She wants to speak, but the police officer raises his hand. I can read the question in her face, but Neil diverts us, for a moment.

'There were other lessons?' he says.

'Yes. He'd draw pictures on pieces of paper, and then we'd have to try and read his mind, and work out what he'd drawn. I'd close my eyes and try to repeat his picture on my own piece of paper.'

'And how well did that work?'

'Surprisingly well. Remarkably well, actually.'

'Who did it best? You or Dowdie?'

'Me. I think it annoyed her, but there was no doubt about it.'

Neil sits up straight. Beyond the window, cars are queued up at the entrance to the industrial park – the drones heading for home. Clouds, the colour of clay, clog the horizon. Mum's fresh cup of tea cools, untouched, on the table.

'You know, this kind of apparent telepathy can be achieved by other means,' Neil says. His voice is gentle – a dad telling his kid that fairies aren't real. He doesn't want to disappoint me.

'With the right skills, someone can manipulate you into drawing what they want you to draw. They use word cues – a kind of subconscious suggestion, so you draw what they're telling you without you even realising that's what's happening.'

'Like Derren Brown? I've seen his shows,' I say. Neil gives a little, impatient harrumph. I don't think he knows what to make of me. Am I a gullible convert, a cult victim – or am I a sceptic? The answer is very complicated and probably I don't know it myself.

'Perhaps you were better at the telepathy game than Dowdie—'

'Because I'm more suggestible?' I interrupt. 'Because I was easier to manipulate?'

'Yes!' Mum bursts out, unable to contain herself. 'Exactly that! My God, you were a little fool! If I'd known what that man was like, I'd have never—'

'Mrs Renalden, please,' Neil cuts her off. He doesn't want motherly passion upsetting his control of the situation.

'Look, it's getting late,' he says. 'We'll wind up for today, but I want *you both to come back tomorrow, so we can continue.' Then he sits forward again, elbows on thighs, hands clasped.*

'There's one more important question,' he says. 'I just need to check. And I'm sure your mother wants to know the answer to this one too. Amber – did James Renault ever behave in a physically inappropriate way with you?'

I stare at Neil, and then at my mother. The room seems cold. Have they switched off the heating, now so many people are going home? I rub my arms and stare through the window at the tight clot of cars waiting for their turn at the mini-roundabout.

'Amber,' Mum says. Her voice contains an unexpected sharpness. Is she angry with me?

'You mean, did he molest me? Was he a paedo?' I am abrupt and my voice is a little mocking and crude. I don't know how else to get the words out. 'No!' I say. 'Why do you have to think that? No he wasn't.' Then, to Mum:

'You think someone's only going to be interested in me to get that*? Why do you find it so hard to believe that he liked me – just for me?'*

'Because of what happened,' Mum says. She's looking at the floor now. Her face looks a little grey and tired. Neil steps in – taking control again.

'Thanks, Amber,' he says. 'I didn't think so, but I had to be sure. There are all sorts of ways this kind of man exerts control.'

He stands up. 'I'm sorry to have kept you both so long. I know it's tough, but it is important. Please come again tomorrow – same time.'

'I can't come tomorrow – I won't get another afternoon off work,' Mum says.

'What about your husband? Can he bring Amber?'

Mum fiddles with her handbag. As it happens, Dad isn't working tomorrow so he could take me. However I don't think Mum wishes to miss my confession. She wants to know it all.

'OK.' She is reluctant, but can see no other way round it. Neil shakes her hand. At the back of the room, the note-taker stops scribbling and the tape machine goes off with a click. The session is over.

Nine

Johnny's pictures floated in my mind as I walked home from his house. The bleak mood of his work overlaid the town, as though I had briefly stepped into his personal world and was seeing through his eyes. A film of sepia shadows covered the roads and cars and houses. I had that feeling again, as I did first walking with Dowdie. A rook on top of the cinema, a plastic bag torn on a rose bush, possessed a particular significance, as though they were more than themselves – and had become symbols of some other, higher order that I sensed but couldn't understand. Some joker had changed the letters on the big sign above the cinema advertising this week's films, so it said *Chav Centre*. A queue of short, bulky, middle-aged women, sweltering in the shade, waited for the bingo hall to open. I was very tired, my nerves strained, but excitement burned inside me. Was this falling in love – my hands shaking, my stomach flipping and the peculiar rush of emotion I felt whenever I recalled a vivid moment of the afternoon?

Although I will be in Year 11 after the holidays, I will confess I had never had a boyfriend, or even been asked out by anyone. It had never bothered me that much. I wasn't part of the cool crowd, all of whom had boyfriends constantly in the frame. I had never been interested in anyone I knew at school, and certainly none had given any indication they were keen on me. I had thought about it from time to time, when I was reading about relationships, or just lying in bed with the lights off and my mind drifting. I'm sure it sounds sad, but the only people I'd had crushes on didn't even exist; they were one step removed even from the pop idols so many of the other girls sighed over. For a month I couldn't stop thinking about Lawrence of Arabia, played by Peter O'Toole. Another time, the man was Louis from *Interview with the Vampire* – the book, that is, not the film. Both times, I imagined them, a second voice in my head, talking with me. I dreamed what it would be like to be out in the desert with Lawrence, or in a grand old southern American house with Louis, or riding with him across our estate. Sometimes I imagined so hard, I could almost conjure them up, their warm physical masculine presence. I know this sounds sad – like I'm some kind of desperate freak, but that is just the way it was. Nothing, shall we say, *untoward* ever happened in my passionate fantasy friendships. Not even a kiss. That was far too alien to imagine.

When I was younger, you see, I'd been very slight and agile. I was a little birdlike creature with a waist my father could put his hands around. I had bony legs and arms, and an excess of physical energy – always running round and jumping about. Then, just a year ago, in a Citizenship class, I had to present a speech on waste recycling. The speech – all our speeches – were videoed and afterwards we watched ourselves on screen. It was a horrible shock. My mental image of myself didn't match up with the girl I saw talking on the television. I wasn't birdlike any more. I wasn't exactly fat, but it was as though a sleeve of flesh had been pulled over me, without me even noticing quite what had happened. I was too big – there was too much clumsy stuff. I felt, obscurely, that some nasty trick had been played on me. I wanted that clean, spare, continent little body back, not this unpredictable mass with its unpleasant emissions and stinks and stains. Some of the girls wore their new bodies with obvious pleasure and delight, baring their belly buttons, revealing their limbs. I just hid mine away, covered it up in baggy black clothes. The idea that someone might one day want to put their arms around me filled me with a peculiar sense of shame.

Except? Except that Johnny had come along, and even thinking about him was a thrill and replaying the events of the afternoon made me hot and cold all over. In fact, the more I thought about it, the more intense my feelings became, like a fire I could feed with my imaginings.

When I got home, Mum was dishing up dinner. She asked me how I was, and what I'd been up to. I told her about Johnny – I just couldn't resist the opportunity to talk about him – and his house, and his amazing artistic skills. Mum was fussing about with some kind of pasta dish and I don't know how much she was taking in.

'Well I'm very glad you've found some nice friends,' she said at last. 'I've had a horrible day. Everything's gone wrong. Nasty customers, late orders, me in the middle of it getting all the blame.'

She did look worn out. When we'd eaten, she and Dad washed up. I knew I should offer to help, since they'd both been at work all day and I'd been (as Dad would say) lounging about and enjoying myself. But I couldn't bring myself to do it. Instead I disappeared to my bedroom, got out my journal and wrote down, in a great rush so I wouldn't forget a detail, everything that had happened. Then I went to the study, turned on the computer and visited Johnny's Deviant Art gallery. I printed copies of two pictures, and one tiny photo Johnny had posted of himself. The quality was poor, on our old black and white printer, but it was good enough to remind me. The picture of Johnny was obscure – a slanting shot of his cheekbone with the inky thatch of hair on top. Still, I cut them out and stuck them in my journal alongside my account of the day. Beneath his picture, I wrote: *The Prince of Sleep*.

I didn't fall asleep for ages. Even with the covers off and the window open, my room felt like an oven. My body sweated and wriggled and itched. I thought about Dowdie and James Renault. I thought about the Amethyst children and the community. But most of all I thought about Johnny, Johnny, Johnny.

Dad woke me up early, so I could get a lift with him to the Community. I felt flat and heavy, exhausted by the fevered night, so I took a long, cool shower and washed my hair.

'You look tired,' he said, as I got in the car. 'It must be hard work, doing nothing all day. You should try working for a living.' This with an annoying, cheery grin. I didn't answer. Dad reached out his big, square hand and planted it on my knee. He gave my leg a squeeze.

'Hardly seem to see you these days,' he said. 'I know you've got your friends now, but I do miss you. We used to be such good pals. When I came home from work you'd climb all over me and you'd talk to me for hours. D'you remember?'

I shook my head. His voice sounded wistful but his reminiscence embarrassed me. They were not my memories but his, and harked back to a past I couldn't clearly remember.

'By God, I'm looking forward to our holiday,' he said. 'I could do with one. It'll be great. We're going back to the resort we went to three years ago. D'you remember? Great for you kids. Lots of activities. You loved it. And lots of lounging by the pool for me.'

My heart plummeted. The holiday. I'd entirely forgotten about it. The last week in August and the first few days of September, returning just before I went back to school. I didn't want to go. How could I leave Dowdie, and Johnny?

Dad continued to enthuse about the holiday and I didn't say anything about my own glum thoughts. How could I possibly get out of it? Unlike Johnny's parents, mine wouldn't leave me at home on my own, no way.

The car pulled up outside the Community. Dad got out of the car, and followed me to the house, keen to speak to his new pal James. I slipped inside, to the kitchen, while Dad and James chatted in the hallway. They were talking about computers, I think. Dad had slipped into his jovial salesman mode and was suggesting the Community might want to install some different kind of system. Eventually, he called out a goodbye and departed.

James followed me into the kitchen. 'How're you doing?' he said.

'OK. Hot, and tired. How are you?'

He didn't just say fine, like everyone else does. He thought for a moment, and said: 'I've missed my Amethyst children – you and Dowdie. I have missed your company, and the qualities you bring to the Community. So – welcome back.'

I smiled, and blushed. I loved his direct way of speaking, but I still wasn't used to it.

'But you look sad about something,' James said. 'What's up? What's the problem?'

I smiled again and stared at the floor, disconcerted he could read me so easily.

'Oh, it's nothing much. We're going away on holiday in about a week, to Majorca. I'd forgotten all about it and I don't want to go. I want to be with Dowdie. When I get back the school term will start and I won't be able to see her so much.'

James frowned. 'Yes I quite understand. Do you think they'd let you forgo this holiday and stay here with us instead? I think I've established a rapport with your dad – I could have a word with him. What do you reckon?'

A golden possibility. I could stay at the Community, with Dowdie. I wouldn't have to leave. Thoughts folded over one another in my mind. First of all, my parents would be really upset I didn't want to go. This holiday, as they would see it, was a rare opportunity for quality time together. They'd also paid for me to go and I think they'd find it hard to understand why I'd miss out on two weeks at a glamorous holiday resort. But I didn't want to go. Why should I go to please them when my dearest wish was to stay? Feelings conflicted, like a physical shredding in my chest.

'Yes, please,' I said. 'Would you mind? Talk to my dad. He likes you.'

James looked away with an odd little smile on his face. 'I'll do what I can,' he said. Then he looked at me again, very directly, and put his hand on the top of my arm: 'I think it's important for you to spend as much time here as possible. This is a critical time in your development. You've made a commitment but you have a long, long way to go and you need the right environment to blossom further. Two weeks away could be . . . a problem. You're vulnerable. You could come under the influence of other, less positive people. D'you understand what I'm saying?'

I nodded. He had a lovely, smooth, grave voice, and the way he looked into my face suggested he could see into my heart and soul.

Then he broke away, and stood up.

'Dowdie will be back in about an hour,' he said. 'Make yourself at home. Perhaps we might do some work together in the afternoon.'

In fact, Dowdie wasn't back for three hours. Perhaps she had inherited her always-late gene from her mother, who it turned out was to blame for the delay, with her shilly-shallying in Glastonbury. I passed the time mooching in the garden and talking with the guys in the workshop, as they laboured over their carpentry. Then I went inside and lay on Dowdie's bed in her little garret room. I fell asleep, for a while, soaking up the peaceful atmosphere of the house. And it was so deliciously cool, the thick walls keeping out the sun's aggressive heat.

I think I sensed their return before I physically heard them, because I woke up with a jump. I lay still for a moment or two, disorientated. Then came Dowdie's voice, distant from the ground floor, shouting something at her mother, and Eliza's strong voice in response. I sat up on the bed, and waited, not wanting to step into the middle of a family squabble. But Dowdie came clomping up the stairs and stormed into the room. She was taken aback to see me – perhaps not pleased.

'It's you,' she said ungraciously.

'We arranged it,' I said. 'Honestly Dowdie, I told you I'd be here when you got back, to meet you.'

Fury filled her face. An almost tangible black cloud hung about her, as though Dowdie's anger gave off a kind of emotional smoke.

'Evil, miserable bitch,' she snapped, striding back and forth in her room. Was she talking about me? It scared me, the intensity of her rage. I didn't dare speak.

'How could she? How could she?' Dowdie strode up and

down in the little room, seeming to fill it up. 'After all this time, how could she think about it? Selfish! She only thinks of herself.'

'Dowdie, what is it?' This offered quietly. I was afraid her anger was indiscriminate – that she might turn on me, shout at me – even hit me. She glanced over and her eyes flashed.

'What is it? My mother, that's what. She's got a *man*. She's got a new man in her life, and guess what? Just 'cos she's got this *boyfriend*, just because she thinks she's *in love*, that gives her the right to turn my life upside down. She wants us to leave here and live with him.'

'That's why you had to go to Glastonbury with her,' I said. All the pieces fell into place and my heart plummeted. Dowdie would move away and I would lose her. A door would close shut on these short, magic weeks together and I would be cast out, once again, into the cold grey world.

'She wanted to *introduce* me to him,' Dowdie said, still pacing.

I said weakly: 'Was he nice?'

'*Nice*? I don't care if he's nice or not – *I don't want to go!*' She stopped, clenched her fists and stamped her foot. She looked like Justin having a strop – but very much more scary.

'I don't want you to go either,' I said. Tears prickled. 'You're the best friend I've ever had. I'm crazy about you. I don't want to lose you.'

Dowdie took two or three deep breaths, clenching and unclenching her fists. Her head gave an angry little shake, and then she dropped down, to sit on the bed beside me. She put her long, slim arms around me and hugged me so hard I thought my shoulders would break.

'I'm not going,' she hissed. 'She can't force me. I'll refuse to go. James'll sort something out. I'll talk to him. I won't go!'

We stayed in her bedroom another hour or more, talking

about Dowdie's – *our* – dilemma. Eliza had met this new man while attending a herbalism course in Glastonbury. New Man owned a smallholding, a couple of miles out of town, and he had plenty of money, accumulated during two decades in the music business. Not a rock star though – some high-flying sound engineer.

'But he's *old*,' she said. 'His hair's grey. He must be *fifty*. And he was all over Eliza – it was vile.'

So we concocted fanciful plans for her escape. She'd come to live with me (I couldn't imagine it – any more than I could imagine us keeping a tiger in the little house at Field View); she'd run away and live wild, off the land (oddly this was easier to imagine); we'd both run away and join a band of travellers, with a little caravan of our own.

'Why can't you stay here, and live with your dad?' I ventured, finally.

Dowdie shook her head. 'It's complicated,' she said. 'Eliza wants me with her. James is my dad – but his name isn't even on my birth certificate. It just says "unknown". They had a big fight and broke up when she was pregnant, and she didn't want anything to do with him. James disappeared, and didn't show up again until I was four. That's when he invited us to come and live with the Community. He was just setting it up then. He'd begun channelling, and the spirits had spoken through him, with warnings and prophecies. The spirits had told him about the Amethyst children, and that his own, lost daughter was one of them. So he came to find us.'

'And where were you?'

'We'd been living in Bristol, in a stinky little flat high up in a tower block. I don't remember much about it, to be honest. Mum had no job and no money. She hated the city and the flat.

So when James came back, and told her about his new path in life and the Community he had set up, she agreed to come and live here. Not as his partner, of course, just as another member of the Community. I was about four then.' Dowdie sighed, and collapsed back on the bed. She covered her face with her hands.

'I don't want to go,' she said. 'I asked Eliza if I could stay here, at the Community, but she wouldn't listen. We hardly ever argue. She always lets me do what I feel's right – but this time she was absolutely adamant. I don't understand, Amber. But I can't go now. I just couldn't bear it.'

She didn't say I was the reason she couldn't go, but she took one hand from her face and squeezed my arm tight.

I'd been bursting to tell her about Johnny ever since I'd met him but now the urge shrivelled away. It was strange. As soon as I was with Dowdie, Johnny's significance dwindled. I felt I had been rather stupid now, to have built him up so much in my mind – to have allowed myself to obsess after so brief an acquaintance. Dowdie was more important – more *real*.

'Let's go out,' Dowdie said. 'Shall we go into town?'

'Into town?' I repeated. 'I didn't think you liked town.' I couldn't imagine her hanging out in New Look or on the benches outside Wilkinsons.

'I feel like a change,' she said, abruptly jumping from the bed. 'And,' she allowed, 'there are some nice places in town. I want to go to a café for a milkshake. I want to get away from here. Specifically, I want to get away from *her*.'

Before we set off, we punked up – war paint and armour in readiness for battle. Lots of black eye-liner, beads and bangles. I had my habitual black, of course, but Dowdie had bright, clashing colours – silky purple leggings, a short red velvet skirt and a light cotton blouse printed madly with paisley. Her hair hung in long, coppery curls over her shoulders and she looked utterly mad and strange and beautiful. I was so proud of her, to be her friend, to be part of the Amber-and-Dowdie duo. Her mood lifted as we prepared.

We left the house without a goodbye and walked through the garden and out onto the road, ready for the hike into town. How quickly the A-and-D enchantment was renewed. As we walked and talked, our magical world wove itself around us again, where colours were brighter and tiny stones gleamed like pearls in our path, where the trees had spirits that whispered to us and at any moment an unseen door might open and lead us into an extraordinary adventure. I don't know quite how it happened. Most of the time we all succumb to the dreary everyday reality, the retail park/traffic jams/jobs/credit cards reality. Maybe the more of us give in to it, the more powerful it becomes and the easier it is for everyone to just sink in. On your own it's hard to believe in any other kind of world – because then you are one against everyone else, and probably you are mad, or everyone thinks you are. So you need at least one special person who steps outside with you, into the same Otherplace, and then it becomes a new reality. And that's where we walked, through the Amber-and-Dowdie world, in our mad clothes, with our cargo of stories and endless silly jokes that no one else would ever understand.

It wasn't quite so hot, that afternoon. Huge clouds trawled across the sky, covering the face of the sun from time to time and plunging us into welcome shadow. Town was busy, as always – pensioners buying vegetables, young mums with pushchairs, a stringy-haired traveller type strumming his guitar in a doorway, and lots of kids of course, school summer holiday kids with nothing to do but hang out in town with their mates and irritate pedestrians with their skateboards and bikes.

We attracted stares and jeers from them but Dowdie gave a proud toss of her head as we passed. We headed for the charity shops and spent an hour or so investigating racks of clothes. Dowdie said she got most of her outfits this way – and she certainly had an eye for how good an unpromising item might look once she had washed it and matched it up with some good companions.

She bought a T-shirt with an embroidered mermaid she said she would cut out and stitch onto something else, and a blouse patterned with yellow roses. I found a string of black plastic beads and a silver brooch in the shape of a half moon. Then we headed for a café, and sat outside it in the shade of a green-and-white striped umbrella. We both ordered milkshakes and admired our purchases.

A male voice said: 'Look at the camera.' Surprised, we both raised our heads, and a camera clicked. Dowdie scowled and snorted. Johnny stepped forward.

'Thank you, ladies,' he said. Then, without asking, he dropped into the seat opposite and took another picture of the two of us – Dowdie with her scowl, and me with a look of shock on my face.

'Hey Amber,' he said, putting the camera on the table.

Dowdie immediately turned to me. 'You know this guy?' It sounded like an accusation rather than a question. It is hard to describe the stew of emotions stirring inside me in that moment. Surprise, to see Johnny, and a mix of embarrassment and thrill to see him again after a night of long obsessing; a dash of guilt (why? Because Dowdie was annoyed by him?) and, I hate to admit it, a flash of jealousy. Maybe I didn't want Johnny to meet Dowdie. They were both such remarkable people, weren't they both bound to like each other much more than they liked me?

'Since Amber's clearly lost the power of speech, let me introduce myself. I'm Johnny,' he said.

But Dowdie didn't look impressed. She folded her arms and glared at him.

'Does he go to your school or something?' she said, still staring at Johnny.

'No. No he doesn't. We only met yesterday,' I said, almost apologetic.

Faced with such open animosity, I think most people would have slunk away, but Johnny seemed immune. He smiled. 'You're Dowdie,' he said. 'I have to say, you don't look in the slightest bit dowdy. In fact,' he picked up the camera and took another picture of her, 'you look perfectly magnificent.'

'It's incredibly rude taking pictures of people without asking their permission,' Dowdie snapped. 'Who the hell d'you think you are?'

Johnny laughed and put the camera down again. 'Sorry,' he said. 'Didn't mean to upset you.' I took the opportunity of his spat with Dowdie to stare at him again. It's strange how memory works. I had thought about him so often the night before his face had warped slightly in my memory, so seeing him in the flesh he didn't quite match up to my internal image. But now he was so *real* – so utterly, unpredictably present. I sipped my milkshake, because my mouth had gone dry. I couldn't think of the right thing to say but that didn't seem to matter because Dowdie and Johnny continued to argue with each other. I began to sense, however, that both were enjoying the argument. Dowdie's eyes were shining. Johnny was goading her a little but Dowdie was taking up the challenge. The air between them crackled with a curious electrical charge.

'Amber tells me you don't go to school,' he said. 'You got some kind of hippie freak parents?'

Dowdie gave me a furious glance and pursed her lips. 'What about you?' she said. 'Posh boy. Bet you go to a public school, right?'

'Guilty, as charged.' He gave a mock bow. 'We're all alcoholic fox-hunting homosexuals, of course. Every last man of us. So what about you? Bet your parents say you're too *special* to go to an ordinary school.'

'I bloody am,' she snapped. 'Presumably your parents send you to posh school so you don't have to mix with riff-raff – so you're better placed to climb to the top of the shit-heap.'

'Ah yes,' he said, with a teasing smile. 'The ascent of the shit-heap. Public school, Oxbridge, a job in the City maybe. The golden path. Aren't I lucky? Not like you. You'll be scrounging benefits with half a dozen kids while your hippie husband lies in bed smoking dope. Isn't it interesting how easily our lives can be mapped out?'

I thought Dowdie might spring at him, physically, across the table, because her body tensed and she squeezed her hands into fists. But something changed and her mood flipped, as though at a switch. Suddenly her body relaxed, and she erupted with laughter. Johnny grinned, and then he began to laugh too. They were so loud people sitting at nearby tables turned and stared. But I didn't laugh. It was as though I wasn't there. Neither Dowdie nor Johnny seemed to notice me at all and all the joy of the morning walk, and the glowing memories of my afternoon with Johnny, seemed to slide away and disappear. I had deluded myself.

When they had recovered, Johnny and Dowdie continued to converse. They were still antagonistic, but the argument had turned into a game. They moved closer together.

'I hate rich people,' Dowdie said. 'Really rich people – the upper class. It's weird isn't it, that they call themselves the upper class – as though they're higher in some way. Upper-class people are the descendants of people who stole the land and pretended they could own it. At one time no one owned the land – how can you? Can you fold it up and put it in your pocket? It was our birthright – the birthright of every human being. But the upper class enclosed it and chased people off and said they owned the forests and only they could hunt in them. It was the beginning of the end. They made slaves of the rest of us. Most of us are still slaves now.'

'You're right,' Johnny said. 'D'you know, my grandfather's brother – my great-uncle – is a hereditary peer. A lord! But don't you wonder how they did it? Maybe those ancestors of mine had more brains and courage than your peasants. After all, the lower orders allowed it to happen, didn't they? They gave their so-called birthright away. They let themselves become slaves. They didn't want responsibility for themselves, so they put themselves in the hands of the strong.'

It was weird, watching them talk from my cool distance. Dowdie was fierce and passionate, totally upfront. She believed every word she said, and her feelings were painted loud and clear in her face. In Johnny, though, I sensed the distance between his words and his heart. He was only speaking to annoy her, playing her like a fish, creating an intellectual argument I was sure he didn't actually believe. Unlike Dowdie, he dissembled. There was a space between his feelings and his argument.

Dowdie was still ranting. 'I bet you've had everything given to you on a plate. You've had a life of undeserved privilege. When I was little we lived in a horrible city-centre flat with damp in the walls, where heroin addicts slept on the concrete stairways. Mum couldn't go out after dark in case she got mugged by kids needing money for drugs.' She said this with some pride, as though her difficult beginning was a badge of honour. There was no mention, however, of the rather more salubrious surroundings she'd enjoyed for the last ten years, at the Community.

But Johnny's expression changed. His eyes darkened. He leaned in to the table and said in a low voice. 'You're a fool if you think privilege is all about money. Children can be needy in many ways, Dowdie, so before you get on your high horse please think about that.' The gap I had sensed between his heart and his words had closed. Now he looked serious.

'I was sent off to preparatory school when I was seven,' he said. 'This was a boarding school, two hundred miles away from home. I was just dropped off, and effectively abandoned by my parents, who never wrote or visited, to sink or swim with a hundred other seven year olds. At the end of the first term the housemaster put me on a train, on my own, and when I arrived home I got out of the train and waited for my parents to pick me up.

'The train got in at two-thirty in the afternoon, and I was still waiting there at the station all on my own at nine o'clock that evening. There I was, in my uniform, holding my bag, not making trouble, just as I'd been taught. Hour after hour, as hundreds of people came and went, walking by me without a word. It was December, nearly Christmas, and bitterly bloody cold. In the end one of the station staff noticed me in the dingy little waiting room and asked who I was and how I was getting home. They tried to phone my parents but they were out – had gone to a party, it turned out, drinking sherry and eating mince pies, having forgotten altogether about picking me up.

'The staff at the station didn't know what to do with me. Should they call the police? Social services? I think they were reluctant to do either, judging by my clothes that I was – as you say – *posh*. In they end they had no choice. It was gone eleven and my parents still out, so a social worker came to pick me up and I spent the night in a children's home.

'The next morning my mother came to pick me up. She was furious and embarrassed, but she put on a good show, apologising and joking with the staff about the *terrible mistake*, and how it wasn't her fault, and how they would sue the school and her poor dear son and all that. They weren't fooled though, the staff. I overheard one of them saying how it wasn't right – that my parents had got away with it, but if some other, more materially needy child had suffered the same way, they'd have been investigated or had their name put on a special register. All the way home, in the car, my mother was livid – as though it were my fault she'd forgotten to pick me up and I had purposely humiliated her in public among people she did not consider her equal.

'As you might imagine, I didn't have such a good Christmas that year. In fact, I was quite glad to get back to school again.'

He stopped talking and sat back in his chair. As the story unwound, I had forgotten about the café and the street, caught up in imagining the cold, lonely, seven-year-old Johnny, waiting in the station for all those hours. He glanced at me, I think the first time he'd looked my way since beginning his conversation with Dowdie, and a brief communication passed between us. He sensed my reaction to his story, perhaps, and my pain on his behalf. And for a moment, I saw how small and lost he was still, beyond the façade of his public school confidence, and the dark sense of humour that allowed him to duck and dive with so much cleverness.

Then the shutters went up. He lounged, a little self-conscious, and picked up his camera. Dowdie was, unusually, lost for words. I could see she was shocked.

'You're right,' she said at last. 'Obviously there are many ways children can be needy. It isn't all about money.'

Johnny doffed an imaginary hat, acknowledging her response. 'Can I take some more pictures now?' he said.

Ten

'Dad, I want to see the house again,' I say. Mum and Justin have just left, for work and school respectively. I have permission to miss the first week of school because of what happened, to help me get over the shock and so that I might, as they say, help the police with their enquiries. Mr Scholes, the headteacher, came round to the house and briefly spoke to my parents, granting leave of absence under these exceptional circumstances. He was kind to me, though as one of seventeen hundred pupils I wonder if he had even known of my existence before everything kicked off – before the newspaper coverage and the reporters ringing him for comments about his pupil's involvement. It's weird missing school – knowing the ceaseless noisy stream of days is continuing without me.

'I want to see the house,' I insist. Dad is tanned from his holiday in Majorca. His forehead and the front of his smooth, bald scalp are a glossy honey-brown. He loves the sun – soaks it up despite Mum's worries about melanoma.

'D'you think that's a good idea?' He's struggling a bit, my dad. He doesn't know what to say or do. He's never been in such a situation before and frankly, despite the show of Dad-ish competence, he's floundering. There's an unspoken suggestion in the air that I've *brought horrible disgrace on the family – that I've messed up. He doesn't know whether to be angry or compassionate. These last few days, he's been an uncomfortable mixture of both. I think he and Mum had been under the illusion that if you always do the right thing, then the universe will do right by you. I wonder how many times he wishes he'd insisted I go on the holiday with them?*

'Please, Dad,' I say. 'We can go on the way to the police station. We've got time. I just want to see it again.'

He sighs. I'm still his number one daughter after all, still the little girl who climbed all over him when he came home from work.

The weather has changed. Overnight, summer has folded up and packed its bags. These first September days are comparatively chilly. We drive along the dual carriageway, then head down the narrow lane to the village. Coarse, dry grass chokes the verges. Weeks of sun have leached the colour from the hedgerows. Unusually, Dad doesn't put any music on.

'Didn't you have any idea, what Renault was up to?' Dad says suddenly. I think he has been working up to the question.

'No – not to start with. Why should I? You met him too, Dad. Didn't you pick up anything?'

Dad shakes his head. Maybe he's kicking himself that he didn't spot anything untoward about James either.

We drive through the village and out the other side. The car pulls up outside what was once the Community. I unfasten my seatbelt and open the door. Dad remains where he is.

'Aren't you getting out?'

'No,' he says. 'I'll wait here. You be quick. We don't want to be late.' He turns on the car radio, and listens to the news. He doesn't even look out the window.

Police tape still bridles the gate. Stray ribbons of the stuff flap around the remains of the house. The thick walls are black, the windows shattered and vacant. I climb over the gate and slowly walk across the garden. The vegetable patch Chris and the others so lovingly tended has been utterly destroyed – burned and smoked and trampled underfoot. The perfume of the fire still lingers on the air. The roof has caved in, the doorway gapes. I peer inside, straining my senses for a hint of James's continuing presence. Where have they gone, the ones who had escaped? Some, I know, like Chris, have been questioned and released. Only a trusted inner circle had known the whole truth.

I hear the car's electric window open and Dad calls out: 'Come on – we've got to go.'

I turn around slowly. This is the last time. I shan't come back again. The burnt walls will be bulldozed. Perhaps, like the ancient armies of the Romans when they defeated and sacked Carthage, our modern authorities will curse this place and salt the ground so nothing will ever grow again.

Eleven

And so two became three. Dowdie invited Johnny to come with us to the Community the following day. He said he'd meet us there – not fancying the walk and having a scooter to transport himself.

I stayed the night with Dowdie, and Johnny was all she could talk about. Half the time she spent slating him, half the time she marvelled over him, his energy, his intelligence. She hadn't mentioned to him (and nor had I) that we were Amethyst children, though that evening, when Dowdie was in bed and I was lying on the camp-bed beside her, Dowdie speculated that Johnny might be one too. He was a misfit, wasn't he? A visionary, an artist?

I had a perverse desire to lower him in her estimation, so I told her, with a critical tone in my voice, about his love of abattoir art and his ugly littering. Dowdie, lover of all things natural, would surely find this behaviour unreasonable and abhorrent? But no – even these were signs Johnny had an unusually mature and unconventional mind. He was a radical, a free thinker. On and on she chattered, often repetitious, and my mood sank lower and lower. It had been inevitable, hadn't it, that

Dowdie and Johnny would like each other more than they liked me? And if I went away for two weeks, on the dreaded holiday, that would be the end of it. Two weeks together, and the two of them wouldn't need me at all. The dream would be over. I had to get out of it – had to persuade Mum and Dad to let me stay at the Community. I wanted this adventure to continue. I needed every last day of it.

Johnny turned up at ten o'clock, armed with his camera. We showed him round the place, the house, the gardens and the workshops. He took pictures of everything, and everyone. Then the three of us retired to the kitchen and drank glasses of homemade lemonade, poured from a tall glass jug Eliza had left for us on the table before she went to work. Perhaps it was a peace offering to Dowdie. Mother and daughter had not exchanged a word since their row the previous morning, and Dowdie had put the issue to one side, trusting, as I did, that James could sort things out.

I watched Johnny carefully. He was curious about the Community, but noncommittal. He asked a hundred questions, but didn't enthuse as I had done. Dowdie tried pretty hard to impress him and they continued their playful squabbling most of the morning. Dowdie seemed to have forgotten all about me now she had a better toy to play with.

James Renault emerged from his office at lunchtime. He was wearing tight black jeans and a vest top that displayed the muscles of his arms and shoulders. I couldn't imagine him working out at a gym, but he was in astonishingly good shape. Perhaps he did hours of yoga.

'James, this is Johnny,' Dowdie said in a rush. 'He's a friend of ours. We invited him over.'

Johnny stood up, and the two eyed each other, James and

Johnny, each making an assessment. James held out his hand. 'Nice to meet you,' he said. Then, to Dowdie: 'You're not supposed to bring people here without asking me first.'

Dowdie blushed, to be admonished in front of us, but she quickly rallied. 'You tell me to use my instincts,' she came right back. 'So I used them. I think Johnny has something to teach us. I wanted you to meet him.'

She was flushed, anxious and furious all at once. Nothing of Dowdie's emotional life remained hidden – her feelings exhibited on her face. James nodded. 'Fair enough,' he said easily. 'So what d'you think of the place, Johnny?'

'It's beautiful,' Johnny said. 'How lucky you all are.' They shook hands for a long time.

'We're having a special ceremony tonight,' James said. 'You'd be welcome to join us. I don't know what you'll make of it, but you'll need to be open-minded.'

Johnny smiled. 'I have a very open mind,' he said. 'About everything.'

James turned to me. 'I have some good news for you Amber,' he said. 'I've spoken to your father about their holiday. I was on the phone to him this morning – making some more enquiries about this system he's trying to sell me. And he said if you'd really rather stay here with us, then you can.'

I could hardly believe it. 'Really? He said that? Didn't he mind?'

'I wouldn't say he didn't mind. I don't think he was happy about it and you should expect them to try and persuade you to go, but he agreed it was your call.'

I threw my arms around Dowdie's neck, then jumped to my feet and hugged James. I was so excited I even hugged Johnny, pressing my face against his hard, bony chest.

'That's fantastic,' I said, jumping up and down like a kid.

'Thanks so much James, thank you, thank you. A whole two weeks here! I can't believe it!'

Dowdie laughed too, and James, and when the rest of the Community came in for dinner the kitchen had the atmosphere of a party. Everyone made Johnny very welcome and finally he seemed to relax. Dowdie sat next to me and the rapport between us was re-established, so for an hour or more I was crazily, deliriously happy. Why did I worry so much? Why didn't I trust my friends? Why didn't I just trust myself?

Slowly the gathering dispersed. Dowdie, Johnny and I were left with the washing-up, though Johnny didn't do much. We spent the afternoon lounging in the garden, talking together, and for a while everything was very natural and happy between the three of us. The workshops closed early so everyone could help prepare for the evening.

'So what's going on tonight?' Johnny asked. 'What kind of ceremony is this?'

'It's the full moon,' Dowdie said. I sensed a note of defensiveness in her voice. She was worried Johnny would mock, but his face was perfectly serious.

'We have a party every full moon, and sometimes if the mood is right, James channels the spirit.'

'Channelling? When a higher being speaks through him?' Johnny said. It was hard to read what he was thinking. I didn't detect any jeering in his voice.

'Yes,' Dowdie said. 'Spirit is what you might call God. But Spirit has aspects, which are entities with names and personalities. One of these entities is called Throne, and he is the one who speaks through James.

'It was Throne who told him to set up the Community in readiness for the upheaval the Earth is facing over the next decades. And it was Throne who told him about the Amethyst children, who are being born into the world at this time to help guide humankind through this period of change and evolution.'

'Amethyst children,' Johnny said, plucking at the grass. 'I've heard of this. There's stuff about it on the Internet – websites and forums and things. James dreamed it all up?'

'He didn't dream it up,' Dowdie shot back. 'It was a revelation. He received the information from Throne.' We waited for Johnny to throw metaphorical litter on the beautiful idea, but he remained thoughtful, still pulling the grass.

'And presumably *you* are an Amethyst child,' he said. 'You're one of these special human beings, right?'

'Yes,' Dowdie said proudly, raising her head. 'And Amber is too.'

'Of course.' Johnny smiled. 'Of course she is. And what about me? Do you think I might be too?'

I stared at him, obliquely.

'You may be,' Dowdie conceded. 'What do you think?'

Johnny shrugged. 'I've no idea. It's a fascinating theory.'

'It's not a theory – it's the truth,' James said. He had appeared behind him. I hadn't noticed his approach, and he startled us, shifting the mood. James sat down in the grass, crossing his legs. Johnny, lying on his tummy, stuck a grass shoot between his teeth and stared up at him lazily.

'We're having solar panels installed right across the south-facing roof, and a heavy-duty wind turbine at the end of the paddock, where the ground is highest,' James said. 'Within a year I reckon we should be self-sufficient in energy terms. We already have a food surplus, which we sell in the shop. We'll be off the grid very soon.'

'Ready for the years of cataclysm,' Johnny said. 'When the sea rises and the oil runs out, when society collapses. You'll be all right. Throne will tell you what to do, and you'll have your Amethyst children to guide you through the troubled times.'

James detected his sarcastic tone and gave a grim smile. 'It's good to question,' he said. 'You shouldn't take anything at face value – that's an attribute of an Amethyst child, you know. Gets them into trouble though. Tell me, do you find it easy to relate to your parents? Do you fit in at school?'

A curious light flared in Johnny's eyes. 'Actually, I have a great family life and I'm head boy at school.'

James shook his head and laughed. 'Liar,' he said, reaching out to pat Johnny on the arm. 'I said it's good to question, but don't let cynicism blind you. Now, Dowdie – I want to talk to you, and your mother. Come inside please.'

Dowdie pulled a face, but she obeyed.

Johnny and I were left alone, on the grass. Nervous now, with just the two of us, I clasped and unclasped my hands.

'What do you think?' I said.

'Of James? He's a smug bastard,' Johnny said. 'I just wonder how he gets off on all this. Power, I suppose. He gets to be king, doesn't he? Ruler of his own little realm.'

'You don't believe it then – channelling and Amethyst children and stuff.'

'It's bollocks,' he said. 'Why – do you?'

Did I believe it? I still ask that question. There were times I believed it absolutely. But faith isn't a constant. It's not a light that switches on and off. It's more like fire that blazes when there's fuel and oxygen, but falters when the damp comes in or the fuel is consumed. It can smoulder quietly and it can be completely extinguished. It can also be rekindled by a stray spark, or fanned to dramatic heights.

'I don't know what I believe,' I said. 'But I do love it here. Everyone is so kind and I love they way they live. It's how I'd like to live. Wouldn't you?'

'Not with smug-face lording it over me, thinking he's got all the answers,' Johnny said. 'D'you think it's a democracy here? D'you think anyone argues with him?'

I didn't know how to answer. The Community had entirely enchanted me and James had won me over, heart and soul. I had never imagined such a beautiful place, nor such thoughtful, generous people. These last weeks had been utterly happy and magical. I was prepared to believe, if that was the key to the kingdom.

'I've upset you,' Johnny observed. 'Take no notice of me. I'm a miserable git. I've never been happy anywhere, that's the trouble.'

I didn't have a chance to talk to Dowdie before the ceremony began, so I had no idea what passed between her and Eliza. She seemed cheerful enough, though, when the food was laid out and the party began.

Other visitors arrived, people connected with the Community who lived nearby. I don't know exactly how many were there that night, but it might have been as many as forty. Even Eliza's new man travelled up from Glastonbury. He looked OK to me – long grey hair in a ponytail, an expensive-looking leather jacket. He and Eliza looked very happy together, though Dowdie ignored them both. When the eating and drinking was done everyone sat in a huge circle in the garden, on the grass, as the moon rose over the horizon, straw-coloured, patterned like an old coin. An owl hooted from the roof of the workshops, and somewhere in the twilight a baby wailed.

A cup was passed from hand to hand. Everyone took a sip.

Silence descended. I'm not sure what the drink was – wine, I think, though flavoured with something else with a tart, flowery herbal taste. I took enough to wet my lips, no more. Beside me, Johnny gulped a mouthful before giving me a rather manic grin.

Minutes passed, and nobody spoke. Darkness gathered around us. The moon continued on its arc, steeped in gold. I felt totally alert, waiting for something to happen. My senses were primed – my mind open. I was aware everyone around me felt the same – that we were all in one single mental and spiritual place. Everyone was focused on the moment, on the here and now.

'Spirit, we are ready,' James said. He was sitting in the circle, his back to the house. 'Throne, come to me. I am your servant. Speak through me.'

It was hard to see him clearly. His face was a pale blur in the gloom. His head tipped back. He took a long breath then he raised his head again, to look into the heart of the circle.

'Children, be prepared.' His voice had altered. It was deeper, darker in tone. I felt cold all of a sudden. The hairs stood up on my bare arms.

'I am Throne. I am a face of Spirit, a true voice speaking to my children in the material world. You are my faithful ones, treading a path through the wilderness, you are the seekers of truth who have cast off the manacles of the man-machine. Your time is coming. All over the world the children who will guide you into the next age are being born – it is your job to find and nurture and guide them. They are many – but they are vulnerable. When the darkness comes, you will be a light. When the battle rages, you must be strong and righteous.

'The death throes of the man-machine will be terrible, but it will be overcome.'

The voice stopped for a moment. James closed his eyes.

'You face a time of testing,' he said. 'The spirit of the man-machine senses how strong you have become. It will try and destroy you. It will try and tear apart everything you have built up under my guidance. Even among you there are those who wish you harm. Be ready for them. Be vigilant and have faith. Keep your hearts strong and your minds incorrupt. I will stand by you, if you, my people, remain true to me.'

James slumped forward. The atmosphere altered, and a tide of voices rose from the circle of people. A woman jumped to her feet and took a cup to James, helping him to drink, pressing the palm of her hand to his face. People turned over the meaning of Throne's words, trying to work out what he had meant with the call for vigilance, with the warning about those who wished them harm. The circle broke up as people rose to their feet and broke off into little groups. The baby, wherever it was, began to wail. The moon glowed with a tinge of red, like a hot coal.

Twelve

The next day Mum and Dad tried to dissuade me. How could I miss out on this precious two weeks with them, the highlight of our family year? Their feelings were hurt but I steeled myself against them. Obviously I preferred to be with my new friends.

'Well, she's nearly fifteen now. I suppose we shouldn't force her if she doesn't want to come,' Dad said. He stared at me, waiting, yearning for me to change my mind, and say that yes, the holiday was more important.

'Oh Amber – are you sure?' Mum pleaded. 'I've hardly seen anything of you these last weeks. I was so looking forward to spending some time together. I mean, you can see your friends anytime, but I don't get that many days off work. If you're really sure, you can stay, but won't you please come with us instead? Think what you're going to miss!'

'I want you to come with us,' Justin said, throwing his arms around my waist. 'Please Amber, please.'

It was tough, holding out against the weight of their wanting. They stared at me – Mum, Dad and Justin – my parents scarcely believing I would rather be with someone else.

'I'm sorry,' I said, my throat tight. 'You'll be OK without me. I really want to stay.'

Mum looked close to tears. Dad put his arm around her.

'OK,' he said. Then, to Mum, with a false cheery note: 'I know it's tough, but she's growing up. It's bound to happen sooner or later. You wouldn't want to drag her there kicking and screaming. Who'd have a nice holiday then?'

'I think Amber stinks,' Justin said. His arm fell away from my waist, and he slouched off to the living room and the television. Dad gave me an unconvincing half smile, and Mum turned away, with a sniff, piling on the guilt. I clenched my teeth.

The rest of the evening I hid out in my bedroom, listening to music and reading *A Clockwork Orange*. Kids give the olds a kicking. It was oddly soothing. At eight o'clock my mobile rang. It was Johnny.

'Can you come over?' he said. His voice was terse.

'It's a bit late.'

'Please. It's important, Amber. Just for an hour.'

I didn't ask permission – simply headed out the front door, calling as I hurried past: 'Just popping out – won't be long.'

Through the open window of the living room I heard Mum sigh and say: 'Isn't she selfish now? Doesn't she care about us at all?'

I took out my bike from the garage and pedalled away from the estate. Johnny's back door was open, so I stepped inside, walked past the apparently housekeeper-ignored mess in the kitchen and ran up the stairs to his bedroom.

'Johnny?' I knocked on the door. 'It's me – Amber.'

The lock turned, and Johnny's narrow face peered through the gap as the door opened. 'Come in,' he said. 'Come and see.'

The computer was fired up; windows open on email, the

Internet, a string of thumbnail pictures he had taken the day before at the Community.

'What is it?' I had a bad feeling, the squeeze in the belly I get sitting in the dentist's waiting room.

'What is it Johnny?'

He flapped his arm, gesturing for me to be patient. The mouse clicked, clicked again. On-screen windows closed and opened.

'Have you checked James out at all?' Johnny said. 'There's a lot of stuff on the Internet about him. Interesting stuff.'

'No. Actually, I've hardly been on the computer at all recently. I've had—'

'More interesting things to do?' Johnny interrupted. 'Maybe you have – but it's always worth having a dig around.'

'Why? To find something bad? Is that what you've done?'

'OK,' Johnny said, ignoring my question. 'Pull up a chair. Renault has several websites. There's one for the shop, for mail order and stuff. There's one about the Community, and then there are a couple of weirder ones where James spouts his theories. He's set up all these information guides and forums for parents who think their kids might be Amethyst children, and how to help them. This one . . .' he clicked on a link from the Community website, '. . . records all the stuff Throne has channelled through him. Boring tosh, most of it. The same kind of rubbish he was babbling last night.'

'You don't believe in channelling?' I said. 'You don't think it's real?'

'No I bloody don't.' He was focused on the screen still. 'But this was just the beginning. I dug around some more, looked at groups, followed some clues and found out a bit more on Renault's past. Look.'

A picture opened on the screen. A scan of a black and white

picture of a rock band – four men in rank 70s style glam outfits. There – yes – the guy with a bass guitar. It was James. He looked astonishingly young, all wide open. Laughter bubbled up inside me.

'He was in a band,' I said. 'So?'

'Look at the name in the caption,' Johnny urged. It was hard to read. It looked like the picture was part of a newspaper story and the letters were partly smeared. The bass player, according to the caption, was James Moore. But the picture – it was definitely him.

'He's changed his name,' I said. 'Is that what you're telling me?'

'Yes. He's changed his name. When I did some more digging using his old name, lots of other things came up too.'

The mouse clicked again, a window opened on a posting to some New Age newsgroup, dated 1999. It was titled: *Moore is Dangerous.* I read on. 'Beware of a charlatan called James Moore. He's rich, but his money has blood on it. Whatever you do, don't have anything to do with him. He is very dangerous.'

I didn't speak. The room seemed very still. Only the cursor blinked on the screen. 'It might not be him,' I said. 'There's bound to be more than one James Moore in the world. And even if this guy is talking about him, we have no reason to believe what he says. People write all sorts of rubbish on the Internet.'

Johnny sighed. 'Do you always see the best in people?'

'What? No! Do you always see the worst?'

Johnny shrugged. 'Invariably. People are shit.'

'I'm not shit. Nor are you.'

'Maybe you're not shit. But what makes you think I'm not? You've just jumped to a conclusion because I've chosen to be nice to you. How do you know I'm being truthful? Maybe I despise you. Maybe I'm setting you up for a fall.'

'Is that how you think?' I stared at him. His face seemed shrunken, his eyes little beads in the white face. His hair was greasy, dropping in his eyes.

'Why d'you have to do it, dig up the dirt?'

'I'm interested in dirt,' Johnny said, turning his attention to the screen. 'Don't you want to know the truth about Mr High and Mighty?'

'The Internet isn't truth. You've no real evidence he's done anything bad. Someone somewhere's pissed off with a guy called James Moore. It wouldn't stand up in a court.'

'Why won't you believe he's less than perfect?'

'Why are you determined he's bad? What about all the other people at the Community. Didn't they seem lovely? Isn't it a great place?'

Johnny looked serious. 'I think some of them are good people,' he said. 'That's why you've got to help me.'

'What do you want me to do?'

'When are your parents going away?'

'Day after tomorrow.'

'And you're going to be staying there, for two weeks. You can sniff around, check him out. Be my spy. I'm going to expose him.'

'Expose what? He's not doing anything wrong! He takes care of people – like Chris.'

Johnny shook his head. 'I'm not getting anywhere,' he said. 'James has strapped his rose-tinted spectacles on you, hasn't he? You're brainwashed.'

I laughed. 'No I'm not. I'm just . . . curious. Interested. And Dowdie's the best friend I've ever had. She's changed everything for me. Did you know, James is her dad?'

Should I have told Johnny this? Dowdie had never said it was a secret but I felt a pang to tell him.

'Her dad? I didn't know,' he said. 'That adds a new dimension, doesn't it? Maybe she can tell us why he changed his name. Why don't you ask her?'

'OK – I will. Then you'll be happy, yes? Anyway – you'll be coming over too, won't you? You'll visit us?'

'Yes – but you'll be . . . on the inside. Undercover.'

Johnny laughed, and the atmosphere lightened. He turned off the computer. Late golden light filled the room, broken by the shadows of the trees. The shadow foliage moved restlessly on the wall.

'Let me take some pictures of you,' Johnny said, reaching for his camera.

'No!'

'Go on. Don't be stupid. The light is marvellous.'

'I hate having my picture taken.'

'Everyone does. Except models maybe. And who knows, perhaps them too.'

'I always look terrible in pictures.' My hand ran over my hair, smoothing the tangles. Johnny, ignoring me, was already altering the settings on the heavy, black camera. Click, click, click. Three pictures of me scowling.

'Sit up straight,' he said. 'Look at me. Now look away, towards the window.'

I did as he said, itching with discomfort. I could feel the muscles in my face tensing up. 'Please,' I said, holding up my hand. 'I hate this. Won't you stop?'

'Stop whining. Just relax will you? Pull your hair forward. Move about a bit. Go on – pose.'

Johnny was remorseless. He became impersonal behind the camera. His voice changed, as he forgot himself and focused instead on the work in hand. He didn't seem to consider me any more – not me as a person – just the quest to find something, to see the right image. This process continued for half an hour or more, as the sun descended and the light slowly changed. He took perhaps a hundred pictures. Then, with a sigh, he put the camera down and lay on his back on the big bed. He let me relax.

'Any good ones?'

'I don't know. Might be,' he said. I sat on the bed, then plucked up the courage to flop down so I was lying on my belly beside him. It made me nervous, to be so physically close, but Johnny didn't seem to notice.

'Why don't your parents take care of the house?' I said.

Johnny shrugged. 'They've got a house in London. That's their proper place. This house used to belong to my grandmother, and my parents inherited it. They come here from time to time, but they're not that bothered about it. I like it here.'

'You don't like them.'

Johnny's eyes narrowed. 'No. They don't like me, so why should I like them?'

'You must be really lonely.' Johnny brushed this away, with a look of irritation, because I'd said something trite and obvious.

'I suppose you'll be doing A-levels when you go back to school. What are you going to do?'

'I'm not doing A-levels. I'm not going back to school,' he said.

'What about your parents? Won't they mind?'

'They've never minded anything up till now.' His face had gone hard and tense, like a lump of wood. My questions landed like physical kicks, I could see. But I wanted to know. Johnny jumped to his feet.

'I'm hungry. Let's get something to eat,' he said. He shook his head and ran his fingers through his sticky-looking hair so it stuck up in pointy black clumps. He looked gawky, like a scarecrow, and a little wired. He wrung his hands, cracked his knuckles, stretched and squeezed his fingers.

'Are you OK?' The room was darkening, the tree shadow obliterated.

'Yes. Fine. Just hungry.' He went out of the door and down the stairs. Slowly I climbed from the bed and followed him to the kitchen. Johnny was rummaging in the fridge, which bled a clinical white glow into the gloom. I turned on the lights. Johnny winced.

'What d'you do that for?' He had some Jarlsberg cheese and a tray of cherry tomatoes in his hand.

'There's a new loaf in the breadbin,' he said, gesturing across the room. 'I'll find us some plates.'

I wasn't very hungry, and nibbled at a piece of cheese. Johnny ate a lot. He also poured himself a glass of red wine. As he tore into his food, I tried another burning question.

'If you have a housekeeper, why does the place look such a mess – except for your room?'

'I told her not to bother,' Johnny said. 'I told her to clear off and leave it. I think she's a bit scared of me. I said – just keep the kitchen stocked and leave the rest. I'll tidy it up myself before the parents get back. I don't want her hanging around the place.'

I imagined it, Johnny wild and dishevelled, giving some diligent, respectable little housekeeper her orders. I expect she crept in with the food supplies too, as keen to avoid him as he was her.

'So what are your parents like?' Johnny asked, his mouth full of food.

'Oh, you know.' I shrugged. 'They're OK. They're pretty upset I don't want to go on holiday with them.' My tone of voice indicated their fault in this but Johnny smiled, and I remembered that his parents were also away on holiday and hadn't wanted him to go along.

'Must be tough,' he said, with the ghost of a smile.

It is very hard to imagine what somebody else's life is like – truly to step into their shoes – but I yearned to know it. Perhaps that's why I liked reading so much, for the chance to live another life, to see through another's eyes, to follow their thoughts, to feel their emotions, even at one remove. That time, that night, watching Johnny eat bread and cheese, in the giant kitchen at the bottom of his gothic town mansion, I longed to be him. I know it sounds stupid when I knew too well that he was utterly lonely and had endured years of need despite his financial plenty, but still I was seduced by the romance of his situation, by his physical beauty, his pictures, his *difference*. That night, I would have sacrificed secure home and affectionate parents to rid myself of my shameful ordinariness.

'My dad likes Level 42 and Dire Straits,' I said. 'Have you heard of them? They're terrible.'

Johnny's ghost smile again. He was still chomping, tearing thick crusts with sharp white teeth. I could see his thoughts (or was I simply hearing my own?) that my worst complaint was my father's taste in music. Johnny shrugged.

'There'll be a whole community of blokes around his age who think that's as cool as it gets,' he said. 'Good for the dad.'

'It's not cool!' I exploded.

Johnny stopped chewing and stared at me. 'For God's sake,' he said. 'What's with you? What does cool mean, anyway?'

So I told him, about Walter de la Mare and Mr Stephenson. Johnny listened intently.

'So why do you like Walter's poems?' he said.

'I like the way he uses words, but mostly, the atmosphere.

There's a kind of magic and sadness in his poems, as though he's glimpsed an enchanted kingdom through a window and though he'll never see it again, he can't forget it either.'

Johnny put down his bread. 'Well I like the sound of that. I don't read much, but I'd want to, from what you've told me.'

'But what about his anachronistic thees and thous?'

Johnny, my sounding board, my new measure of cool, tipped his head to one side.

'Does that stop you liking him for the reason you just told me? Why do you have to worry what your English teacher thinks? Why do you have to look to the people around you to get a measure of what's the right thing to think or like or do?'

Then he dropped his head back, and sighed. 'But what do I know,' he said, 'I ignore what everyone thinks. I haven't any friends and the boys at school all call me an emo fag. Don't listen to me.'

'You have got friends,' I jumped in. 'What about Dowdie and me?'

Johnny's head dropped forward and he smirked. 'Ah yes, Dowdie,' he said. 'What a curious threesome we are.'

'You like her though, don't you?'

He raised his eyes, looked into my face. 'Of course I do,' he said softly. 'She's so passionately herself. Even aggressively so.'

'The opposite of me then,' I said, infected with self-pity.

Johnny's face softened. 'You'll be OK. You just need more faith in yourself,' he said. Then for a minute or two we were sitting in silence. From the hall I could hear the ticking of an old clock, and distantly, the sound of a passing car. We both jumped when my mobile rang. It was Mum. I noticed, guiltily, it was nearly midnight.

'Where the hell are you?' She was furious. 'I want to go to bed. It's late and I've got work in the morning.'

'I'm on my way,' I said, getting up from the table and heading for the back door. 'Sorry, I didn't realise how late it was. I'll be back right away. You go to bed – I've got my key. I'll lock up. I'm very sorry.'

But Mum just hung up. 'I've got to go,' I said.

Johnny jumped to his feet. 'I'll walk you back,' he said. 'Make sure you're safe.'

'Are you sure? You don't have to. It's a long way.' Of course, I did want him to walk me back, wanted to stretch out every moment in his company. I wouldn't have him for long, after all. Doubtless he would be packed off back to boarding school, despite his protestations, and Dowdie maybe gone to Glastonbury. How could this happen? How could I go back to what-once-was?

Thirteen

We're back in the room with Neil, the note-taker and the tape recorder. Today, however, Dad is sitting in Mum's place and Neil has a primrose-coloured shirt and black cufflinks. He and Dad shake hands, man to man. I notice how Dad's presence alters the dynamic in the room. Neil is brisk and businesslike rather than protective. Again I wonder, is this how he's trained to act?

'Well, Amber, I'm sorry to drag you in again but we've still got more ground to cover. I reckon we should get this wrapped up today if we press on,' he says. 'I reckon you should be back at school next week.'

School. In a million years, a million miles away, I would be back at school. I shake my head, dismissing the possibility. Dad leans back in his seat, legs thrust forward, arms folded. I sense he doesn't much like Call-Me-Neil. Perhaps the policeman, with his faint perfume of expensive aftershave, is too smooth for my bluff father's liking. Then again, maybe Dad doesn't like to be on the defensive. He didn't foresee the cataclysm. He failed to protect me.

Neil sits on the front of his table, his hands clasped in front of him.

'So, Amber, your parents went on holiday on August 20, and you stayed behind at the Community.'

Dad interrupts. 'That's right. I'd met up with Renault several times – even thought we'd do some business with him. He seemed straight up. How was I to know? I mean, I wouldn't leave the country and let her stay with just anyone. Of course not! We trusted him.'

Dad's babbling. Neil holds up his hand to stop him.

'Thank you, Mr Renalden. Thank you. There was no way you could have known,' he says. But Dad is not to be stopped.

'And all this weird stuff – about the Amethyst children and the nonsense he was filling her head with. I had no idea! She didn't tell me about all that. Of course if I'd known I'd never have agreed. But Amber didn't tell me anything!'

He's looking at Neil as he rants, but I realise my dad is actually talking to me. He's angry I kept so much from him.

'Have you got children, Neil? It's easy when they're little – but just you wait till they start growing up. You've no control any more. They do their own thing and only tell you what they choose to let you know. You want to keep them safe, but how can you when they're not straight with you?'

'Please, please,' Neil interjects. 'Mr Renalden, I need to hear what Amber has to say.'

Dad glares at me, but he shuts up. I lick my lips.

'What do you want to know?' I say.

'What was it like, staying at the Community?'

I close my eyes, and the place rises up in my memory. Johnny didn't come over the first few days. It was just Dowdie and me, as we were in the beginning. She set up a camp-bed in her room so we were together from the moment we woke, till the moment we fell asleep at night.

'It was fantastic,' I say. 'It was a beautiful place and I loved everyone there. We helped out a bit, walked a lot, read books, and talked all the time. I was really, really happy. I never wanted to leave.'

'Were there any tensions in the group, do you think? Any rows?'

'James and Dowdie's mum argued a lot. Dowdie was adamant she wasn't leaving but her mum was very keen to take her away.'

'Did you have any suspicions about why Dowdie's mother was so eager to get away – and to take her daughter?'

'There was nothing suspicious about it,' I snap. 'Dowdie's mum had a new boyfriend and she wanted to move in with him. And what mother wouldn't want her daughter to come with her?'

Neil sighs and moves from the table.

'You're trying to work out how much Eliza knew,' I say. 'You think she might have known about James's plans.'

'They had a relationship once,' Neil says. 'They had a child together and he invited her to come and live with him again. I think he wanted to protect them.'

'Yes he did – but not as . . . lovers. It wasn't like that.' Had he questioned Dowdie's mum? What had she told him about me?

'So, everything in the garden was rosy,' Neil says. 'When did that change?'

'When Johnny came over,' I admit.

'Johnny had already briefed you, I think, on what he'd found out about Renault. Johnny didn't like him.'

'No,' I say. 'Johnny was determined not to like him. He wanted to catch him out.'

'Why do you think Johnny didn't like him? Everyone else did – the people at the Community, you, your dad. Why didn't the spell work on Johnny, d'you think?'

'Johnny's a negative kind of a person,' I say. 'He's had a lot of problems. I don't really think he likes anyone – not any adult anyway. He thinks the world's shit, and he saw James as another manifestation of this shit.'

My dad winces, hearing me use this kind of language, but I've stepped beyond his reach.

'But you liked James – and you liked Johnny. How did you reconcile that?'

'It wasn't so hard,' I counter. 'Why should I not like them both? Did I have to pick sides?'

'It just seems odd, that's all. What did James make of Johnny?'

'He tried to win him over – told him he was an Amethyst child. Offered to help him – offered the Community as a new family. Johnny didn't refuse him. He was never rude, never even said he didn't believe it. But he also made it obvious he was only playing along.

'After a few days James took me to one side and warned me that Johnny was a bad influence – a poison.

'"I'm going to have to ask him to leave," James said to me. "He's a talented individual, and without doubt he's an Amethyst child. But we've found him too late. His circumstances have corrupted him and his heart isn't open to change. I don't want him here any more because I feel he's having a bad influence on you, Amber – on you and Dowdie – and you're both too special to lose."'

'And what did Johnny think of the ban?' Neil asks.

'He looked pretty pleased, actually,' I remember. 'He'd been rejected again. Thrown out. He said it confirmed something for him, something about James and the Community.'

'What did it confirm?'

'That you had to conform to James's system of belief, of course. That you had to sign up to his personal vision of reality.'

'And did Johnny's banning change how you felt about James?'

I think about this for a moment. It had disappointed me. I had loved the Community at first because it embraced people who didn't fit in with the ordinary world. Now I had seen it had its own rules – that you could be a misfit even among this particular tribe of misfits.

'Yes it did,' I concede. 'It's just occurred to me now that Johnny did it on purpose – for that very reason. I think he got himself excluded so I would agree to snoop on James – to make me angry with him, to show me he wasn't perfect.'

'So that's what happened. Johnny was sent away, and you agreed to investigate. Johnny was clever, wasn't he? At that point you chose sides. You joined Johnny over James.'

'No! That's not right. It wasn't like that!' I've painted myself into a corner. It's television police drama time again, and I'm the criminal the clever policeman has talked into confessing.

'I agreed to help Johnny 'cos I thought that would prove to him nothing was going on! I thought I would show him that James was just what he said he was! Why do there have to be sides?'

My conscience is guilty. Even now, even knowing what I do, I harbour a loyalty to James. He has a powerful hold. He believed everything he said – about the Amethyst children, about the apocalypse and the need to prepare for it. He created a reality that was more than the drab, random world of jobs and governments and consumers and pensions. There were storms ahead, in James's vision, but there was also meaning and purpose, and a path we could follow. He was a dark angel pointing the way into a promised land, where I wasn't a faceless nobody, but an Amethyst child, prophesied by the voices of the spirits. We were part of something. We were going somewhere.

So – the question again – did I really believe him?

Neil interrupts my thoughts. His voice is cold and hard.

'And when you found the guns. What side did you take then?'

Fourteen

We stood outside the Community house, Johnny, Dowdie and I. Johnny was sitting astride his scooter, his helmet in his hands. Nobody knew what to say, but we were reluctant to let Johnny go.

'You shouldn't have to leave,' Dowdie said. 'I don't know what his problem is.'

'Well, he can't stop us seeing each other altogether,' Johnny said. His voice was light. 'You two can come over to my house.'

'You shouldn't have to go!' Dowdie repeated. 'Who does he think he is?'

Johnny snorted: 'The Messiah, obviously. The main man. The king, the chosen one.'

'He's not the Messiah,' I said softly. 'He's a very naughty boy.'

Johnny exploded with laughter, and I laughed too, suddenly caught off balance. Dowdie, who hadn't grown up watching films, stared at us. She didn't like to be left out, and she scowled.

'What?' she demanded.

'It's a line from a Monty Python film,' I said, choking back the fits of hysterical laughter. But Dowdie just flapped her hand and turned the other way. Johnny and I laughed again, helplessly. It was strange to laugh at James. Some part of me enjoyed it, the tearing down of an idol. Another part was stricken with guilt. James had been good to me – taken me in. Standing with James, the horizon widened. You were part of a bigger reality. That was the deal, wasn't it? Yield to him, and in exchange, become part of his world. Except that Johnny was immune to his spell, or else didn't want it.

At last he stuffed his head into the helmet, started up the scooter and rode away. We could hear it pop-popping, even after he had disappeared into the village. The dusk, like a grainy, pink smoke, settled over the house and trees. Dowdie sighed.

'I'm going to my room,' she said. 'I want to be on my own.' Her voice was abrupt. Then, remembering her room was also my room now: 'I can't get away from you, can I? You're around me all the time.'

I stood, hurt and helpless, not knowing what to say. I couldn't believe it. She'd never been mean to me before. Why take it out on me? It wasn't my fault Johnny had been sent away.

She turned away, with a toss of her head, and marched into the house. I was left alone, by the front gate.

Over the house a dozen swifts plunged and circled. Far away, my mum and dad and brother would be sitting at a table eating a late meal. Were they missing me, I wondered? And that moment I ached for them, to be safe and cared for, to know where I belonged.

Slowly I turned towards the house. I couldn't go up to Dowdie's room, but the other Community members were about. Some were sitting in the garden, drinking and chatting. Chris the gardener was on his own in the kitchen, engrossed in a book. He looked up at me, said hello, but turned his attention to the page again. In the study, James was talking to Diane. I was about to withdraw, not wanting to intrude, but James waved for me to stay.

'Wait,' he said. 'Just wait a minute, Amber. I want to talk to you.'

So I sat down. My nerves were frayed, my confidence undermined. I wanted everything to be all right with Dowdie. I ached to be her friend again.

James and Diane talked for more than a minute. They were discussing Eliza's decision to leave, and her desire to take Dowdie with her. I felt uncomfortable, listening in, but James had told me to stay and I didn't dare walk out. James said he had no choice but to let them go – that he had no power to keep either Eliza or Dowdie. Diane protested. She said they were key members of the Community and shouldn't be lost. She urged James to assert his rights – to have a DNA test to prove he was her father and seek legal advice on gaining custody. But James, to my surprise, did not want to take this path.

'I don't want to get involved with the courts,' he said. 'I want to get out of all that – away from it, away from Babylon. I've washed my hands of it. I have to sort this out myself, Diane.'

Diane sighed. She didn't say anything for a moment. She just stood up and put her hand on his arm, a gesture of comfort. James reached out his own hand, gently touched the side of her head, and kissed her cheek. I was quiet as a mouse, but Diane glanced over. She patted James on the shoulder, and went out of the room.

'Goodnight Amber,' she called as she left.

James turned to me, and smiled. I can still remember it now, that feeling, when he focused on you and it felt as though no one knew you better, or cared for you as deeply. He wasn't afraid to look at you intently. His eyes, an astonishing blue, seemed to penetrate the layers of my personal fears and disguises, to see the real essential me beneath them. The me that was hurting, cast out by Dowdie.

'Come on,' he said, patting the chair beside him. 'Come and sit here.'

He leaned towards me, a power like an electric current circulating his bulky body. How had I ever thought he looked ordinary? There was nothing ordinary about James, nothing about him like any other person I had met.

He leaned over the table, his head propped in his hand.

'I expect you're angry with me, for sending Johnny away,' he said.

'No, I – well, I don't know. It's up to you,' I babbled. Trying to say the right thing, not knowing what the right thing was. It was no use trying to dissemble.

'Be honest, Amber. I know you're very fond of him. Well it hurt me too. Do you believe that? It hurt me too. But it was for his own good – do you understand?'

I didn't answer, because I didn't understand. James continued:

'I did it for his good, and for yours. Johnny's a damaged young man. You can see that, yes? He carries his hurt – it's like a bruise on him. Like a burden he's carried so long it's bent him out of shape.'

I nodded. 'Yes.'

'I want to help him, Amber. Do you believe that? I want to take that burden from him. But he's got to be willing. He's resisting change. He doesn't want to let go. He's put up so many barriers nothing can get in.'

My feelings were getting the better of me. I clenched my teeth together and looked away from James. I didn't want to cry.

'I don't want him here again until he's prepared to be open. You know what I'm talking about, don't you? You're a very bright girl. You understand.'

I didn't answer, not trusting my voice.

'I suspect he's already tried to turn you against us – against me,' James said. 'Amber – is that true?'

I couldn't speak. Whatever I said would betray one of them. So I just shook my head, eyes blind with tears.

Softly James continued: 'What's he told you?'

'Why did you change your name?' I blurted.

James raised his face, and looked up at the ceiling. He laughed. 'Is that it?' Then, straight at me: 'Because I became a different person,' he said. 'My life changed. I haven't always led a virtuous life, Amber, that much I will admit. I was a sinner, as they say. But I had my Road to Damascus moment.

'I had a revelation. Throne spoke to me, and lifted the veil on the future. Throne raised a mirror, to show me who I was and where my purpose lay. Johnny's told you I'm a charlatan, no doubt – warned you I'm a crazy? I can see his thoughts written all over his face. He's just a kid, Amber. Just a damaged child playing games he's not old or wise enough to understand. This Community isn't about me. I'm just a messenger – a signpost for you and all the other Amethyst children struggling to cope, waiting for their time to take us into a new world.

'I wanted to create a haven and a resource for you and the others. There are so many Amethyst children out there – misunderstood and isolated. You and Dowdie are just the beginning – the torch-bearers. I have a website, you know, a way for us to reach out to the families of other Amethyst children – all over the world. So many worried parents come to me there. They recognise the characteristics of the Amethyst child in their own sons and daughters, and they find me – and I can offer them advice and encourage them to take heart, to let them know they are not alone. And like Dowdie, you will learn to identify others like yourself, in the town and at school. I want you to find them.

'Here at the Community we have a safe place when they want it – where you can gain strength and understanding, where you and they will be protected when the time comes. And it can be a haven for Johnny too, when he's ready.'

'But Dowdie's going to leave,' I said. 'I heard what you were saying.'

James shook his head. 'I can't stop her mother taking her, no. But Dowdie will be sixteen in not much over a year. Eliza won't be able to hold her for long. That's Dowdie's strength. She does want she wants. She won't be contained or bridled for long.' He smiled. 'She's her father's daughter.'

'I don't want her to go,' I said, thinking of her in a strop in her bedroom, cutting me out. 'I can't manage without her for a year.'

James shook his head. 'We'll still be here. I will be here. You won't ever have to be alone again.'

Would life be different, knowing James was behind me? I imagined going back to school, moving among the herd of other kids, negotiating my way through the social tribes, through exams and decisions about the future. Even without Dowdie it would be different if I knew I had a life beyond it, and that school wasn't the be-all and end-all.

James patted me on the shoulder and told me he was going to bed. So I took a book to the kitchen and read with Chris and some of the others. We didn't speak, but it was easy and companionable. After about an hour, Dowdie came down. Her face was very pale.

'Come on,' she said, abrupt, as though I had kept her waiting. 'Come upstairs. Bring some drinks will you?'

We sat side by side on her bed. The light wasn't on so the room was gloomy, one window-shaped patch of moonlight illuminating the floor.

'I've got to go with my mother,' Dowdie said, fiddling with a thread on her jeans. 'I've got to go to shitty Glastonbury with Eliza and lover boy. We're going next week – when you go home.'

'I know,' I said.

'He says he won't interfere.' She thumped the bed. Her eyes glittered. 'I won't know anyone there. I won't have any friends.'

I didn't respond. Was this as near as Dowdie would get to telling me she didn't want to leave me either?

The following morning, unpredictable Dowdie was cheerful again. She woke me up early, eager to get away from the Community. We packed sandwiches, fruit and drinks to take with us. Dowdie wanted to walk ten miles or more, far away from town and over the chalk downlands to the Wansdyke. Outside the air was fresh, the grass covered with a fine dew, in which we left our footprints. We had Max with us, and in a golden field full of stubble he sniffed out a huge hare, which bolted away with the dog in hot but useless pursuit. I hadn't been this way before. It was an astonishing, magical day. Every turn, every gateway, seemed to open onto a dazzling new scene. Lanes winding through patches of woodland, fields full of chalk and flints, diving dry valleys carved into the downland, blue distant views from the high scarp-face over the low-lying quilt of pasture and wheat and barley fields. At times we walked in silence. Sometimes we talked, mostly of the past – memories of our childhood, dreams we remembered, books we had read and enjoyed. The talk was a pleasure; the times of quiet were easy. The landscape unwound beneath our feet, and every corner turned brought some new delight – a particular bright flower, the curve of a tree.

We stopped to eat in the shade of a willow tree, which arched over a pond. The water, a coin of dark green glass, was fringed with lush grass, pocked on one side by the hooves of cattle. Max dabbled in the shallows, sending water insects skittering over the surface. Threads of sunlight pierced the canopy of leaves.

Dowdie ate slowly, lying in the grass on her belly. I took off my shoes and dangled them over the water.

'What is it with you and water?' she said. 'You're always staring into water. It's like your default mode.'

I smiled. 'I don't know. I just like it. Water's soothing.'

'Maybe you think if you look long enough, you'll see something interesting.'

'What, like an answer?'

'There's never an answer. Every answer's just another question.'

'Like the Community? I thought that was the answer.'

'And now . . .?'

'And now it's a hundred questions.'

Dowdie sighed and rolled onto her back. 'I wonder what Johnny's up to.'

'I was thinking that too.'

I touched the surface of the water with my toes. The cold was biting. Deep down, in the murk, a dappled fish moved. We had a long walk ahead of us, back to the Community, and I was already tired. But I didn't worry too much. It was impossible to worry, in the cave of shadows, by the jewel of a pond.

'Is this it, then?' Dowdie said. 'You, me? Is this the end?'

I didn't answer. How could it end? I was happy. The moment would last for ever.

Dowdie ran screaming round the house. Eliza had gone to Glastonbury while we were out to make preparations. When she returned, she would take Dowdie with her. This much was relayed by Diane, who now stood in the kitchen doorway with her hands over her ears as Dowdie screamed.

'She knew this was happening,' Diane said to me. 'Why has she flown off the handle now?'

I shook my head. Perhaps because the date was set and because she'd hoped James would find her a way out. Her mood had changed in the last hour of our walk. We were tired then, and depressed by a sense that everything was coming to an end. Dowdie had marched in silence, head down, anger seething inside her. It made me afraid. There was never anything reasonable or moderate about Dowdie – it was one of the reasons I liked her so much. But it was scary, watching the storm brew, sensing the pressure of her rage.

'Where's James, where's James?' she screamed. 'Why isn't he here? Where's he gone?'

'He's down at the shop,' Diane said. 'Dowdie, please, will you stop shouting? He'll be back soon. You can talk to him then. Please – this screeching isn't helping anybody.'

'I want to talk to him *now*. Get him back here *now*,' Dowdie shouted. Her red hair jumped around her face as she stamped her foot. Diane hesitated, not knowing what to do. Dowdie shrieked again. Her body was taut, as though at any moment she might lash out with a kick or punch. Would she do it? Was she capable of it? Diane clearly didn't think it worth the risk.

'I'll call him,' she said. 'Wait there, Dowdie. Try and calm down, will you? Please?' She hurried into the office.

Dowdie was breathing deeply. Her face was flushed, her hands balled into fists by her side.

'Sit down,' I said. 'He'll be here soon.' I don't think Dowdie even heard me. She gave no sign of it, as she burned with anger. She kept her eyes fixed straight ahead of her and didn't move or speak till James arrived, twenty minutes later.

'Dowdie,' he said, stepping in through the front door. 'For

goodness' sake – what are you playing at?' His voice was calm and mellow, his demeanour relaxed. He walked towards her, holding out his hand.

'Come on,' he said. 'I know you're angry and upset. Come and talk to me.'

Without a word, Dowdie let him take her hand and lead her away to the study. I stood where I was, not knowing what to do, but James glanced back at me.

'You too,' he said. 'This involves you doesn't it?'

James ushered us inside then shut the door. He gestured to the chairs, but Dowdie refused to sit.

'Now, what's the problem?' he said.

'What's the problem?' Dowdie exploded. '*What's the problem?* What the hell do you think it is? I told you I didn't want to move to Glastonbury and you said you'd sort it out. You said not to worry. Mum's busy making her plans, and still you tell me not to worry. Now it turns out you're not going to help me after all, and she's disappeared to make her final arrangements, and I've only got four days left to go. That's my problem, OK?'

Her voice was loud and aggressive. I shrank back in my chair but James didn't flinch.

'I'm sorry, Dowdie,' he said. 'I couldn't talk your mother round. She wants you with her.'

'But you're my dad. You have a say in the matter too.' She jabbed the air with a forefinger.

'I have no legal claim on you.'

'You could have – if you tried. Get a blood test – go through the courts.'

'No!'

Even Dowdie was pulled up short. I'd never heard James raise his voice before.

'I won't get involved with all that. I'm out of it. You must understand, Dowdie – I want nothing to do with the system.'

'Even when you could use it to get what you want?'

'Even then.'

'Not even for me?'

His face struggled momentarily to contain some emotion. 'Not for anyone,' he said. 'Dowdie, you won't be far away. You can come and visit us. And in another couple of years you'll be able to do whatever you like.'

'That's it then,' Dowdie said bitterly.

'Don't say it like that.' James sounded irritated. 'It's a change, but it's not for ever.'

He held out his arms, offering a hug, but Dowdie backed away. She didn't look at James at all but walked past him out of the room. I heard her feet drumming on the stairs. James sighed.

'Go and talk to her,' he said. 'Tell her you'll go and visit in Glastonbury. That'll make her happier.'

I nodded and went to walk past him but James held my arm.

'I do love her,' he said. 'More than anyone. I want her to stay – to keep her safe. But there's nothing I can do right now.'

Dowdie was lying on her bed, her face pressed against her pillow. At first I thought she was crying. I knocked on the open door.

'Can I come in?'

She made no response. I sat on the floor; my back propped on the wall. I couldn't think of anything helpful or comforting to say.

I think I must have drifted into sleep for a while, exhausted by our walk. When I opened my eyes, Dowdie was lying on her back, her eyes wide open and staring at the ceiling.

'What time is it?' she said.

'Half eight. Did you sleep?'

'Yes. I was thinking and thinking – and then I woke up.'

I wriggled against the wall, and stretched out my legs. Beyond the window I could see Chris and another man taking feed to the animals in the paddocks beyond the garden. The swifts circled. Max was lying on his back in a last patch of sunlight, paws in the air.

Dowdie sat up and wrapped her arms around her knees.

'Maybe Glastonbury won't be so bad. There are lots of alternative types living there. It's got a big pagan community – and it's a beautiful place,' I said reasonably. 'I could come down and stay with you some weekends. You could come and stay with me. We could talk on MSN every night.'

But Dowdie didn't take any notice. 'We could run away,' she said. 'We could head for a city – find a squat. Then we'd be together. I've got contacts. I could find somewhere. It would be an adventure.'

'Surely living in Glastonbury would be better than living in a squat,' I said. 'You're not serious are you?'

'Yes I am serious. Will you? Will you run away? I can't do it on my own – but with you, yes.'

It is hard to describe how her question made me feel. For a moment I was tempted. What would it be like, to live in the enchanted space Dowdie and I created together? But it was only a moment.

'I can't run away,' I said. 'What about my parents?' And my life and my future? I had read about running away. Cold, boredom, drugs, poverty, abuse. I don't think Dowdie wanted to run away really – she just liked to play with the idea. My refusal got her out of having to do it – but she could use it to blame me too.

Dowdie sighed. 'You think he's wonderful, don't you.'

'Who?'

'James. You think he's it. Well he's not.'

'You've always given me the impression . . . well, you thought he was it, didn't you?'

Dowdie had hero-worshipped her father. She was proud of him, the leader and messiah. He wasn't like ordinary people – he had taken a stand. Now, when she had most depended on him to save her, he had let her down. He was in for a verbal kicking. And so, it seemed, was I.

'You're so easily taken in, Amber. You believe everything people tell you. You think everyone will be nice to you if you're nice to them. You need to sharpen up a bit.'

'Why are you taking it out on me? What have I done?' Her words were knives, designed to hurt. Suddenly I didn't want to be stuck at the Community. I wished I had a mobile so I could phone home, so I could be with my safe, reasonable parents. Of course I had no mobile and my parents were out of reach.

'I'll show you. Later, when everyone's gone to bed, I'll show you, Amber. It'll make you think again.'

So we stayed up. I hadn't washed since our walk and my skin itched. Her room was hot. I opened the window, but the air outside did not refresh. And I was so tired, aching for sleep, which Dowdie denied me with her bitter ranting. James was this, her mother was that, the world was doomed, fate kicked you in the teeth, nothing was fair, everyone she knew was shallow, useless and unreliable. She repeated herself, creating endless circles of the same words till my head ached. I wanted her to stop – to shut up.

She didn't stop talking until midnight, when she decided everyone must be asleep. We crept out of her bedroom and down the stairs. Dowdie led the way into the kitchen and turned on the light. Max stirred in his basket by the door, yawned and blinked sleepily. He didn't bother getting up.

'I want a drink,' Dowdie said. 'And I'm hungry.' In the unsparing electric light she looked very tired now, all energy drained out. She rummaged in the fridge for cheese and salad and made us each a sandwich.

'I'm sorry for going on at you,' she said, sitting at the table. 'You know it's not you, don't you? I don't mean to get at you.'

'I know.'

'I just can't bear it. I feel so helpless and angry.' Her hair tumbled forward over her cheek, and she pushed it back behind her ear. She ate slowly, thinking hard.

'But I think you should know. If you're going to be here when I'm gone it's right you know everything. What I'm going to show you – only a few of them here know about it. Just my dad's closest friends – the ones he most trusts. I only found out by accident. He doesn't realise I know. When I was little – a kid – I was always poking around, and I saw what they were doing.'

'What?' I said. 'I don't understand. What were they doing?'

Dowdie didn't answer. She finished her sandwich and drank a glass of milk. I couldn't eat much, but I downed my milk and then a glass of water. In a little decorated mirror on the wall I could see my face – old-looking, greasy and greyish. I could hardly see straight I was so tired. The walls leaned away. I grabbed the chair.

'Come on,' Dowdie said. Her voice was sharp.

'Dowdie – I – I don't know that I want to see. Maybe I'd rather not know.' What was she planning to show me? What? I knew it would be bad. Did James have child porn on his computer? Was he a drug dealer? I felt strangely disembodied, as though my limbs had turned to smoke. I could hardly trust my legs to carry me.

'Come on,' she repeated. 'And be quiet.'

She led the way to the office. It was locked, but Dowdie had a bunch of keys in her pocket and she opened the door. The monitor was turned off, but the stack beneath the table had a quiet electrical hum. I had expected her to load up the computer, but she dropped to her knees instead and pushed aside a large rag rug. This revealed a wooden hatch in the floor. The hatch had a serious mortise lock, which Dowdie also unlocked. She flipped the hatch open. A long flight of metal stairs led down into the darkness.

'I'll go first,' she said. 'I can turn on the light.'

I followed her down. The cellar was huge – the size of the house above – and divided into separate rooms. It wasn't damp or earthy, as I would have expected. The walls and floor were lined with concrete. Three metal filing cabinets stood in the first room, along with a dozen orange gas bottles, each nearly two metres tall. In the second was a mountain of food. Boxes and crates of tinned food, crammed in from floor to ceiling. The use-by dates were scrawled on the outsides of the boxes, along with simple descriptions of the contents. Baked beans, corned beef, prunes, apricots, dried milk powder, kidney beans, flour, tuna, rice, pulses, tomatoes.

'There's enough for three years,' Dowdie said. 'When everything goes to pieces – when the oil runs out and the economic system breaks down, when people haven't enough to eat, with the farm and the gardens and this much in store, the Community will survive. We're planning ahead.'

I felt enormous relief. Was this it? An underground larder?

'Of course,' I said. 'It makes sense.'

But Dowdie wasn't finished. She led me through another door into a much smaller room, this one stocked with equipment. Hand tools, torches, a crate full of batteries, lanterns, binoculars, all sorts of knives.

'Do you know what this is?' She gestured to a waistcoat lying on a shelf. I had seen them before, on television, worn by soldiers and armed police officers.

'It's a bullet-proof jacket,' I said.

'*It makes sense.*' She repeated my words. 'If we have a store, we shall have to defend it, don't you see?' Then she put her shoulder to a metal cabinet and slowly pushed it aside.

'Look.' She pulled me forwards. 'Hidden – there?'

Between the false back of the cabinet and the wall, a narrow space accommodated three large guns.

How quiet it was. I'd seen a million guns on television and computer games – but in real life, never. It was a shock – a confrontation. I forced myself to breathe, and breathe again. On telly a gun was banal – in reality, it was terrifying. I couldn't tell you what sort they were, but I knew what they could do. Heavy, glinting, passive for now but capable of dealing death. Engineered to shatter bone and body. Honed for killing. Perfectly still, they threatened.

'This is just the beginning,' Dowdie said coldly. 'There are another fifty all around the house. When James renovated the place he sealed them into the walls under the plasterboard. No one would ever find them unless they pulled the house apart. And who's going to do that? There they stay, until the day they're needed.'

'Why are you telling me? Why are you so keen to stay here if you know about the guns?' I said.

'I'm not worried about them. They won't ever be used – unless the time comes when we have to defend the Community. My father isn't like other men. He's not one of those docile cattle who do as they're told and suck up to the boss and sell their souls to the system. But you – I bet it worries you.'

Fifteen

Dad's face is sweaty, though the office isn't exactly hot. As I describe the cache of guns they seem to materialise in front of us, potent and dangerous. Neil's face is very serious. My dad lets out a shocked snort. Breaking off from my account, I turn to the window. Outside, an elderly man is cycling along the road on an old-fashioned bike. Starlings perch on a telephone wire, and beyond the hedge a dozen black and white cows are grazing. It is a tranquil scene, observed from our box of a room with its fizz of tension and remembered fear.

Policeman Neil asks me questions about the guns – what they looked like, exactly how many, details about the others apparently hidden in the walls. But I haven't much detail to satisfy him. I've already said everything I know.

We take a break for a few minutes, perhaps as much for Dad's benefit as mine. He is restless and impatient, finding it hard to keep still on his chair. I think he wants to push Neil out of the way, to protect me from him even though he didn't protect me from James. Poor Dad. He's tried so hard to be a good parent, but here we are, at police headquarters.

A man arrives with a tray bearing drinks and biscuits. Neil

hands Dad a cup of strong black coffee, into which Dad spoons three large teaspoons of sugar. I only want water and even that tastes bad. It doesn't refresh – instead its flavour is sour and metallic. I take the opportunity to stand up and wander up and down the room, stretching out my legs. I try and focus on the future – tomorrow, next week, next summer – but I can't see beyond the end of the interview. There is still so much to tell and it is the hardest part.

Behind me I can hear Dad arguing with Neil, some small complaint he's making into something much bigger. I wish Mum had come today. Her brand of worry is easier to deal with – quieter at least. Dad has to be assertive but it all comes across as so much bluster. Neil tries to reassure. I turn round, and in a loud voice say:

'I need the loo.'

Dad is drawn up short. Neil nods. 'Sure. Jim – will you show her the way?'

Of course I already know the way, having visited the toilets on my previous visit, but presumably I am not allowed to just wander unaccompanied through police headquarters. They want to keep an eye on me. Stolid Jim, who brought the tray of drinks, follows me through the door and along the corridor to the women's toilets. I wonder if he'll actually step inside, but no, without a word he stops by the door.

I am glad to be alone, even in the contemporary institutional-style police station toilets. Clean, tough, practical and unadorned. Six cubicles, three sinks, two electric hand-dryers. Virtually vandal proof – unless you had a sledgehammer of course, and who's going to take a sledgehammer into a police station?

There I go again. Listen to me. My mind gets snagged on details. I am clutching at straws. It's a weird expression, isn't it? So familiar it makes no impact, but I think about it now. The drowning man clutches at straws. I see him in my mind's eye, this poor man. It's dark, and the sea's cold and black. He dips under the water, struggling desperately and grasping, grabbing, catching at useless shreds of straw that can't possibly save him. There's no hope for him. He's going to drown. Oddly though, the straw will survive. It will float away on the surface of the water, perhaps for thousands of miles across the ocean. And here in the police headquarters, these exemplary, ugly toilets will endure while a tide of lives damaged and broken by robbery, murder, rape, wife beating and child abuse will pass in and out. Why do trivial things last longer?

No good, no good. I'm still standing here, in front of the screw-fixed mirror, and Jim outside will be getting impatient. I am paralysed by my brain's over-activity. I can't stop thinking. Quickly, before another train of thought carries me away, I step into a cubicle and pee. It seems I was bursting to go but hadn't really noticed. My body and mind have become a little detached, I think. The circuits have gone awry. Now I notice how much more comfortable I am, to have an empty bladder.

I wash my hands. Briefly I exchange glances with my reflection. I have dark roots showing and a brace of spots on my forehead, looking particularly lurid in the harsh electric light. I stare, while the tap runs on.

'Miss? Are you all right?' Jim's patience has run out. He knocks on the door.

'Coming,' I say. 'Just a minute.'

Back in the interview room, Neil is sipping his coffee. A window's been opened, refreshing the stale air. Dad looks a little calmer. He's munching a chocolate biscuit.

'Are you ready to begin?' Neil asks. 'We're nearly there now. But take it slowly. I want to know every detail from here on. Every step.

Every word. You saw more than anybody. You were the closest. Don't leave anything out – even if it seems unimportant to you. Do you understand?'

'Yes,' I say. 'I understand.'

Dowdie fell asleep almost immediately but I lay on the camp-bed, wide awake, the image of the guns branded on my mind. Branded, yes. Like a bright light burnt on the retina. I couldn't shift them. Couldn't get them out of my head.

It had been a long, exhausting day. Dowdie seemed to have achieved some kind of emotional satisfaction revealing the guns and the stockpile of food. She was angry about the move, furious with James. It was revenge on her father, to betray him by showing me the contents of the locked cellar. She wanted me to be angry with him too. But she hadn't thought about what it would do to me.

Dowdie's breathing slowed and deepened. I got up from my bed, and in the gloom I watched her sleeping. She was lying on her back, her arms spread wide. Her face was pale and looked almost childishly young.

What should I do?

The question echoed over and over again in my mind. I was out of my depth. Not just out of my depth but thousands of miles from the coast and entirely alone, without hope of rescue.

What should I do?

Mum and Dad were far away, doubtless enjoying their stress-free holiday with nothing more to worry about than sunburn. Why hadn't I gone with them? Then this wouldn't have happened. I wouldn't know about it. I wouldn't be stuck in this agonising, terrifying place.

What should I do?

I wasn't tired any more. There was no way I could sleep. Every atom of my body, every mote of thought in my brain was alert.

I pulled on my clothes, quietly, so as not to wake Dowdie, left the bedroom and slipped downstairs. The house was silent. In their various rooms, the Community members were fast asleep, locked in their own little worlds of dreams or lost in oblivion. I thought how much I had loved the atmosphere of the house – its tranquillity and air of freedom. Now I knew about the cargo of guns packed behind the plasterboard and stowed in the cellar, and the house was a different place. Why hadn't I sensed it? Surely the guns, dealers of death and breakage, seeped out a poisonous air I should have detected?

By the open kitchen door, Max shifted in his basket and whined.

'Don't get up,' I whispered. 'It's OK boy. Stay there.' I crept past him, to the front door. The heavy black key rested in the lock. I turned it, expecting at any moment to be stopped, for a hand to reach out and grab me. But nothing happened. I opened the door and stepped out of the house.

Moonlight spilled over the garden. The night was still, the forest of cabbage and lettuce all silvered, like a fairy-tale enchantment. They rose up in my mind now, all the folk tales I'd devoured. Perhaps James would seize me and turn me into a nightingale and lock me in a cage to keep me quiet, and instead of warning about guns I would sing only jug, jug, jug. Except that nightingales don't say jug jug. Perhaps they did in the Germany of the Brothers Grimm. Maybe, like Bluebeard, James would kill me for looking in the locked room. He was like Bluebeard – all masculine charm, and murderous power.

Stop it. Stop it. I was getting distracted. I had to think clearly. No use wondering about fairy tales when escaping a house full of monstrous guns. I ran down the path without looking back. It would be dangerous to look over my shoulder, wouldn't it? Fatal to have second thoughts.

It is hard to describe my flight from the house that night. I was tired – so tired – but wide awake now, buzzing with adrenalin. Lucky for me the moon was full and bright, so I could see where I was going. I kept away from the country roads and the cars full of potential rapists, and ran along the lanes and footpaths I had walked with Dowdie so many times. In the fields a long black moon-shadow ran ahead of me. In the lane by the spinney overhanging trees blocked out the light and I blundered in the darkness. I fell several times, bruising my hip and scraping the skin from my knees and hands. It seemed to take hours, this jaunt of a few miles. The journey seemed to take on a life of its own, a spiteful personality. It played with me – stretching out fields, scratching at my face, turning gateways around, offering paths in the wrong direction, raising trees to stop me, fences to obstruct, ditches to trip and drown in. I fought my way, through the dark places and the pools of dappled light. I wouldn't be stopped.

At last, like a mirage, the town appeared before me. Perversely, it was the town that appeared unlikely and unreal, after my flight through the fantasy land. I crossed the sweep of the bypass, embracing the first of the new housing estates illuminated with numerous street lights. Then I headed down the main road into the town centre. I don't know what time it was – maybe two or three in the morning. It would be light in a few more hours. Hardly anyone about. A cat crossed my path, something struggling in its mouth. One solitary car swooped by, its driver obscured by darkness. It was so very quiet.

Johnny's bedroom light was on. I could see it, dimly, through the trees in his front garden. Perhaps, the prince in the tower, he was the only person in the town to have escaped the enchantment of sleep.

His back door was, of course, unlocked. I went inside, through the kitchen, along the hall, and pounded up the stairs to his room.

'Johnny! Johnny! Let me in!' My voice sounded strange. What would he think, to have me landing on him in the middle of the night?

The lock turned and Johnny opened the door. He stared at me.

'Amber? What are you doing? Is everything OK?'

He stepped back, so I pushed my way inside. His computer was on, and the printer was busy.

'Can I have a drink please?' I said.

'Sure. What d'you want?'

'I don't know. Fruit juice? I'm really thirsty. I ran all the way here, from the Community.' I could see the questions bubbling up inside him, but he resisted them for the moment.

'Of course,' he said. 'Sit down, will you? I'll be back in a minute.'

I sat at the desk, and stared at the computer screen. He was logged on to his Deviant Art gallery. The blue bar along the bottom of the screen referred to his email account, Google, and a website called Terminus. I put my hand on the mouse and clicked through the pictures in the gallery. One of his latest additions was a picture taken at the Community – James among a gathering of other members, now adorned with a halo. The lighting and colour had been adjusted, to make the picture resemble a Byzantine-style religious icon – white, two-dimensional faces and a smattering of gold leaf. Best of all, in his original shot, Johnny had captured a look of intense piety on James, and rapture in the faces of his followers. It was cruel, and funny. Already other Deviant Art members had posted enthusiastic comments beneath the picture.

'I've made some cheese on toast as well,' he said. 'I'm starving. Have some if you want.'

He saw the picture on the screen and grinned. 'What d'you think?'

'It's . . . disturbing,' I said.

'Good. Art should disturb.'

'I don't mean disturbing in a good way.' I was thinking of the guns. I had bolted here, pell-mell through the night, to tell him about the guns. Now, faced with the real flesh and blood Johnny, I couldn't bring myself to tell him. Not yet. If I told him he'd go straight to the police, wouldn't he? Is that what I wanted? What other option was there?

'Perhaps any disturbance is good,' Johnny said.

'If I saw a murder, I'd be disturbed. Would that be good?' I was antagonistic, and didn't know why. Johnny had welcomed me in the middle of the night (with freshly-squeezed orange juice, cheese on toast with mustard) and still I felt prickly.

'Perhaps it would be good to see a murder,' Johnny jumped back. 'Maybe it would make you appreciate your life more.'

'You don't mean that. Don't you appreciate life anyway?'

Johnny stared at me for a moment, his eyes suddenly unfocused and diffuse. Then he gave himself a curious little shake, and picked up a piece of toast.

'Eat it. Before it gets cold,' he said. So I ate, and the heat of the food and the mustard's spice warmed my stomach. The juice was so cold and fresh I felt my mouth and throat absorbing its store of sunshine and life.

The atmosphere changed then. All the worry seemed to drain away. The outside world receded, and all that remained was Johnny in his bright, warm room. And I realised that more than anyone – even more than Dowdie – I felt at home with Johnny. I wasn't afraid of him; I didn't feel the need to impress him or to pretend anything. It came over me, in a wash of feeling, that I could say whatever I was thinking and he would understand what I meant.

'Why have you come?' Johnny said. 'I mean, in the dark, at this time of night.'

Words struggled in the front of my mind. An apocalypse played out, in an instant. Don't tell him yet. Not yet.

'I had a massive row with Dowdie,' I said. 'About her leaving. She's so angry with James but it spills out on everyone. She hates everyone.'

I felt my conscience sting, talking about her like this with Johnny. He didn't pick it up though. He was thinking about something else.

'I've done you some pictures,' he said.

'What pictures?'

'From the photos I took last time you were here.' Johnny looked a little nervous now, as he shuffled papers from the printer's out-tray. He was worried I wouldn't like them.

'Let me see.' I lay down on his bed, on my tummy. He stretched out alongside me so his shoulder was touching mine, and presented me with three pieces of glossy paper, splashed with printed colour.

I looked at the first. The colours resolved themselves into a picture.

'Oh my god,' I said. 'Is that me? Johnny, is that how you see me?'

I looked at them, slowly, turning from one to another. Then my eyes filled with tears and I couldn't see them any more. The colours blurred and swam.

'Hey,' Johnny said. 'Hey, I didn't mean to upset you.'

'You haven't upset me,' I said, though the words stumbled on the blockage in my throat, and I suddenly had to sniff. A fat, stupid tear dropped from my cheek to the first of the pictures. I wiped my nose on the back of my hand, clumsy like a little kid, and wiped my eyes with my palms.

'Here – I'll get you a tissue,' he said, all gallant now, jumping from the bed. He looked – amazed.

I sniffed again, and stared at the pictures.

Johnny had used the photos he took of me and turned them into something else. I could see it was me in the pictures, but I didn't recognise myself at all. It jarred, this discord between the Amber I saw in my unflattering mirror every day and the girl who stared out from the picture. For she wasn't the Amber I knew. She was someone else.

In the first picture, he'd used my favourite poem as a theme. How clever of him to remember – to have bothered to remember. My face (curiously not like my face, though it was) stared from the heart of the picture. Behind it, a woven collage of cobalt and turquoise. In dark gold, an antique script unravelled across the top . . . *If I were Lord of Tartary* . . . Hints of images in the pools of blue – peacock feathers, the golden-glimmering bodies of fish and a tiger's burning stripes among the slim, dark stems of fantastical trees. Perhaps if you didn't know the poem you wouldn't even see these images, rising like smoke from the fire of colours. But I could see them, the whispered pictures, the ivory bed, a golden throne. The girl's face (my face) was white and flawless, soft like ground almonds. Her eyes stared from the picture, ice-cool, and in the coils of her white hair hints of jewels glittered.

The second picture was another version of the first, except the background had receded and darkened, and the face glowed with a brighter light. The girl's eyes and her perfect Cupid's-bow mouth were a crystalline violet. The shadows playing over her face were mauve. Was this someone else? Amber the Amethyst child?

The third picture was very different. This Amber was sombre and melancholy. A little sultry too. It was almost monochrome, just a hint of indigo among the bare, black trees massing in the background. It was a wintery place, where Amber lay, on her side, upon a grainy stone tomb. She was dressed in black, but her long white hair trailed down the sides of the tomb and became long tendrils of mist, that wove through the trunks of the trees.

I stared at the picture, soaking it up, wanting to absorb every tiny detail of it – wanting to remember it for ever.

'I thought you'd like that one.' Johnny was standing by the bed, holding out toilet roll. 'You brought out the goth in me. I thought it'd look a little clichéd. But actually, I think I did a good job. Kept the colour very discreet, and the mist works well. Took me bloody hours.'

I took the toilet roll, pulled off some tissue and blew my nose.

'I love them all,' I said, choking up again. 'I can't believe it. I can't believe it's me. It doesn't look like me. That's not what I'm like.'

'Of course it's you.' Johnny said.

I struggled to explain. Johnny's Amber looked like me, except . . . except what? Johnny's Amber didn't look small and scared and ordinary. That's why she wasn't like me.

I started to cry again, giving up all resistance. The events of the long day, Dowdie's anger, the shock of the guns, the frightening journey in the dark, like so many heavy waves beating over my head. I had held out so long. I'd been so happy to send off my parents, to cast myself adrift on the world without them – and now I was flailing about in the water. I was drowning. How did Johnny manage, without that – without the support of his family?

I don't think he knew what to do. He sat on the bed beside me, his skinny body all hunched and uncomfortable, while I lay curled up in a ball, making his black bedspread all soggy with tears and snot. At last, when I stopped, all wrung out, he tried to take the pictures away but I hung onto them.

'They've upset you,' he said.

'No they haven't. It's not the pictures. I love them, Johnny. I love them. I just wish I was like her – like that girl.'

'You are her, you dope. Isn't that what happens in your head when you're dreaming about that poem? I know it is. I've seen it in your face. Why can't you let it be you?'

My eyes filled again but I didn't succumb to my tears.

'Why are you so unhappy? You don't have to be unhappy,' he said. Johnny was nonplussed. It was odd – he was so cool and dry on the outside, while I was so moist and teary and doubtless horribly blotchy, but I could see how unhappy he was. My paddle in the shallows of sorrow was nothing to the depths in which Johnny moved. He was damaged, as James had said. He was like a Russian doll, full of broken layers. Inside him was the little boy his parents had forgotten and left for hours at a railway station. He had no one.

The room was very quiet. Johnny sat with his hands pressed together between his thighs. I wiped my face with some tissue. The room was a little box, and nothing else existed. Just the two of us. Just this little theatre where we acted out our drama. Neither of us spoke for a few minutes, caught in our own thoughts. Then Johnny gave an abrupt little sigh.

'I got my GCSE results,' he said. 'They came in the post this morning. They're late. I think the school sent them to my parents' house in London, and the house-sitter has only just got round to forwarding them to me.'

I stared at him. He looked very small and shrunken.

'How did you do?'

Johnny shrugged. He stood up, strolled to his desk and picked up two scrunched-up pieces of paper.

'See for yourself.'

I smoothed out the pages on the bed. Johnny had taken eleven GCSEs. The highest grade he had achieved was a single D. The others were Es and Fs.

'I failed them all,' he said.

'You didn't fail them,' I said, blabbing, wanting to say something good. 'I mean – you don't fail GCSEs.'

Johnny shook his head. 'There isn't one of the necessary A to C grades,' he said. His voice was like ice. He didn't want my stupid cheery comfort.

'I failed on purpose.' He was staring at the floor, head bent forward. 'During the examinations, I didn't write anything. Or if I did, I wrote nonsense. Blah, blah, blah.'

The moment stretched. I struggled for the right thing to say. But how could anything be right?

'Why? Why did you do it? To get back at them? Your parents?'

Johnny propped himself on his desk, and folded his arms. 'Would it get back at them? Will they even care? I don't know. Maybe. When one of their friends inevitably asks how I did, I suppose it might dent their egos for a moment. Then again, they'd probably just lie.

'I don't know why I did it. I just couldn't be bothered. That's all it was. I didn't care enough. I didn't want to play the game. Why should I?'

'But what are you going to do? What about your A-levels and all that stuff?'

'Don't know. Don't care. What does it matter?' He lifted his face, and again his eyes were full of the horrible diffuse darkness I'd seen before.

'What about your photography – your pictures? You care about that. Wouldn't you like go to college for that?' Hark at me. I sounded like my parents.

But Johnny shook his head. He was shaking me off. I didn't understand. So much annoying noise. He was on the outside now, the little-boy doll, standing at the railway station while the hordes of faceless, careless people moved past. I didn't think then – didn't make a conscious decision. I stood up and put my arms around him. He was so tall my face pressed against his hard, bony chest. His body was very cold and stiff, like a piece of wood. Without moving, he seemed to resist, pushing me away. But I kept my hold, clinging on like a kid, squeezing tight. But Johnny wasn't made of warm, living flesh and blood. He was a coffin full of iron chains, broken rods, smashed gears, snagged wire, needles, poison and grit. If I held him, wouldn't I hurt myself? But I didn't let go. Outside a car passed the house, and then another. The computer rattled into life, making some autonomous little adjustment. A milk float hummed on the road. Morning was coming. How long could I bear it, to hold him tight and have him push me away? I had my eyes squeezed shut, my cheek pressed against his ribs. I liked the smell of him, the unfamiliar odour of boy, the perfume of night and sleeplessness.

Johnny made a little movement, and I thought at last he would physically push me away. He lifted his arms. Then he laid his hands on the top of my head. I could feel the weight of them, the shape of his fingers pressing lightly into my hair. So we remained for another while. Then his hands slid to either side of my face. His thumbs brushed against my cheeks, and gently he dipped his head and pressed his lips against my mouth.

It wasn't like I'd expected. A kiss. Isn't that when the orchestra strikes up? Of course I'd imagined what it would be like to kiss him. Not like this. It is a weird thing, to put your mouth against someone else's, to have your face against theirs. My mind dissolved in a storm and my body seemed to light up. All along the front of me, where I touched Johnny, I felt a kind of burning.

After a few seconds, Johnny drew away, but his arms were around me. Everything about him had changed. The stiffness had gone. His body was soft and warm and pliant, all resistance dissolved away. He stared into my face.

'Why did you do that?' he said.

I tried not to be shy. How could I not be, when we had just kissed like that?

'I don't want you to be so unhappy,' I said.

'What does it matter to you, that I'm unhappy?'

'Of course it matters. You're my friend.'

Johnny looked away, over the top of my head. 'A friend you kiss,' he said. 'So you feel sorry for me.'

'I don't – I mean, I do. But that's not it. That's not why.'

He took my hands. 'I'm tired,' he said. 'Lie down beside me.' The pictures were still on the bed, where I'd left them. Johnny pushed them onto the floor.

'Don't worry. I'll print them up again, on proper paper. Then you can keep them,' he said. 'They disturbed you, didn't they? I told you art should be disturbing.'

Johnny turned off the light, but it wasn't entirely dark because the first pale threads of daylight crept in through the window. The room was full of shadows. We lay down side by side, on our backs. Johnny kept hold of my hand. Our fingers interlaced. Outside, in the trees, a blackbird began to sing.

'It was very kind of you,' Johnny said. 'Very kind. But you're that sort of person, Amber.'

'I wasn't being kind.'

'Ah – it was an act of cruelty?'

I couldn't see his face, but I smiled.

'Why do you have to play this game?' I said.

'This game? I don't know. I don't know what to say. I'm scared.'

'Of me? Or 'cos of your results?'

'Everything. Life. It's a long battle. An endless line of fights and wounds and insults and bruises. It wears me out. I'm only sixteen and I'm tired of it already.'

For a moment Johnny was quiet. Then he said, abruptly: 'At least James Renault's chosen a more original game. I'll give him that much.'

Johnny's voice was very hard and cold. I didn't like it. But I wanted to hear what he was thinking. His hand, warm and holding tight, did not seem to belong to the voice.

'That's what it is? James is playing a game?'

'Of course. But like I said – everyone plays one. It might be the get-rich game or the family game, or the politics game or maybe even the crime game or the drugs game.'

'So what's my game?'

'I expect you'll pick up the game your parents play. That's what most of us do. Study hard, get a job, buy a house, have kids, teach them the game.'

'You make it sound like it's not serious – if it's a game,' I said.

'Perhaps it isn't serious, not really. Just that people make the mistake of thinking it is. I dunno. Maybe that's where I'm going wrong. You have to believe your game's serious, or what else is there?'

'Is that why you messed up your exams?'

'I didn't want to play,' Johnny said. 'So what shall I do instead?'

The question hung in the air, and I didn't know what to say. It had been the strangest night of my life, and lying beside Johnny in the twilight I tried to stay awake, to savour the unexpectedness, the weirdness, but sleep caught at me, dragged me down into the dark.

I don't know how long I slept. There were no dreams. I was so very tired.

Then, a screaming. I was way down, fathoms deep, and to begin with the screaming came from far away. Gradually, stealing through the darkness, the noise grew louder. A horrible, piercing human noise.

I woke with a jolt. Smashed, obliterated by sleep, it took an instant to remember who I was – and where –

Dowdie stood at the end of the bed. She was screeching and ranting. I couldn't make sense of what she was saying. Johnny lay beside me, our hands still clutching each other.

'What are you doing, you treacherous bitch! What are you doing? How could you do this to me? I thought you were my friend but you're just like all the others! How could you, how could you? And with him? I thought I could trust you, Amber. I thought you were my friend but you went off with him, you cheap little slut, you ran off after him! You make me *sick*, how could you?'

She looked terrifying – like a witch. Writhing Medusa hair, face burning with fury.

The shouting proceeded. The same words and phrases over and over again. For a while I lay there helpless and disorientated beneath the violent, verbal assault. I could feel her accusations bodily, her words like knives. I let go Johnny's hand, climbed clumsily from the bed and stood up straight.

'Dowdie – please. Please stop shouting. Dowdie – listen to me. Please. Everything's OK, honestly.' Did Dowdie think I'd spilled the beans? Was she worried that in a fit of conscience I'd told him about the guns? Was she jealous, to find me so intimate with Johnny, or afraid he'd take me away from her? All of them, I think. All out of her control. I felt a horrible, plunging guilt.

I glanced at Johnny, which seemed to infuriate her all the more. But Johnny shook his head and went out of the room, leaving me alone with Dowdie. At his departure, strings of tension relaxed. Dowdie's voice dropped. She stepped closer and grabbed my arm.

'Have you told him?' she said. 'Is this why you went running off? To tell him about the guns in the cellar – to unburden yourself?'

'No! No I didn't tell him.'

'So why did you come here?' Her sharp fingers dug into my arm. I pulled it away.

'I was scared,' I said.

'You were scared,' she repeated, cold and derisory. 'So off you ran. And now – you and him?'

Johnny was back, with a cola can in his hand. He stood in the doorway. Dowdie gestured towards him.

'Who are you with?' she said to me.

'This is stupid. Why do I have to make a choice?'

'Who are you with?'

In the doorway, Johnny shook his head and backed away.

'Go back to the Community,' he said. 'Go on. Take her home,

the madwoman. Sort it out. I'm not messing things up for you, Amber.'

But I didn't want to go – didn't want to leave him.

'Come on,' Dowdie said ungraciously. 'You heard him. He doesn't want you here. Come home with me.'

Johnny nodded. He wanted to be rid of me – and rid of Dowdie. So I had no choice. Did I?

Seventeen

We didn't go straight back. Dowdie said she wanted a drink, so we headed into town. I had no money on me but Dowdie had a fiver from somewhere so we went to the coffee shop. She bought us fruit juices and a Danish pastry to share.

Once we were out of the house, Dowdie's mood altered. She became very fey and bright and brittle. She didn't talk about Johnny to start with, instead joking about the office drones coming in for their morning fixes of caffeine. We were sitting by the plate-glass window, overlooking the marketplace. Fat, doughy clouds ploughed across the sky, but it was still hot. I stirred my drink with a straw, in a daze, hardly taking in Dowdie's comments. She was trying, though – trying to buck me up. Then she said:

'I'm sorry I shouted. You know I was trying to help you, don't you? Had to get you away from him.'

I looked up at her, still turning the straw in the glass. I don't know what I felt. Tired, mostly. Hardly awake. Mentally, I was still caught up in the events of the previous night. Physically too – my nerves replayed the sensations of the kiss. I could remember it perfectly, a recording ingrained on the flesh of my mouth. The present morning was unreal.

'Hello? Are you paying any attention to me?' Jokily, Dowdie waved her hand in front of my face, close enough to irritate.

'Don't,' I said. 'Please, don't. I'm really tired.'

'Do you understand what I'm saying? Are you listening? He isn't good for you, Amber. Steer clear.'

'I thought you liked him. I thought you were, well, a bit keen on him?'

Dowdie flinched. Emotion congested in her face. She blushed and shook her head. You're like your dad, I thought. That same way of turning things around, trying to make me believe everything you do is for my own good. Well I'm tired of it – tired of having my strings pulled. She didn't answer my question. Instead she said:

'I shouldn't have shown you. I'm sorry. There was no need for you to know.'

I was wary of what she might say next – how unguarded she might be. On the table next to us, two middle-aged women in smart blouses and bulging suits glanced over.

There was no need for me to know? Well, I did know. She couldn't take that back. But my parents were away for another week and I had nowhere else to go, except the house full of hidden guns. Could I cut them out of my mind? Could I somehow pretend to myself that they weren't there, snuggled behind the plasterboard, stocked up with the tins and boxes?

'How do you manage it – not worrying?' I said.

'I'm not like you,' she said, shrugging. 'I'm not caught up in all this.' She gestured, at the people in the café. 'It doesn't mean so much to me. That's not virtue on my part,' she reassured. 'It's just how I've been brought up.'

I indicated the café, the marketplace, as she had done. 'This isn't your game,' I said. 'So you don't play by the same rules.'

Dowdie smiled. 'Just so.'

'And what about me?'

'What about you? I can't tell you where you belong. That's your choice.' She didn't look like she was offering a choice – her face was fierce.

She polished off the pastry and we left the café. The High Street was busy. Women with pushchairs, elderly couples out shopping, the perpetual gangs of kids loitering. Dowdie didn't ask me what I wanted to do, merely set off in the direction of the Community. If I went back now, wouldn't I be complicit? Wouldn't I be saying I accepted what she had shown me, that I was OK about it? What else could I do, for now at least? I could ring my parents – and say what? I'm having a lovely time, and by the way, there's a hoard of guns in the cellar. Could I abandon Dowdie and stay with Johnny? But Dowdie had only a few days left at the Community in any case. She would be moving to Glastonbury. Shouldn't I stay by her side for these last days? Think about it. Those guns had been there for a long time – and nothing bad had happened. The only difference now was my knowing about them. Couldn't I live with this knowledge for a few days, till Dowdie left and my parents came home? I didn't know what would happen then – what I would do – but everything would be so much easier. I wouldn't be on my own.

I picked up speed, so I was side by side with Dowdie. She looked at me.

'So you're coming,' she said. 'You're with me?'

I nodded. 'Yes.'

She smiled. 'I knew you would be. This has been a testing time, hasn't it? I do understand it's been hard for you. I thought you'd get through it.'

'Have you forgiven him?' I said.

'Who?'

It flashed in my mind she thought I was talking about Johnny. I added: 'Your dad – for letting your mum take you.'

Dowdie shrugged. 'I haven't gone yet.'

It was quiet at the Community. I could hear someone working in the office, but the door was closed. It seemed everyone else was out – tending the shop, in the garden or down in the workshops. I don't know where James was. It was a relief not to see him – how could I look at him now, knowing about the guns? Wouldn't he see through me?

We went straight upstairs. I went to the bathroom, took off my clothes and had a long, cool shower. The water sluiced away layers of sweat and dirt and dust. I washed my hair, using Dowdie's nettle and tea-tree shampoo, and brushed my teeth. Then, all fresh and clean, I lay down on the camp-bed in Dowdie's room. Dowdie was on her bed already, reading a book. It was nearly midday. Far away I could hear a cow lowing. I thought of Chris tending his tomatoes and courgettes, and Diane weighing out organic brown rice in the wholefood shop. Dowdie had told me only a trusted few knew about the guns – so what about them, Chris and Diane?

'Dowdie,' I said. 'Does your mum know?'

Dowdie sighed, turning a page. 'I don't know,' she said. 'I didn't dare just come out and ask her. Sometimes I think she does. Other times – well, I'm not so sure.'

'Weren't you tempted to tell her?'

Dowdie snorted. 'No. I was scared that she'd take me away.'

'But she is taking you away.'

Dowdie shook her head, as though she was refusing to accept this would happen. Something would turn up. If she wanted something badly enough, she'd find a way.

The rest of the day passed quietly enough, though inside my head the same difficult thoughts turned over and over. My fears about the arsenal under the house were intermittently interrupted with remembering the kiss with Johnny, and the long, painful ache of wanting to be with him again. Dowdie was a little distant, disappearing into a book for a couple of hours, scribbling notes in a journal. I sensed I wasn't entirely forgiven.

That night, falling asleep, I dreamed about Johnny, searching for him and losing him, never managing to keep him in sight. The mood of the dream was melancholy, Johnny a shadow I could never catch. Then the dreams dispersed and I sank into a deeper sleep, everything forgotten.

When I woke, very early in the morning, a thin, golden light filled the room. The air carried a weight of dust and static, heralding perhaps another day of thwarted thunderstorms. Dowdie was still asleep. I rolled off the camp-bed, and lying on the floor on my belly, peered out of the low window and over the garden. Dull, ochre cloud clumped over the tree tops. Drowsy cows huddled in the bottom corner of the paddock. Like a picture, everything was still. No breeze to stir the trees. Even the irrepressible chickens were silent.

'Dowdie,' I said. 'Dowdie, wake up. Look outside.'

But Dowdie didn't stir. Slowly the cloud shifted, breached by spears of early sunlight. The window framed the scene, a bottle of landscape, tawny like a distant Renaissance landscape.

Then, improbably, something did move. An ant with a black carapace, an ill-fitting, deviant thing. The invader crept behind a rose-bush, surveyed the scene, and then trotted across the garden. It crouched behind the carpentry workshop and gestured to some unseen companion.

All thought stilled. I was conscious of my blood drumming,

and a coldness spreading from my fingers and hands, along my limbs. A kind of darkness filled the room, though my eyes were open. I wanted to call out to Dowdie but the connections between my will and body were momentarily severed.

A second ant, similarly black and armed, scuttled across the garden and took up position beside the hen house. There were others, I could see, moving in pattern. Insects with a group mind, powered by a single will.

'Dowdie,' I croaked. 'Dowdie! Wake up. Quick.'

On her bed, she rolled away from me, her movements heavy and lazy. She mumbled something.

'Dowdie. For God's sake. Please – wake up.'

'What? What is it?'

'In the garden – they've come, Dowdie. Armed police.'

Dowdie sprang to her feet, stumbling over the camp-bed. She pushed me out of the way and leaned towards the window. She peered out, scanning left and right, then she caught her breath.

'You did tell them!' She whipped round and grabbed me by the hair. 'You liar! You miserable traitor! You told them!'

'I didn't tell anyone!' I pushed her away but Dowdie was electric with rage and wouldn't let go. We rolled against the camp-bed, and I lashed out with my feet. My scalp burned, as her hands tore away, taking strings of hair. She drew back her hand and punched my face, on the cheekbone close to my eye. A bright pain dazzled.

'It wasn't me!' I shouted. 'Get off me! It wasn't me!' We rolled impotently on the floor for a few seconds, struggling against each other. But Dowdie was bigger than me, heavier and less scrupulous about causing hurt. She kicked at my shins, with her bare, bony feet.

'Stop it! Stop it!'

'Of course it was you – who else? Who else?'

'I didn't tell anyone, I swear. I swear on my mother's life. I didn't tell anyone!' I had to get her off me, had to stop her hurting me. I bucked my body, dislodging her, and scrabbled out of her reach.

Dowdie was breathing heavily. 'Then how do they know?' she said. My face throbbed, where her knuckles had hammered me.

Then, from downstairs, we heard a heavy pounding on the front door. The house, so still just minutes before, suddenly seethed with life. The nest had been disturbed.

I glanced at Dowdie.

'What shall we do?'

Dowdie shrugged. 'What can we do?'

'Is your mum here? What about James? Where is everyone?'

'How do I know?'

I crouched down by the window again. I could see half a dozen officers. Doubtless others were positioned all around the house. I racked my brains. How did the police know?

A second pounding on the door. I ran past Dowdie and down the stairs. Everyone was gathering in the hall – a milling mass of bewildered people were moving around in the hall and living room, most still in their night clothes, including Chris and Diane, and Marie with her two little children. I couldn't see Eliza or James.

'Shall we let them in?' It was Chris who spoke, just out of bed, in a pair of shorts and a T-shirt. His face was white, his hands visibly shaking. A hubbub rose, so many confused, frightened voices. A second man shook his head.

'Wait. Wait for James. He'll know what to do.'

'Where is James? Why isn't he here?' The older man with long grey hair spoke up.

Outside, the oppressive noise of a helicopter. It circled around the house. We could see its insect legs through the window. The little children cried out and pressed their faces into their mother's nightie.

All the others just turned to each other, all in a panic, not knowing what to do. They were leaderless – useless. An argument started up, and Diane tried to soothe.

'I'll – I'll – I'll let them in,' Chris said. 'We haven't done anything wrong. This is just some mistake.'

The others looked at one another again, wanting reassurance.

'Why are they here?' a dreadlocked woman bleated. 'What's going on?'

'I'll open the door,' Chris said. He lifted his arm to draw back the lock. But the office door suddenly banged open. There was James, all dressed, apparently calm, his hands in his pockets.

'Leave it, Chris,' he said. 'Step away. It's OK.' His voice was level and reassuring. They let out a collective sigh of relief, all of them, to see him. It was almost tangible, the passing over of responsibility.

'James – do you know why the police are here?' Diane asked. 'Shouldn't we let them in and see what they want? We haven't got anything to hide.'

A heavy weight thudded against the door, a different sound to the earlier banging. It was a very thick, sturdy front door but even so, it would probably break on the next blow.

'They're going to break down the door,' Chris said. 'Please, James, what shall we do?'

James glanced over his shoulder, and nodded. Two men stepped out – carrying guns.

The sense of shock was palpable. I don't think any one of the other residents knew about the Community's hidden cache – none but James and the two men – except for nosy Dowdie, and unlucky me. They all stared, utterly stunned. No one said a word. Chris collapsed to his knees and moaned, covering his face in his hands. Then Marie broke the spell. She grabbed her children and dragged them away, up the stairs and along the corridor. Perhaps she hid them in a cupboard.

'What's going on? Where have they come from?' somebody called out.

I stared at the two men. I'd seen them before, at the Community, but didn't know their names or anything about them. Truth be told, I hadn't seen them much. Not at meals, not working in the gardens or the workshops. They'd been around, at the ceremonies, sometimes late at night talking to James. Now one stepped to the window at the front of the house. He opened it, and stuck out the nose of his gun.

'Keep away from the door,' he called out to the police. 'Step back – all of you. Leave the door!'

I couldn't see what was happening outside but the attempt to break the door down stopped abruptly. Presumably the police officers fell back to some safer position.

James hadn't moved. He stood with his hands in his pockets. All the others stared at him like sheep. I don't think they could believe what was happening. Outside a megaphone started up but we didn't listen to the voice of the negotiator. We were tuned, every one of us, to James.

'Could you tell us what's going on?' Diane's voice was steely. 'Where do those guns come from? Why are the police here?'

James didn't attempt to explain. He beckoned to the other armed man, who moved to the far side of the front door. Why hadn't Dowdie come down? Was she still in her bedroom, hiding out?

'This is my house,' James said. 'I'm not letting the police take it. We've been sold out. Someone's betrayed us. The guns were never intended to be used – they were our insurance policy for the future, when we might need them to defend ourselves, and what we have. They were for your future protection – and for your children.

'You came here to live with me, to be part of the Community. If you want to leave now, that's your choice. If you choose to abandon me and everything we've worked for then do it now.' He looked around the room, at every one of us. We had all, old and young, signed up. We had taken our places in James Renault's grand design – signed on the dotted line. We had all said, at one time or another – *I believe*. Would they all abandon him now? Would they betray him? Or had James betrayed them, with his secret store of guns and ammunition?

I could see the conflict in the faces of his disciples. Chris, rescued by James from a miserable life on the streets, was still on his knees with his hands on his face.

James focused on me. 'Where's Dowdie?' he said. 'Where is she?' His voice was abrupt and angry.

'She's – she's upstairs in her room. Do you want me to get her?' Rage briefly revealed itself in his face before the mask of calm reasserted itself. Did he think Dowdie had betrayed him? Perhaps he knew she had discovered the guns and thought she had exposed him as an act of revenge for letting her down. I remembered her shouting and screeching at her father. Unreasonable, burning with anger, thoughtless of the consequences, would she have called the police? For a fleeting moment I thought perhaps she had. But my face throbbed – reminding me of her violent fury when she saw the police in the garden and thought that *I* was the Judas . . .

'She didn't do it,' I said. 'It wasn't her, James. It couldn't have been.'

He didn't reply. Instead he gestured to his two lieutenants.

'Stay where you are,' he said. 'Make sure they can see you, but be careful – they'll have marksmen. Make sure nobody leaves without my say-so – you understand? We've got some time. They'll send in a negotiator. We've got to think what we can do.'

James was brisk. He turned away and ran up the stairs. As soon as he was out of sight the others clutched each other and began to murmur. Diane put her arm around Chris and helped him to his feet.

'Come into the kitchen and sit down,' she said. 'I'll put the kettle on. Don't worry, Chris. Everything's going to be OK. There's just some kind of misunderstanding.'

But Chris glanced at the guns. It was hard to know how they could be misunderstood. The helicopter circled again, very low and loud, and Chris began to sob. Diane manoeuvred him into the kitchen. Some of the others followed Diane. Several young men remained in the living room, peering out of the windows, trying to work out what was happening. I could hear an anxious argument between them – a throwing of blame, an angry raising of questions.

I wondered how long James would leave them. When he was present, everyone looked to him. In his absence, perhaps some kind of rebellion might happen. The others might muster enough strength between them to decide what they wanted to do. A whispering started up. The young dreadlocked couple were ashen-faced, holding onto each other, weakened, as though the stuffing had been kicked out of them. Nobody took any notice of me – they were all too terrified. And what should I do? Could I sneak out a window without James or his men noticing? Was I in trouble because I was part of the Community and shared its collective guilt? I didn't think I was afraid, but my entire body was shaking.

Just a few minutes later James ran back down the stairs. He glanced out the windows. Then he looked at me.

'Amber,' he said. Then, very slowly: 'My little star.'

His charm had polarised. The intimate warmth had switched to a rage just as powerfully frightening. I could sense it, emanating from him.

I tried to move out of his way but my body was slow responding to the shrilling voice in my brain. James grabbed my arm and dragged me into the office. A woman called out in alarm – Diane, I think. And somebody else shouted: 'What are you doing? What has she done?'

The trap-door was open, the rug folded back. I struggled and panicked but James was very strong and determined. He pushed me through the hatch so I fell onto the narrow stairway.

'No! No!' I shouted out. 'It wasn't me, it wasn't me.' But James was relentless. He pushed my desperate scrabbling hands away and closed the trapdoor above my head. I banged the door with my fists, but I heard the lock turn, and all sound from the house was cut off.

For a few minutes I gripped the stairs, mind in a maelstrom, struggling to draw breath. It was utterly dark, entirely silent. My senses reeled, deprived of impressions to hang on to. My mind seemed to fall into pieces, knocked off balance by the plunge from the hectic siege to the utter nothing of the black pit under the house. I clung as tightly as I could, overcome by vertigo, afraid I would fall away into some unplumbed depth.

Time passed. I'm not sure how long. I think I might have lost consciousness for a couple of minutes. A faint or a weird sleep, I'm not entirely certain. I just remember waking up.

Inside me, everything had changed. I felt very calm, and my mind was clear. Slowly I shifted on the stairs. My muscles ached, arms and thighs and deep in my belly. The underground bunker had lights – if I could remember where the switch was. I groped along the wall beside the stairs, sliding my hands over the cold, smooth surface. There it was. The lights buzzed on, illuminating the first room with its filing cabinets and ranks of bottled gas. It was odd but I thought of Johnny and the night before in his bedroom. I was in a lit room again, a little space where a drama might be played out. But this particular stage set was just for me. There was no dialogue yet. The action was taking place off-stage, above my head in the house. Perhaps fighting and gunfire and death. But it was hard to credit so much could be happening just centimetres away. The bunker seemed another world. How easily we are deceived.

I wandered through the cellar into the second room with its larder of food. At least I wouldn't starve to death – or not for a very long time. In the smallest room I checked for the secret place behind the cupboard, where the guns had been hidden. This place was empty now. Presumably these weapons, closest to hand, had armed James' lieutenants. There were, however, other things I could use to protect myself if I had to – screwdrivers, knives, hammers. I picked up a screwdriver, weighed it in my hand. Would James kill me? Would he come through the trapdoor with a gun in his hand and take his revenge? I gripped the tool's smooth, balanced handle. What use was this against bullets? I turned it in my hand, raising it to my shoulder like a weapon. An image flashed into my head – how it would feel to thump the long, iron shaft into a living body, and the strength it would need. Would I have the guts to do it, when face to face with someone intent on hurting me? Hard to tell. I couldn't imagine doing it. I opened my hand and the screwdriver fell with an echoing clatter onto the worktop.

An unexpected and crushing sense of boredom assailed me. What could I do? God knows what was happening in the house, but I was locked out. They were managing without me. Where was Dowdie now? Would she rescue me? Presumably she had told James I knew about the guns and then denied contacting the police herself – thus putting the blame on me. But did Dowdie believe this? She had to know it wasn't true. Gripped by a peculiar calm, I speculated that obviously James's possession of guns did not make him a murderer. He anticipated an apocalypse and had stockpiled the weapons to defend his people. It was a rational thing to do, under the circumstances. Rational, that was, if you believed what he believed.

But I didn't want the guns. They weren't part of the story. Or, as Johnny might have said, the game I was playing. Perhaps, deep down, this meant I hadn't really believed what James had told me, about the spirit Throne, and being an Amethyst child. There was no logical reason why the apocalypse shouldn't happen of course – what with the oil running out, terrorism, climate change, environmental breakdown. It wasn't just James who believed it. Even the serious papers quoted experts claiming the human race could be largely destroyed over the next century – *my lifetime* – because of wars, hunger, and climate chaos. And so many nights I'd spent awake, scared and worrying, fear in my guts, looking for an answer, waiting for someone to tell me what to do, while everyone else plodded on in a hypnotised, complacent dream . . .

I wandered back to the first room. There were no chairs, nowhere to sit, so I propped myself against the wall. It was cold in the cellar, and in my T-shirt I shivered, the pale hairs on my arms standing up. Uselessly I stared at the ceiling. I yearned to know what was happening.

Time stretched. I think hours passed. My mind worked

endlessly over the same thoughts for ages. Then at last a kind of numbness followed, and my head was light and vacant. I dozed for a bit, uncomfortable against the cold wall, then jumped awake from a dream that Dowdie was standing beside me, aiming a pistol at my head. Sleeping again, I dreamed of my parents and little Justin, running across the fields to rescue me. I can't tell you how it felt to see their faces, even in a dream, and how empty I was on waking, to find myself alone in the cellar.

The whole day went by, and night drew on. Even below ground I could sense it. Perhaps it was just the ticking of my biorhythm or a change in the taste of the air. All around the cellar, in its bed of dirt, night creatures were moving. I imagined them, worms and beetles, scurrying and scuttling through the sponge of earth, feeding and breeding and hunting. I stood up, and pressed my palms to the wall, and then my ear, in case I could hear them, all the living things outside my sterile concrete prison.

What I heard was the turn of a key. The hatch door opened, feet landed on the staircase and then the hatch was shut again – locked and bolted from the inside. I heard all this – because I didn't turn around. I had my eyes tight shut. I didn't want to see.

A hand landed on my shoulder. I could smell him, the aura of heat and fear and masculine sweat.

'It's just you and me now,' he said.

Eighteen

James pulled me away from the wall.

'I didn't do it, I didn't tell anyone, it wasn't me.' I didn't even have time to think. The words spilled out in a babble. James didn't answer. His hand was still on my shoulder. The other hand he raised, with finger to his lips, to shush me.

'Leave it,' he said.

'But it's true! You don't believe me, I didn't tell anyone. I never had a chance but I wouldn't have anyway.' One part of my mind watched the other, blabbing, part in horror. Shut up, it was saying. Don't be so weak and craven. Take control of yourself. The blabbing part wouldn't listen.

'Don't kill me. Don't hurt me. It's not my fault. I would never tell anyone, not ever. You must believe me, please believe me.'

James didn't move. He kept his finger to his mouth. The cool part of my mind observed how pale he was, how a sheen of sweat glistened on his forehead. His breath smelled bad, but mine did too, sour with fear – I could taste it. The pistol, just like the one I'd seen Dowdie carrying in my dream, jutted out from a pocket inside his jacket.

My voice, with a life of its own, continued to plead while my mind wandered. What had happened today? Where were all the others? What happened to Dowdie? The hand James held to his lips had blood on it, congealing around the fingernails.

He was patient, waiting till the stream of words had dried up. Then he lowered his finger. His other hand remained on my shoulder.

'It's just you and me,' he repeated. Some of the strength had gone from him. He turned away from me. 'They've all gone,' he said.

'Gone? What – dead?' The words seemed to choke, filling my throat like stones.

'No!' he snapped. 'No one dead. One injured – a bullet wound in the arm. The others – they left. All of them. Not one had faith enough to stay.' He smelled of anger, a dangerous, suppressed burning, though his voice was cool and matter of fact. He wasn't looking at me when he spoke.

'It was getting dark. The police got impatient. In the end a marksman fired through the window. Matt was hit. The bullet shattered his upper arm. There was blood everywhere.'

James considered his stained hand. 'That was it. Everything changed. All the others – all of my devoted followers – headless chickens. Screaming and wailing. They fell apart. I lost them then. They decided to leave the house – to surrender. By then I was effectively holding them, in a crowd, at gunpoint. Men, women, children. What could I do? Shoot them all? So I let them go.'

James fell silent, apparently deep in thought.

'And now you're going to let me go too.'

James sighed heavily. He didn't answer. Instead he drew out the pistol from his jacket. 'They'll know I have a hostage,' he said. 'The others will have told them. So I'm sorry, Amber. I'll have to keep you a while longer, to give me space to think. I need a little more time.'

He had always seemed so self-contained before – so much in control. Now I saw the storm roiling through him.

'They just left me!' he erupted. 'Just pissed off, like that, after all I'd done. Did they have such little faith?' He turned abruptly and marched up and down the room, still talking and cursing under his breath.

'Somebody – *somebody* – sold me out. All the useless nobodies – how could they! The very first sign of trouble, and they're gone. None of them had any conviction.' He banged the wall with his fist.

I was afraid. He was struggling to control his anger. Perhaps he would hit me next, or worse.

'Such pathetic little people. Such sheep.'

I didn't answer, just huddled close to the wall, hoping he wouldn't take any notice, that I wouldn't become the focus of his burning rage. But it was coming. He turned on his heel and strode towards me. He reached out his left hand and grabbed me by the throat. His strong fingers pressed against my neck and he shoved me hard against the wall, almost lifting me from my feet. Stunned, struggling to breathe, I couldn't speak or fight back. Instead, on the tips of my toes, I tried to stand to relieve the pressure on my throat.

James brought his face next to mine. So close I could see the pores of his nose, the grey, pouchy skin beneath his eyes. The pistol was still in his right hand and slowly he raised it to my head. He pressed the end of the cold metal barrel to my temple. My body felt like water, without any strength. I choked, hardly conscious now, the thunder of blood in my ears so overwhelming I could hardly hear what he said.

'Did you betray me, Amber? Did you?' His lips continued to move, but he was far away now, receding into a red haze. Was this the end – was I going to die? My feet kicked out, in a feeble panicked spasm. My thoughts fizzed.

Then he let me go. My legs gave way, my liquid body pooled, helpless, on the floor. I came too, coughing and coughing. I rubbed my neck, feeling the bruised imprint of his fingers.

James sighed. He considered the pistol, and then put it back in his jacket. Then he proceeded to the second room, rooted around for a box and drew out a plastic bottle of water.

'Want one?'

I sat up, my throat still hurting. Was this a trick? Would he try and hurt me again? Instead he handed me the bottle, which I opened and drank. I hadn't realised how thirsty I was, though it hurt to swallow. The water didn't take the bad taste from my mouth.

'Don't drink too much,' he said. 'There's no loo down here. You'll have to use a bucket to pee.'

'How long are we staying?'

He shrugged. 'As long as it takes.'

'To do what?'

'For me to work out what to do.'

Everyone else was outside. Matt, presumably one of the men with guns, would be tended by ambulance staff. Probably the other gunman had surrendered too, faced with such overwhelming odds. All the others would be taken away and cared for. Dowdie was safe. It was over, for all of them. All except James and me. And what would happen to me?

James opened a second box and took out some kind of muesli bar. He threw it across the room to me and pulled out several more. He ripped open the wrapper and began to eat. He looked friendly now, almost relaxed. It was as though the last scene hadn't happened. Just moments before he'd held a gun to my head. How could I second-guess him?

'There are chairs in the other room,' he said. 'Didn't you find them? Go and have a look. Might as well make yourself comfortable. And – if you're cold – a pile of sleeping bags at the bottom of the cupboard. Didn't you look? Where's your sense of initiative?'

I thought back to the moment I'd spent brandishing the screwdriver. It was still there on the worktop. I could pick it up now, couldn't I? Rush at James before he had time to reach for his gun again. I went to the little room and sure enough half a dozen chairs, folded like umbrellas, were stacked in the corner. I took two and set them up in the first room. The sleeping bags were rolled up in green drawstring nylon bags. I tugged one out, picked up the screwdriver and dropped it inside. Wearing my little T-shirt, I had nowhere on me to hide it.

It was entirely odd, our little scene. James and I sitting on our camping chairs, munching muesli bars, me with a sleeping bag draped over my shoulders. If we'd been outside, in a field or by the sea, we could have been father and daughter on holiday, sharing a companionable silence after a day's summer fun.

But I was a hostage. James had a gun. Just minutes before I had feared he would kill me. Outside, unseen and unheard, the police were waiting. Did my parents know yet? Had someone found them, contacted them?

'I'm sorry it's all gone wrong,' I said. 'I was so happy here. I don't think I've ever been happier.'

James looked up, his train of thought interrupted. His head jerked.

'What? You were happy?' He still didn't look at me, talking as though to himself.

'Everything will be twisted now. Everything will be made into lies,' he said. 'They'll say I was barmy – some nasty little power-hungry cultist. They'll crucify me.' The metaphor, so unthinkingly apt, made him laugh, briefly.

'Perhaps, it would help if you would tell me what you are planning to do now.' I was cautious, afraid he might get angry again. Instead he looked at me with a surprisingly gentle smile.

'Ah Amber,' he said. 'My Amethyst child.'

'You – you still think I am one?'

'I know you are. Don't you?'

'I don't know.'

James shook his head. 'Doesn't this prove it? Did you think it would all be crystals and rainbows and dolphins, little girl? The Amethyst children are warriors. You'll have to fight. This is just the beginning.'

'Is that what we're going to do? Fight the police?'

James smiled. 'You think that's what I want? Would you fight beside me Amber? Would you risk their bullets?' He looked at me – intent, searching. For a mad moment, I would have said yes. Even now, after the gun. He was so grave and strong – the most real and sincere person I had ever met. But that was an illusion, wasn't it? His conviction was so infectious. I could feel it reaching out to me again, an invisible hand.

'I don't want to be shot,' I said. James raised his head and laughed.

'Well said. Neither do I. Then again, I've no wish to be locked up and paraded through the courts. I can't see a way out. What shall I do?'

'What does Throne say?'

'Throne has already told me what to do,' James said. His voice dropped. He leaned forward in his chair, turned his hands over, and stared at his palms.

'What? What must you do?'

James ignored the question. 'D'you like school, Amber? I hated it. That's why I don't want any of my Amethyst children to go. It kills you. Stamps all the life out of you and fills you with fear. I left as soon as I could.'

'You were in a rock band,' I added. 'I saw the picture, on the Internet.'

'I tried all sorts of things. Never kept at anything very long. Not all good things either. I was in the army for a couple of years. Served in Northern Ireland. I didn't know what to do when I came out. So I travelled a lot. Then I joined a private security company, for an oil business in Nigeria. I hung out with some dodgy people.

'Then I left the job and got involved in some bad stuff, Amber. Things I don't like to remember. I lived in Africa for several years – Nigeria, Uganda, the Sudan. Anywhere there was trouble.

'D'you know what I ended up doing? I worked for arms dealers. I was the on-the-ground man doing the dirty work for smart men in suits who took the money and handed over guns, no questions asked. I made the contacts and did the deals, with some very nasty people. I was the lowest link in that particular food chain – I was the one out in the field. I hurt people. I lied and betrayed. But I made a lot of money. I took plenty – but that was peanuts compared to what the suits raked in. D'you understand what I'm saying?

'That was me. That was what James Moore did. So I wanted to leave his name behind.'

I didn't know what to say, so I said nothing. He didn't seem to need a response. He just kept talking.

'And then one night everything changed. I was staying in a filthy little town, out in the desert, in another war zone. Nearly everyone had abandoned the place. The only people left were those with something to gain from the fighting – rebel soldiers, mercenaries from over the border. It was just a heap of beaten up shacks and burnt out vehicles, a few half-starved dogs and desperate types hoping to sell the soldiers something, to make a little money.

'I had a meeting set up with the local war-lord. The boss had sent me instructions to collect a deposit on a consignment of assault rifles. It was a long drive. Hundreds of miles, and nothing but heat and rock and red earth. My driver, Seth, was my guide and translator. He was the nearest I had to a friend, and he wasn't much of one. If it came to it, he'd save his skin first, just as I'd save mine.

'We were both off our heads. We took drugs constantly. Cocaine takes the edge off things. It soothed the nerves and killed the boredom. That surprises you, that we were bored? There was so much waiting. Days of it, with nothing to do, hoping for a message. And of course drugs stopped you feeling too much.

'Seth was a top driver, even off his face. He was whip-thin, but strong as the devil and handy with a knife when he didn't have a gun. He drove for eight hours straight, without a break. In the late afternoon we arrived at a village, for the meeting. Three jeeps were parked up, and half a dozen men were waiting. They took us to a shack where the top man was sitting at a desk. It was comfortable inside, but camouflaged by the miserable exterior. They had a generator rigged up. He had electric light and a television hooked to a satellite dish.

'I'd dealt with this guy before. There'd been no problem and I didn't expect one now. I had, simply, to receive a down payment. Of course you are always afraid. We were two, and they were more than twenty, all heavily armed. So much went on above my head, so many arguments and deals, I could never be certain I wouldn't be shot to pieces – or worse.

'So it proved. As soon as we got inside the head guy started shouting at Seth. I have no idea what they were saying, and Seth didn't have time to explain. I could see how frightened he was, the sweat bursting from his face. I tried to interrupt, to find out what was going on, but the man just pulled a gun and blasted Seth in the guts.'

James stopped speaking. He rubbed his face with the palms of his hands, and took a deep breath.

'There was so much noise. Everyone was shouting. Seth dropped to his knees, clutching his belly, but there was blood everywhere. His whole body was shaking. He looked up at me, powerless, appealing for help, but what could I do? Everything happened so fast. The guy was shouting at me now and I didn't know what he was saying. Presumably there'd been some mix-up or betrayal. My own bosses had stitched him up or let him down. Maybe it was just some misunderstanding, the wrong word said to the wrong person. They were angry and I was alone.

'The soldiers were all waving guns and I knew I would be shot, just like Seth. I didn't even think – I pushed them out of the way and ran out of the shack. I just left him, Seth, curled up on the floor. I couldn't help him – couldn't help us both.

'Somebody fired and I caught a bullet in the thigh. I was so wired, so afraid for my life, I didn't even feel it. I ran to the jeep and started it up. They were all around me, the soldiers. I kicked them away. They could have killed me, I'm sure, but perhaps they wanted me alive, some kind of bargaining tool. In any case I was lucky they didn't just open fire, and I managed to drive away.

'Of course they came after me but I had a head start. In the end I don't think they were that bothered. They chased me for an hour and then just lost interest. I wasn't worth the trouble. Not that I was out of the woods. I didn't know where I was, and pretty soon the Jeep ran out of petrol. If the deal had been done, they'd have refuelled it for our journey back.

'So there I was, all alone in the middle of nowhere, days from help. My leg had started to hurt. Blood soaked my clothes, and flies were everywhere. I was still half out of my head. Night came, very suddenly. There are no twilights like you get in England. The sun flames up on the horizon, and then in a moment, darkness covers the desert. It gets cold very quickly, bitterly cold. I huddled up on the seat of the dead Jeep, freezing, the throbbing pain obliterating anything else. I knew I would die. I had no supplies, no help and no direction.'

'But you didn't die,' I said.

'I didn't die. That long night it seemed my mind came to pieces. I suffered for hours but in the end the pain and cold disappeared. I stretched out on my back and stared at a sky burning with stars. They are never the same in England. Perhaps we have too much electric light or pollution, or the atmosphere is more opaque. There in the desert the stars blazed, rivers and seas of stars. The light seemed to fill my entire mind, obliterating my thoughts and filling me with a sense of the most absolute peace. It didn't matter any more if I lived or died.

'Time expanded. I had no sense of a past or future. I was leaving my body behind. It was a broken parcel I didn't need. But I didn't die. I heard a voice. It was Throne, reaching out. I felt his presence all around me, pushing open doorways into my mind. He showed me, in an instant, how empty and stupid and wasteful my life had been. And then he stretched out his hand to reveal what was to come and what I had to do next. He told me about the troubles we face – and how could I dispute them? I'd spent the last years stirring the cauldrons of war. He showed me the path to take and a vision of a new generation of children who would make good our mistakes and take us into a new era.

'When I woke up in the morning, a boy was standing next to the Jeep. Half a dozen white goats were clustered around him, nibbling the shrubs among the rocks. The boy thought I was dead because he jumped back and screeched when I opened my eyes. But he was my saviour. He went for help, back to his village. It was miles away. He'd come this way on a whim, but it was no coincidence. He'd been sent to save me – driven by a sixth sense. When I looked into his eyes I recognised what Throne had revealed to me.'

'He was an Amethyst child?'

'When you know – it's impossible to miss, Amber.'

'And you saw this in me, too.'

James took another swig from his water bottle. A question teased. Did I dare ask it?

'How do you know it was real – the voice – and not just some kind of hallucination because of the drugs and shock and stress?' I said.

'I know it was real. Maybe those things made me open to the voice. Most of the time our minds are full of clutter and distraction and stupid chatter but then my mind was clear for the very first time.

'The desert's special. It's the place for divine revelation. No comforts, no distractions. So many prophets have seen the face of God in the desert.

'And in any case,' he added, 'I've heard Throne many times since. It didn't just happen once.'

James looked very old and tired. All the vital life he'd possessed in abundance had drained out with the story. Was it true, his vision? Or had he lost his mind on that long night alone in the desert, dying, with a bullet in his thigh, a kernel of insanity embedded in his brain. Or perhaps it was true – all the stuff about spirits and channelling and Throne sending messages. James was entirely sane and the rest of us were labouring under a delusion. How could I ever know the truth of that? Reality is democratic then. Reality is what the mass of us agree to. I guess that's the compromise we have to live with. But it doesn't make that reality more *real*.

Of course James might be lying. Maybe he'd made the story up, but I didn't think so. It would explain how he had the money to establish the Community and the contacts to stock his armoury. And he had lived in a war zone. He knew how a home might need to be defended.

We were quiet for a long time. James was lost in thought. As he told his story I had forgotten about the army outside, but I thought of it now. How long would they wait? What would they do next? It was hard to read James's mood. He was still sitting in his camping chair, his legs stretched out in front of him. He seemed hardly present in the bunker, perhaps lost in recollections of the past he had retold.

'James – James, what are we going to do?'

He lifted his head. 'It won't be long now,' he said.

'What won't be long?'

But he flipped his hand in front of his face and declined to reply. I didn't want him to lapse away again so I persisted.

'Why have you told me all this?'

'Why d'you think? I want you to know.'

'Do they all know? The others?'

'No,' he said. 'Some of them know some of it. But the rest – why would I tell them?'

'So why me? Why now?'

'You're being stupid, Amber. Why ask me questions when you already know the answer?'

Because I don't like the answer, I responded in my head. I don't want to say it because then it will be real.

'There is more to tell you, Amber. Another reason I can't go out.' He looked small now, almost apologetic.

'What?'

'This place.' He gestured with his arm. 'What I've done to create it. What I've done for you.'

A painful twinge of alarm. 'I've never asked you to do anything for me,' I said.

James looked at me sideways. I was being stupid again, and disingenuous. I had asked for his shelter.

'What have you done?' I said, dreading to hear.

He sighed, looking at his feet. 'It doesn't let you go, the world I was part of,' he said. 'Do you think a place like this could really run on the proceeds of a healthfood shop and a carpentry business? I knew we still needed money – lots of it.

'There was another deal. I wanted it to be the last. Hoped I wouldn't need to be involved again. But they have so much on me, the suits. They talked me into it, half threatened, and I was tempted – on your behalf, I was tempted. But it was dodgy – right from the start. So much leaking. People I knew we couldn't trust.'

'What do you mean? What are you saying?' I think I knew. But I needed him to spell it out.

'I think that's why we have such an army outside. If someone did betray me, it was only the trigger they needed. They were watching already. They were waiting.' He frowned and pressed the heel of his hand against his forehead. The confession continued.

'A huge consignment. The usual small arms, landmines,

grenade launchers. But more than that. Information. The most dangerous resource – and the most valuable. Information on the creation of biochemical weapons, for an unspecified client on the border of Afghanistan. It is a complex business – a game for cold minds. There is never a direct chain from manufacturer to customer in these kinds of situations. Instead, they create a web of phantom links, some real and some simply imagined, so a trail can never lead back to the men behind it all. No one trusts anyone. The deal is always a series of feints and bluffs and tests. And I was part of it, part of this shadow play. Right at the heart of it.

'I have the documents here,' he gestured to the locked filing cabinets, 'which I have been paid to take on a winding route to our client's contacts. The information they need.

'I knew it was getting dangerous. I knew the set-up was leaky. But I hoped – just hoped – I could get it over and done with. Odd things weren't right. You develop an instinct for this stuff – learn to know who you can trust. I was afraid they were on to me. And I was right, evidently.'

He raised his eyes to my face. 'I can't leave,' he said. 'I'm destroyed.'

A sense of cold horror, rising in a dark flood, as I absorbed what he was telling me. James Renault, my idol, the voice of sanity, was still immersed in a world of war and killing. The Community was a perfect lie. Its foundations were stained and dirtied by the very things I feared most; that I dreaded.

'I didn't ask you to do this for me,' I said. 'You didn't do it for me. I don't want it. It's a lie. Everything you told us is a lie.' I was shaking again, hot and cold at once. I couldn't keep my hands still. It was as though the ground beneath my feet was falling away. James had seemed like an answer and now had revealed himself instead to be the very worst kind of man. A liar, a purveyor of death, a part of the murderous game of power.

But James didn't seem to hear me. He rose from his chair and stepped towards me. He knelt at my feet. I was alarmed – mortified. He took my right hand and held it between his.

'I was granted a space of time to put my life in order,' he said. 'I've served as a signpost for the ones who will follow – for you and Dowdie and all the hundreds of Amethyst children who have been born over the last ten years. But I always knew I was living on borrowed time. Throne gave me a chance to put things right with the daughter I lost, to set up a home for the people who find it hardest to survive these last days. Since that night in the desert, I've been a dead man on leave, Amber.'

I looked down into his face. His hands were warm, his face was bright and clear. The horror of what he had done had washed away, with his confession. He had loaded it on me instead. Now he looked like my little brother Justin – guileless, wide open.

'What about me?' My voice was breaking. I had a profound fear I would never get out of the cellar.

'Don't be afraid!' he said. 'Don't you see? You're the next one, Amber. This is just the beginning. I knew it, as soon as I met you. Throne wants you to be his mouthpiece. Be ready for him. One day he will open your mind.'

My lips were cold and clumsy. James was appealing to me and frantically I searched for the right answer – what I needed to say to persuade him to let me go.

'He will talk to me?' I said. 'He told you so? You're going to let me leave so he can talk through me?'

James nodded. His face possessed an eerie calm that frightened me more than his rage when he had slammed me against the wall.

'Do you understand now? Will you take this on, Amber? It's a sacred trust. Will you promise?'

I would have promised anything – anything at all.

'Yes. Yes I promise. I'll do what you want, James. Please let me out now. Please let me go.' I couldn't help it – I began to sob. Helpless tears spilled over my face. James reached up and put his arms around me.

'It's all right,' he said. 'All will be well. Let it happen, Amber. Don't be afraid.'

I cried for ages. James didn't speak. He held me tenderly, like a father. In the end my tears stopped, leaving me utterly empty. I sat up straight, and a voice came through me.

'It's time,' I said. 'Unlock the hatch. Let me out.' This new voice didn't quiver or plead. James drew away. He fumbled in his pocket for a key, and without another word he proceeded up the steep stairway to the hatch. He unlocked it, and folded it open.

I had expected the upstairs room to be light, but the trapdoor revealed a dark square. James stepped back and I climbed up the stairs, not looking back. Everything was silent, and for a moment I wondered if the police had just given up and gone home. Then looking through the window I saw fierce spotlights, moving over the exterior of the house, torches, the movements of men and the mass of vehicles beyond the garden. I closed the trapdoor and heard James lock it behind me. Slowly I stood up straight. I felt perfectly calm.

The windows were open, and the air was warm and perfumed with summer. I took a deep breath, walked to the front door and drew back the bolts.

When I stepped outside, everyone froze, instantly on the alert. I felt their eyes on me, and the gun sights too. No one spoke. I pulled the door shut and stepped down the path. One step, two.

As my eyes adjusted I could see better the police cordon all around the house and the faces all turned towards me. The night was peerless, combed with stars. The soil itself smelled sweet.

A firm, masculine voice called out: 'Put your hands in the air!'

I complied, still walking. A short, burly policeman stepped forward to meet me. He held an arm out, in welcome.

Then they closed around me, patting me, asking me questions. Was I hurt? What had happened? Where was James Renault? Was he armed? I didn't answer, scanning the crowd.

'Where's Dowdie?' I said. 'Is she OK? Where is she?'

Then they all shut up. 'Dowdie?' one said.

'Dorothy – the daughter,' another answered. Then the cry went out, people calling her.

'She is here,' the first man said. 'She wouldn't go without you. She's been waiting.'

And there she was, her pale, beaky face pushing through the policemen towards me.

'Amber! Are you OK? Did he hurt you? Where's my dad?' She looked strange, eyes wide, her face very tired and drawn. We clung on to each other, like little kids.

I heard the first policeman suggest to his colleague that they move in on the house.

'No!' I shouted. 'No – don't go near it. Keep away. You don't know what he's going to do!'

Dowdie, still clutching my arm, turned to me sharply. The policeman pushed his way over.

He looked into my face and said, very serious, 'What is he going to do?'

'He's got a gun. He's not coming out.'

The policeman considered. Some kind of discussion began, but I couldn't hear exactly what they were saying.

An ambulance medic came over to find out if I were hurt. She gave me a blanket to wrap around me and gently suggested it was time for us to leave. Indomitable Dowdie stamped her foot and told the medic she wasn't going anywhere until she'd seen her father. The woman pursed her lips.

'I don't think it's a good idea,' she said. 'You both need to rest. Why don't you come back later?' As if there would be a later. 'Honestly, there's nothing you can do here. You can see your dad when this is all over.' She talked to Dowdie as though she were six, and Dowdie glared.

Then it happened. A huge, suppressed whump and the ground shifting beneath my feet. A shockwave pushed us away from the house, and a ball of flame filled the interior of the downstairs room, blasting out the windows. Glass burst from the wooden frames. Shouts and cries rose from the assembled army of police.

Dowdie howled. She tried to run towards the house but the medic pulled her back. The woman must have been tougher than she looked because she kept her grip while Dowdie lashed out and struggled to get free.

'Daddy! Daddy!' Dowdie's voice carried over the noise of the flames and the shouts of the police. She kept on and on while the medic tried to drag her away. Moments later a second explosion nearly knocked me off my feet and sent the fire shooting through the first floor and out of the windows. A tide of heat blasted over us.

I don't know if that second boom affected my ears but everything seemed to go quiet. I was dimly aware of motion all around me, of police and firefighters busy at their task, of orders shouted out. So much hectic activity and me, forgotten for the moment, standing perfectly still while the storm lashed around. A forest of flames, tearing at the house, scorching my face and the front of my body. Sparks spiralled towards the stars. Smoke thickened the air, catching in my throat.

I don't know how long I stood there. In the end the woman medic came back. Over the dull and distant din her voice was distinct.

'You shouldn't be here. Your friend wants you.' She had a bruise on her cheek, quite likely inflicted by Dowdie. I remember thinking, in an oddly rational moment, this was not a good way to treat someone trying to help you.

'OK.' I nodded.

The house burned. The firefighters trampled the garden, as they struggled to put out the blaze. Chris's treasured vegetables were smashed underfoot.

'It's time to go,' the woman said.

'Time to go,' I repeated, still staring at the house, burning like the end of the world.

Nineteen

We were taken in an ambulance to the community hospital in town. Nobody spoke. Dowdie wouldn't even look at me, wrapped in her blanket, eyes fixed on the floor. My face burned and a constant ringing sounded in my ears. A paramedic accompanied us in the ambulance and a policewoman was sitting up front with the driver. We arrived at the tiny A&E unit and all trooped inside. It seemed we were the only customers and we had to wait for ages before a nurse came along to check us over. She looked very tired.

I had lost track of the time but the clock on the hospital wall said it was nearly two in the morning. The nurse was taken to one side by the policewoman and the paramedics. They conferred in low voices, glancing over at us from time to time. Some kind of commotion started up just outside the door and Eliza burst in. She ran across the room.

'Dowdie! Dowdie!' She threw her arms around her daughter. 'My God, what happened? You could have died – they told me – are you hurt? What happened?' Eliza's voice broke. Tears spilled over her face. Dowdie pressed herself against her mother and began to sob.

I felt very cold and alone then, to see Dowdie embraced by her mother while I sat all by myself. The kindly paramedic, the bruise shining on her face, patted me on the knee. Of course Dowdie had lost her father and mine was only a few hundred miles away, but I envied her then for her mother to cling onto.

The policewoman stepped over. She gestured towards Dowdie's mum.

'We're trying to contact your parents too,' she said. 'I understand they're out of the country – on holiday. One of the other residents gave us some details.'

I nodded.

'Of course it'll take them a little while to get back, even if they get the first plane. But be patient. They won't be long.' She wasn't very old, the policewoman. A plump, blond girl with bobbed hair and a freckled nose.

The ambulance staff departed and the nurse took Dowdie and her mother to a curtained cubicle along the corridor. I stared at the walls. The waiting room was a bare, functional place – a dozen chairs, and a poster on the wall about childhood immunisations. My eyes were stinging.

The policewoman told me to call her Shirley, and asked me how I was feeling. I shrugged. She was patronising but trying to be kind. I leaned back in my chair, wishing my ears would stop ringing. The hospital didn't seem entirely real, as though the major part of myself was still caught underground, in the cellar, or standing outside the house and staring at the fire. I could still feel, in my bones, the whump of the first explosion. I closed my eyes and inside my mind the hectic flames rose up.

Far away, a clear, cold voice said: You know who called the police. Who else could it have been? Who else would do such a thing?

And a second devastating thought followed on. It was a trapdoor opening inside me, and a falling, falling, falling into the darkness.

Of course. Of course. I was hollow inside, all cold dread. My bones ached, my mouth tasted of ice.

Johnny had overheard us, hadn't he? Standing outside the door while Dowdie and I were speaking.

And when I'd surprised him, the website he was visiting. *Terminus*. A Latin word, meaning the end. Like Terminator, or terminal illness. I hadn't seen the page address, just the single title word in the bar at the bottom of the screen. I remembered the screwed-up exam slips, the self-inflicted failure, and the look of disintegration in his eyes.

I knew what he had done and now I realised what he was going to do – unless I was already too late.

'May I have a drink please?' I said abruptly.

Shirley sat up straight. 'A drink? I don't know. I mean, I don't think you're supposed to have one until the nurse has checked you over.'

'That's only if you're having an operation,' I said. 'Please. I'm so thirsty my throat hurts.' My voice was rational, but inside my head, a screaming.

Shirley sighed. 'I think they've got a machine along the corridor. We passed it on the way in. I could do with a tea myself. Look, I'll go and check it out. You wait here, OK? I'll see what I can do.'

She got up and walked down the corridor, pushing her way through the heavy double doors. I jumped to my feet. I'd have to find another way out, to avoid her. I tiptoed past the cubicle where Dowdie's mum was talking with the nurse and ran through the dimly lit hospital. It wasn't a big place, and in the depths of the night it was very quiet. Once I encountered another nurse, a young man, sitting at a desk in a pool of light, but he didn't notice me. I turned left and left again. A sign announced a café on the right so I went inside. Surely this would have some kind of exterior fire door? The room was calm and empty, all the chairs pushed tidily against the tables. Perhaps by now Policewoman Shirley would have come back with my drink and already they were looking for me. I had to hurry – had to find a way out. Sure enough, a door opened onto a paved area behind the hospital. It had some kind of opening bar which I pushed, stepping out into the chilly night air. Distantly an alarm bell rang. I closed the door behind me and ran away from the hospital across the car park and a patch of lawn and flower beds, towards the centre of town.

It is about half a mile from the hospital to Johnny's house and downhill most of the way. I ran across the main road, and clung to the shadows at the edge of the path. I hurtled through the dark, dodging pools of dusty light from the streetlamps, allowing the hill to tug me down, down, at such a pace I thought my heart would burst. I expected pursuit but I saw no one. Of course they would have no idea where I was heading. And what would I find when I got there? Horrible images crowded the fringes of my mind but I wouldn't let them in; I wouldn't shine the light of my attention on them.

I pushed my way through the gate in the wall, and the house loomed over me. The moon, a silver egg, perched on a high turret. Orange light from a street lamp dusted the stained-glass window with its multitude of panes. I crunched across the gravel to the path and the back door. I had rushed here and now on the doorstep I was afraid to go inside. The kitchen light was on and looking through the window I could see the perpetually untidy room had been transformed. The table was clear, the sink empty, the tiled floor swept and mopped. Everything was in its place. I grasped the door handle, expecting it to open, as always, but on this singular occasion the door was locked.

Dread swallowed me up, like a coffin of stone. I couldn't think – couldn't draw breath. I stood there, unable to move, while seconds ticked past, while Johnny was inside . . . What now? What now? I forced myself to breathe, bending over with my head to my knees so I shouldn't faint. A sensation of cold filled my belly and I was afraid I might be sick. If I'd had a mobile on me I could've called for help. But who would I call and would they get here on time anyway? I couldn't waste a minute. I might already be too late. I had to think. Had to act right away.

Through the glass in the door I could see the back door key in the lock, on the kitchen side. If I broke the glass I could get inside. It went against every instinct, to break something, but panic breached any reservations. Quickly I looked around the garden for something I could use. What about a stone? I pulled my sleeve over my hand, picked up a chunk of rock from a garden border and whacked it against the glass. It didn't shatter right away. There were two layers, and the glass was toughened to protect it against criminal attacks. But I didn't give up. I hit the spot again and again. It was horribly noisy, the impact of the rock crunching on the glass, and I was afraid someone would hear. But at last the glass gave way. Carefully I slipped my hand inside and turned the key.

The fact that Johnny apparently hadn't heard me battering his back door didn't add to my meagre remains of hope. Standing in the kitchen, breathing in the fumes of pine-fresh cleaning chemicals, I wondered if I shouldn't just back out now, and use the house phone to call the police so they could sort everything out. This was too much for me to deal with. Who was Johnny, anyway? This boy I had known for just a few weeks, whom I had met perhaps a dozen times. I didn't need to be involved. I could just walk away.

Something shifted in the house – a movement of air. The kitchen door moved a little, bringing with it the faintest perfume of Johnny . . . Did I imagine it? A mere thread of scent that sewed itself into my brain. Vivid memories flamed into life – lying on his bed, the pictures he had created, the sensation of pressing myself against his chest, and the sound of his voice. I closed my eyes for a moment, hanging on to the thread, savouring the memories of the previous night. How long ago it seemed, how many weeks and months and years.

Without making any conscious decision I opened my eyes, pushed through the door and ran up the stairs towards Johnny's room.

'Johnny! Johnny! Let me in! It's Amber. Please – let me in now!'

I could hear nothing from his room. No sound of movement. Not a whisper. I hammered on the door with my fist and turned the handle, but of course it was locked.

'Johnny! I know you're in there. I know what you're thinking! Please, let me in. Let me talk to you.'

Still nothing. I noticed a section of the stained-glass window on the landing was open, allowing a breath of night air. This, then, had stirred the house and pushed against the kitchen door. I waited a minute or two then banged again.

'Johnny – I'm not giving up. I'm not going away till I've seen you. I'll just keep on shouting. Let me in for God's sake. Let me in!'

I don't know why I thought he was still alive. Maybe it was simply blind optimism. He made no sound, gave no indication of his living presence. But shouting, calling, begging him to speak to me, I was certain he could hear me. I wasn't going to give up.

He made me wait a long time. I don't know for sure how long it was but it seemed like hours. When my hands were too bruised to bang, I sat with my back to the door and carried on calling his name. Through the open window I watched the stars traverse a tiny patch of night sky. And though my face burned, my body began to shiver with cold. I had no energy left but still I kept talking to Johnny.

In the end I wore him down. He turned the lock.

'Johnny!' Standing in the doorway, while I was sitting on the floor, he was tall and pale and gaunt. I scrambled to my feet.

'Johnny, I thought – I was afraid – I came running here from the hospital because I knew what you were going to do.'

He didn't speak. Shadows had sunk in his face. I couldn't read his expression. He backed away to let me inside. The room was dark, but I turned on the light. Everything was tidy, as always. Everything in its place – the Damien Hirst photos on the walls, the impersonal computer and its glossy accoutrements. In the light, Johnny looked grim. His lips were very white and he had spots on his cheeks. His skin had the dry, matt quality of paper.

'Amber – I wasn't expecting to see you again,' he said. His voice was calm and measured as though everything was under control.

'It all kicked off at the Community. James is dead, Johnny. He was killed in an explosion. He did it himself. He didn't want them to catch him.' My words came out in a rush.

Johnny didn't respond. His face gave nothing away.

I said: 'I know you told the police.'

He raised his head, just a touch. His expression didn't change.

'You overheard us – me and Dowdie.'

Johnny shrugged. 'It doesn't matter.' He sat down on the bed, hands clasped in his lap. I sat beside him.

'I thought . . . I thought,' I had to force myself to say it, 'I thought you were going to kill yourself, Johnny.'

'I was,' he said. 'I am.'

'Why?' A distressed bleat, like a three year old. How could I help him?

'Why?' He gave a short, painful laugh. 'Why not?'

'What were you going to do? I mean, how?'

'I was going to hang myself. A nylon cord, from the banister. They are appropriately sturdy and high. Only, you've interrupted me.'

He was matter of fact. We might have been discussing a school project.

'Aren't you glad – that I did interrupt?'

'No.' Only his hands moved, restless on his lap. The rest of him was perfectly still.

'Why?' I repeated. 'Is it because of your results?'

'My results? That was just the final straw. The logical conclusion. I just can't bear it any more – this reality. This place. My life. It's just too horrible and painful to be endured. It's my choice, isn't it? If I don't want this any more, can't I open the door and step out of it?'

I didn't know how to answer. I could feel the pain emanating from him and didn't know how to stop it. I wanted to take him outside. Somehow, I had to get him away from the house.

'Life could get better,' I ventured. 'I know things are bad now – that they've been bad a long time. But it could change.' I was leading him across a marsh and every sentence I said was another stepping stone on the way. The trouble was, I didn't know which stones were stable, which words to choose to lead him out. What if I said the wrong thing, and sent him under?

'No it won't,' he said. 'Everything is well and truly messed up.

Everything. I've seen what's on offer, what's ahead, and there's nothing I want.'

'I don't want you to go,' I blurted.

He moved then, turned his head to glance at me. Then he stared at his hands again.

'Your face is red,' he said. It was the first time he'd properly noticed me.

'From the fire – at the Community,' I said.

'You're right. I told the police. Now James is dead.'

'That's not your fault. That was—'

'His choice?' A hint of a smile then.

I took my chance. 'Can we go out, Johnny? I need to walk.' In truth I longed to sleep, but I wanted to get him away from the place. If I could alter the chemistry of his mood, if I could entice him away from the house where he'd planned to die, perhaps his feelings might change. But Johnny didn't answer. His mind was tied up. He couldn't see beyond the bleak walls of the present.

'Why did you do it – ring the police?'

Johnny glared at the carpet. 'Because James was smug. Because I hated his certainty – his self-righteousness.'

He bit his lip, still staring at the ground. Then he added: 'And he didn't like me. He threw me out. I didn't turn him in for a parking offence, Amber. He had a hoard of guns, for Christ's sake. He was dangerous.'

'What about Dowdie? Did you think what it would do to her?'

'I didn't think about anyone – but him.'

James Renault, representative of all lying, useless adults, victim of Johnny's final act of revenge. His useless parents, of course, were too far away to hurt, perhaps sleeping off a night of indulgence in their idyllic Greek apartment. They would be hurt if he died, surely. Was that part of his motivation too, for this spiral of self-destruction? The botched exams, the suicide – a final finger to them?

'Johnny – please. Will you come out with me?'

'If I do that, I won't go through with the plan.'

'No, not tonight. But you don't want to now anyway. I've already messed it up. So why not come for a walk?'

Johnny shook his head, irritated. But irritation was a better feeling than his deadly despair, surely.

'There'll be other nights, if that's what you want,' I said. 'What difference will one more day make? Have one more day. Just in case you change your mind.' My voice was light. I stood up, trying to galvanise him into moving. And he did move. He got to his feet.

'May I borrow a jumper? It's chilly in the dark. I know it'll be too big, but I can't stop shivering.'

Johnny looked at me closely then. He saw how my teeth were chattering. Something like concern crossed his face.

'What's wrong with you?' he said. 'Are you in shock? Bloody hell, Amber, you look terrible.'

In shock? The events of the day unreeled before me. Guns and police, a hostage in a cellar with a pistol to my head, the explosion and fire, the hospital and my subsequent escape. A race through the night and break-in to Johnny's house to stop him . . . to stop him . . . I couldn't bear to think of it now. In shock? Yes, I think I was. I was cold inside, all the vital organs of my body like lumps of stone. My eyes were gritty and sore, and I stank of sweat and smoke. Johnny's face, though, staring at me, truly seeing me for the first time that night. I burst into tears, my teeth still chattering, tears running down my cheeks.

He found me an old zip-up hoodie, once black, now a faded charcoal. It was too small for him, still too big for me. I had to roll the sleeves several times. Downstairs he spoiled the kitchen's perfect cleanliness by making me a large mug of hot chocolate and a plate of toast. I couldn't eat the toast, my stomach still clenched like a fist, but the drink warmed me up. And seeing Johnny bustle about, all concerned; that helped even more.

I apologised for breaking the door, as Johnny scooped up the broken glass with a dustpan and brush. He said not to worry about it, that he'd tell Mrs Pugh, the housekeeper, a burglar had tried to break in. Suddenly everything was blissfully ordinary and mundane, as though nothing terrible had happened, or could ever happen. I knew this was an illusion – that James was dead and Dowdie was crying, that Johnny was only one small step away from the marsh. The police would be looking for me, and far away my parents were panicking, packing bags and heading home, abruptly bringing their longed-for holiday to an end. But I didn't want to think about it too much. Just now, in this space of time, here and now, I focused on Johnny.

We left the house, and Johnny didn't lock the kitchen door. Useless to do so anyway, with the glass broken. It was still dark, but the summer dawn wasn't far off. We wandered through the deserted town centre, past the shop windows and their garish displays. At the top of the High Street a CCTV camera swivelled to follow our progress, two black hooded figures with nothing in particular to do. Through the paved marketplace, and on to the parish church, its spire like a blade against the scatter of stars. The little graveyard was silent, spangled with crisp packets, plastic bottles and soggy paper dropped by customers from the fish and chip shop down the alley. Above our heads, gargoyles leaped from the stonework.

Then, across the road and down the steps to the path by the river. Johnny sighed. He took hold of my icy hand. His hand was large and warm.

'The police will be looking for me,' I said. 'I ran away from the hospital. I realised – I had to see you.'

Johnny shrugged. 'We'll go and see them later.'

Down on the river, something scurried and plopped into the river. A rat, probably. Peeing Weil's-infected urine to poison the swimmers.

'So tell me what happened,' he said.

'Are you sure you want to hear?'

'Yes. Don't spare me. Tell me everything.'

'OK – but first tell me what you said to the police. I couldn't believe it – they were like an army. You must have sounded convincing.'

'I phoned them up. I didn't give them my name. I refused to speak to anyone but the chief inspector, and told them I had information about illegal firearms. I was so sober and serious; I didn't want them to think I was some stupid kid. So I gave them James's name, and his original name, told them he had a whole load of guns stashed at his house. I told them I used to be a member of the Community – gave them the impression I was some lackey James had pissed off. That's not exactly a million miles from the truth.'

'Well they must have believed you. I would have thought they'd send round a couple of constables with a search warrant. But they went all out. They sent a battalion, and marksmen and a helicopter.'

Johnny looked down at the path. 'So how did it all kick off?' he said. 'Start at the beginning.'

So I told him. He listened attentively, not interrupting. When I described how James held me hostage he squeezed my hand. Had Johnny, so focused on his act of revenge, not thought how his revelation might endanger innocent people? For we might all have been killed, one way or another, by gunshot, or burned up in the explosion that tore the house apart.

I recounted James's story about his arms dealing days, and his vision in the desert. And how he passed on an inheritance to me, claiming I was the torch bearer now for all the Amethyst children. How one day the spirit Throne would speak through me.

Johnny laughed to hear this but he ushered me on to tell him the rest, the hospital and my flight to his house.

When I concluded, we were a mile out of town. The river wound lazily beneath us, at the bottom of the bank. Darkness was ebbing. In the hawthorn bushes a blackbird began to sing.

'Poor Dowdie,' Johnny said. 'This whole thing – worst for her.'

'And bad for the others – losing their home, and James, and all they believed in.' I looked up at Johnny. 'Losing their game?'

Johnny shook his head. 'I think the game is more robust than you think. James believed it, didn't he? Right till the end. Maybe this will prove to them the truth of what he said – the seriousness of their situation. James is a martyr.

'Do you think Dowdie knows it was me who told?' he said.

'I don't know. She might work it out – like I did. It would be hard to pin blame though. If she hadn't told me, none of this would have happened, so maybe it's her fault. It was James's decision though, to fill the house with guns. It was his fault. I don't blame you, Johnny. If my parents had been at home, I think I would have told them what I saw. It was too much – too serious.'

'You just wanted peace and harmony and home-grown vegetables,' Johnny said. 'Weaponry wasn't part of the picture, am I right?' He was back on his treadmill again, the defensive veneer of teasing and chilly jokes.

'No.' My eyes filled with tears again but I didn't want to cry. 'I wish you wouldn't.'

'Wouldn't what?'

'Tease all the time. Can't you just be straight? Can't you be real?'

Johnny looked away. Over the horizon, the rising sun glittered on streamers of cloud. Pink like salmon, and pale gold, like wine. Soon it would be hot again.

'I can't help it,' he said. 'That's my—'

'Your game?' I broke in.

'It's what I do. Survival technique.'

'So I'll have to get used to it – see through it.'

'If I stay around, yes.' A dark smile, then. It was a warning. He was still in danger. I had stopped him tonight but nothing essentially had changed. Could I help him keep going, one day at a time?

'There's going to be a lot of shit for us in the next few weeks,' he said. 'This is the lull before the storm.'

A ripple of relief for me – that Johnny imagined himself surviving the next few weeks. Was the threat receding?

'I know. What d'you think will happen?' I said.

'Police, parents, newspapers, an inquest, maybe some kind of court case if any of Renault's companions are charged.'

'Then I'll need you, to help me through it.'

'Will you? Amber, you're laying traps for me.' He was mocking again. Would he not be serious, even about this? But he was serious, beneath it all. I would have to learn to see through it. It wasn't easy.

We crossed the footbridge where I had met Dowdie and later, first spoken to Johnny, just a few weeks ago. Dowdie. I'd been so worried about Johnny I'd hardly thought about her. Was she still at the hospital? Perhaps her mum had already whisked her away, to her new home in Glastonbury, far away from the guns and the fire. Far away from me. How she must be hurting, to have lost her dad.

Further along the path we came to Mortimore's Wood. It was a dingy little copse where kids from the nearby estate came to light bonfires and strew beer cans. The river wove through the trees, brown and sluggish, its dirt banks spoiled by plastic bags and sandwich boxes. A few late dog roses twined the trees, and scarves of perfumed honeysuckle.

'So how does it feel to be a prophet of the New Age?' Johnny said.

'What?'

'You know – the inheritor. The mouthpiece for Throne. How are your channelling skills?'

'Don't be silly. I can't channel.'

'You don't believe it. You're too intelligent for that.' It sounded like an order, not a question. Johnny was lost in thought for a moment. Then he said: 'Why did he pick you?'

'I don't know. He threw me in the cellar because he thought I'd betrayed him. Then I think he told me the rest because I was the only one left.'

Still Johnny brooded. His face seemed to close, taking him far away when I wanted him back with me.

'You've got to think what to do,' I said, eager to pin him to a future. 'Why don't you just tell your parents you're not going back to that horrible school and go to college here in town instead?'

'What – and do photography?'

'If you like. Retake your GCSEs.'

He grimaced. 'What a prospect.'

'Isn't there anything you really want to do?' I said.

'Not really. Why – what about you?'

'I want to try and make things right with Dowdie again. She's my best friend, Johnny. She's changed my life. One day I want to go to India. I'll write books.' I blushed then, looking away from him. 'And I want to have more time with you.'

It was hard to say out loud but when I looked again Johnny was smiling.

'You poor sap,' he said. 'Fallen for me.'

But he was still smiling.

Twenty

The tape is turned off, and the man stops scribbling. Dad is staring at me. Neil gives a brief, approving smile.

I haven't told him everything of course, despite the stern instruction. I didn't say it was Johnny who called the police, and I made no mention of Johnny's suicidal intentions. Instead I told them I ran away from the hospital because I was afraid I was in trouble, and lacking parents to flee to, headed for a friend's house. I think Dowdie must have told them to look for me at Johnny's.

Perhaps you think that irresponsible of me. For his benefit, shouldn't I raise it with his parents, or health professionals, so they can give him the support he needs? That might be true. Still, I'm not going to do it. That is our secret.

Neil smiles. The official interview is at an end. The atmosphere in the room lightens.

'You were very brave,' he says. 'It must have been terrifying, trapped in the cellar with James Renault.'

'I wasn't brave,' I say. 'I had no choice.'

Neil raises his hands, to push away my denial. 'You were brave. You kept a clear head and managed to get out of there.'

I glance over at Dad. He looks very tired. He gives me a faint smile.

'Can I take you home now?' he says. Then, to Neil: 'Have you finished with her?'

Neil nods. 'Yes, thank you.'

As I stand up I say: 'It was the gas bottles in the cellar, wasn't it? That's how he made the explosion.'

'Yes. We're not sure of the details – everything was so thoroughly destroyed. Possibly he fired the pistol at the bottles, or more simply leaked the gas out and ignited it. Either way, he would have died very quickly. I don't think he suffered.'

Dad moves closer. 'What happens now?'

Neil stands up too. He is an inch or two taller than my father. 'We'll be pressing charges relating to the possession of illegal firearms on two men, but I can't give you the details yet. It seems none of the others had any idea the guns were there – except Dowdie, of course.

'There'll be an inquest into the death of James Renault. The whole situation has received such wide coverage in the press – as you well know – I think some kind of inquiry or investigation will be proposed. You know the kind of thing – why we didn't know about their stash sooner; if it was handled properly, etcetera.

'Frankly I think it could have been a lot worse. One man died, but there was the potential for dozens of casualties among the Community residents and our police officers.'

I can see Dad isn't entirely satisfied with this answer.

'So,' he persists. 'This Renault guy. He was just some kind of religious nutter? It doesn't seem right people like him are allowed to walk the streets. I mean, I've read the papers. He had a criminal record, right?'

Neil sighs. 'He served a prison sentence, yes. An assault charge, years ago, when he was in the army. But he served his time, Mr Renalden. How were we to know? Did he seem like a religious nutter to you?'

Dad winces. He knows he can't take it out on the police. He was fooled too. After all, he liked James Renault. Still, he wants some kind of resolution. Perhaps if James wasn't burnt to a crisp my father would be able to punch him – or at least give him a piece of his mind. Instead he is faced with Detective Inspector Neil Ripley, who is too clever and slippery and doesn't offer him the same opportunity to restore his male pride.

Neil holds out his hand and grudgingly Dad shakes it.

'Amber may well be expected to attend the inquest,' Neil says. 'We hope the coroner will be satisfied with the written statement from our interview, which we'll type up and Amber will have to sign, with your consent. But he may ask for her to be there, in case of further questions. Someone will be in touch about that at a later date.'

He turns to me. 'It's been a pleasure to meet you, Amber – and thanks for all the help you've given us. I know it's been hard for you and I appreciate all the time and thought you've invested in this. Are you better now?'

'Yes, thanks. Much better.'

'And your friends?' Dowdie was interviewed by the police days ago. I don't know what she said. We were asked not to confer or share notes.

'I haven't seen Dowdie for a bit. Johnny's OK.'

Neil gives me a look then. It is inquiring, and almost playful. I realise he knows – or at least guesses – that Johnny made the fatal phone call to the police, triggering the siege at the Community. If he had asked me directly, what would I have answered? I am not a good liar.

But he doesn't ask me. It wouldn't make so much difference to anything anyway. Maybe that's why Neil is prepared to let me off the hook.

'Back to school, then,' Neil says.

'Yes, come Monday,' Dad pipes up. I grimace.

'Best of luck.' Neil pats me on the shoulder. 'I know it won't be easy.'

We say our goodbyes and leave the police headquarters. I take a deep breath. I feel a little easier now. The sensation of pressure in my chest has lightened. I can move without causing myself quite so much pain. I feel that one day soon I might, after all, be able to leave this behind.

Dad puts his arm around me as we walk to the car but there is some awkwardness in the gesture. Although I know he still loves me, on one level I don't think he has entirely forgiven me for putting us through this – the ruined holiday, the police, the endless reporters phoning and knocking on the door, the whole package of cults and guns and death . . . In some way I am not his perfect little girl any more. I am spoiled goods.

I hope this will change. I don't like it, this feeling of breakage. I want everything to be healed again.

Twenty-one

When the police came to Johnny's house, he and I had just returned from our walk and were sitting in the kitchen, drinking coffee. Johnny made jokes about handcuffs and arrests but the police officer – it was Shirley again – was gentle and considerate, reassuring me I wasn't in any kind of trouble and that they just wanted to talk to me and make sure I was OK. She said my parents were expected home in a couple of hours.

I stood up, to go with them, but knocked over my coffee so an entire mugful spilled over the table and dripped onto the floor. My clumsy hand felt twice its normal size and my fingers wouldn't work. I tried to clutch the chair, but the room tilted wildly, throwing me off balance. Johnny stood up, eyes wide, and reached out a hand but my legs gave way and I sprawled on the floor. He and Shirley were calling out but I couldn't understand what they said. Then I was lying on my back, faces peering over me. Their faces blurred.

The events of the next few days are pretty hazy. I blacked out for a while. Then there were ambulance people, a mask on my face, and a remote sensation of being lifted and moved. I was taken to a hospital. Then an indeterminate time of waking and drifting, lying in a clean, hard bed in a pale room while strangers bustled in and out. Once I woke to find a young, dark-haired nurse putting a luscious cool cream on my face, with gentle fingers. Another time I think I saw Johnny, sitting by the bed, looking vaguely comical.

I don't know for sure what was wrong with me. The doctor said I had some kind of brain fever but they couldn't be certain what caused it. Most likely it was shock and exhaustion – stringing myself out to the limits of my endurance. I had suffered some kind of nervous collapse.

So many long, long dreams, mostly replaying the events of the previous few days. The discovery of the guns, the flight from the Community at night, the struggle with James in the cellar and the long hours with Johnny. The dreams were exhausting. Sometimes events warped out of my control. I would not be myself, but one of the other main players – Dowdie, James or Johnny. Once I dreamed I was lying in the desert while a tide of stars crashed over my head in waves, and a clear voice spoke out of the wilderness, telling me not to be afraid, and that all would be well.

Then, at last, I woke properly. My mother was sitting by my bed. She had a book in her hand, but when my eyes opened she raised her face and stared. It is hard to describe what it felt like, to see her familiar face. There can't be any face more engrained in my memory than my mother's, nor so comforting. And yet, these last days I had gone so far from her, across so many oceans and ages and continents, it was like I was seeing her for the first time. These two conflicting sensations jarred in my head.

'Amber? Can you hear me?' Mum leaned forward. The book dropped from her lap to the floor. I opened my mouth to speak, but my voice just croaked. The nurse came in, the one who had anointed my burnt face so tenderly.

'Is Amber awake?' she said.

'I think so, yes. May she have a drink?'

I croaked again, and failing to produce a word, decided to smile instead. I unwound my hand from the covers and reached out to my mother. She seized it between both her hands and tears filled her eyes. Her face, full of emotion, went very pink. Then the nurse returned with a cup. She helped me sit up and sip the water, but Mum kept hold of my hand.

'Amber, are you OK? Thank God you're awake. I was so worried. My lovely, perfect girl, I'm so happy. I'm so glad you're back with us.' She began to cry properly then and sniffed loudly, fumbling in her bag for a tissue.

'Your mum's been waiting by your bedside every day,' the nurse said. 'And your dad, and your little brother, and your friends. You've had so many visitors.'

Then she stood up straight. 'So how are you feeling?'

I nodded. 'OK,' I said. 'My throat's still dry, and I feel a bit shaky. But otherwise, I'm fine.'

The nurse nodded and smiled. 'The doctor will want to speak with you in a bit.' She left the room. Then it was just Mum and me. We looked at each other. There was so much to tell I didn't know where to start. She moved from her chair to sit on the side of the bed, put her arms around me, and pressed her teary, snotty face against mine.

Two weeks later we drove down to Glastonbury, Mum, Dad, Justin and I. It was a day trip for them, but I would be staying over at Dowdie's tonight and Mike, Eliza's new man, would drive me home the day after. I hadn't seen Dowdie since I came out of hospital, though she'd emailed me a few times, using Mike's flash computer. Apparently he was pretty well-heeled. Mum and Dad were being very bright and cheery about the trip and Justin was annoyingly happy, happy, happy. Mum and Eliza had actually become quite friendly over the last couple of weeks. Though they'd only met once, when Dowdie came to visit me at the hospital, their experiences had drawn them together and they'd been talking on the phone almost daily. The Mothers of Daughters of Siege, Dowdie branded them in an email. Their pally behaviour seemed to be getting on her nerves. Mum had been saying annoying things like: 'Eliza seems a very sensible woman, for a weirdo type.'

It was a still, warm day, the sky overcast. It took about an hour and a half to drive to Glastonbury, and the roads were busy. Dire Straits was blaring but Mum turned the volume down just a little bit. I stared out the window at the passing villages and fields. I was nervous of seeing Dowdie, afraid she would be spiky. She'd seemed OK by email, but in person she might be different. I was afraid of her grief and anger. I was worried she would blame me for her dad's death, because I hadn't persuaded him to step out of the cellar to safety.

We drove down a steep hill to the Somerset levels. The Tor appeared on the horizon, far away. The car wended along narrow roads to the town. We parked up and headed for the arranged rendezvous – a café near the town centre, cosied up to a witchcraft store. Eliza and Dowdie were late, of course. Dad bought drinks while we waited. Then they stepped through the doorway, resplendent, like fairy queens. Eliza's river of dreadlocks was laced with red. She was wearing a green velvet dress over a white embroidered shirt. Fat rings adorned her fingers. Polished chunks of amber hung from her ears. And Dowdie didn't let the side down. She was dressed in a riot of colour – orange, green, black, silver. Layers of clothes, a belt with a clasp like a silver fish, and her dark red hair spilling over her shoulders.

Mum and Dad were agog. Justin cheered and waved. Eliza held out her arms and embraced my embarrassed mother. Dowdie looked me up and down.

'You've lost weight,' she said.

'I know. When I was ill. You look great.'

'Thanks. So do you.'

The lunch was weird. It was a curious meeting of worlds, but credit where it's due, once they got over the shock of her outfit Mum and Dad loved Eliza to bits and they talked for hours. I realised they were more flexible than I thought. Eliza showed us round the town, and then guided us along a maze of narrow lanes to Mike's place. It was a huge converted barn, set in a couple of acres, with a mighty double garage and an orchard. Mum and Dad were – once again – agog. I think they'd expected a hovel in an organic potato patch.

Mike was utterly charming. He showed us round the house. Dowdie had a beautiful bedroom overlooking the orchard and one of the garages turned out to be a recording studio. Dad and Mike talked about music from the good old days and the rest of us trooped back to the kitchen. Dowdie and Eliza had also adopted Max. The dog was ensconced in a basket by the back door.

We'd avoided The Subject all day, but finally, nursing a cup of tea at the huge pine table, Mum said: 'So, did you really believe all the stuff James Renault said, about his spirits and the Amethyst children?'

My mum was an expert on Amethyst children by then. She'd read all the articles in the papers and checked it out on the Internet. The Amethyst project had a life of its own. James might be dead but his violent end had simply spread the word more widely. Websites had been set up by other believers. Parents had established Internet forums where they could discuss how best to raise their Amethyst children. Nothing relating to James's final dark confession ever made it to the newspapers though. Call-Me-Neil asked me to keep the story to myself. They were still investigating other strands of this disturbed web, he said. The operation was covert. If I wanted to help them defeat this insidious arms trade, I would keep quiet, so the web's particular spiders wouldn't disappear for good. The journalists trawled through his previous convictions, hinted at his sojourn in Africa working for security companies, but never picked up his involvement in the illegal arms trade. Then again, all concrete evidence of his final, most appalling project had been destroyed by the explosion at the house. There was nothing more to go on.

I wondered how all that would square with the parents of the Amethyst children? Sometimes I longed to tell them, to break up the party. Then again, I didn't want to damage the hunt for those evil purveyors of war weapons. Best to sit tight on this one, for now at least. In any case, there were so many honest people engaged in the Amethyst project, like Eliza. Despite its soiled beginnings, could it evolve into something good?

'I do believe it still,' Eliza said. Mum blinked. This is not the answer she had expected.

'I'm writing a book on it. Since I was so close to James, because we lived on the Community, I'm in the best position to write something.'

'I think it's nonsense – if you'll forgive me,' Mum said. 'After all that happened. Can't you see it's dangerous?'

Eliza was shaking her head. 'No it's not. James made a mistake. He was one gifted but flawed individual. He thought he was acting for the best and he opened our eyes to a worldwide phenomenon. The world wasn't ready for him, that's all. The world destroyed him.'

I was afraid Eliza's admission would change my mother's feelings about her and that I wouldn't be allowed to stay after all. I pleaded, internally, for Eliza to change track and reassure her. Instead Mum said:

'So you truly think Dowdie – and, and my Amber – are special children?'

Eliza smiled. 'Patently,' she said. 'How could you doubt it? But don't worry. I won't brainwash her. We haven't got any guns. I tell you what – I promise not to mention Amethyst children while Amber is in the house. How about that.' Then she laughed. Mum hesitated for a moment, and then she laughed too. The atmosphere lightened.

After tea, Mum, Dad and Justin said goodbye and drove away. Dowdie and I mooched around her garden.

'What's it like, without your dad?' I ventured. Dowdie kicked at the grass.

'Stupid question. What d'you think? It's tough. I miss him, Amber.'

She wasn't looking at me, staring instead at the purple clouds above the horizon. I didn't know how to answer. Nothing I could say would stop her missing him. Although it was hard to understand, I missed him too.

We were slightly awkward together all evening. Our conversation was stilted. Carefully, we turned over memories, like stones, to see what thoughts and feelings might lie beneath. I asked her about all the other Community members, especially those who had become friends – Diane and Chris. Apparently Diane was also in Glastonbury, staying with friends for a while. Eliza had kept in contact with others, too. They had dispersed all over the country – to family and friends, looking for a way to rebuild their lives. Only Chris had disappeared without a trace.

Perhaps he was squatting somewhere, or living on the streets. We worried about him.

'So you and Johnny – you're an item then,' Dowdie said. Her tone made this a criticism.

'I suppose so,' I said. 'But sometimes, with Johnny, it's hard to tell.'

This made her laugh, and then I laughed too. Did she suspect it was Johnny who had called the police? Surely, if it had occurred to me it would have dawned on her too, that he had overheard her yelling at me that time at his house. Oddly for upfront, unreserved Dowdie, she didn't take this up. She never asked me. Was this a consequence of her own guilt? After all, she had, in a fit of rage, betrayed her own father to me, and it was her fatal lack of self-control that led Johnny to find out. In any case, once she had ascertained I was going out with Johnny, she didn't talk about him any more. She avoided the subject altogether – blocked him out of her consciousness. It was as though he didn't exist.

The following morning, the unease melted away. We woke up early and walked into town. The sky was a brilliant autumn blue. Scarlet rose hips and fat purple blackberries bejewelled the hedges. Everything seemed strange or marvellous or wildly funny. The old Dowdie-and-Amber alchemy was restored. Our senses were heightened and the world shone. You think I had forgotten how selfish and unreasonable she could be? Of course I hadn't. But it was still worth it, to be in this place we create together.

There was something about this alchemy that attracted others too. We were sitting on a bench in the town centre, when a tall black guy, with dreads down to his waist and a dozen necklaces strung around his neck, sat down right beside us and engaged us in a lively conversation about ley-lines and his quest to walk from one side of the country to another following the energies he could sense in the surface of the Earth. Later, in the café, a very smart elderly lady, white hair pinned in a bun, told us about her new volume on witchcraft and asked our opinion on the effects of genetic engineering on England's natural flora.

At midday we decided to climb the Tor. I realised I had not entirely recovered from my illness because the steep climb wore me out, though Dowdie was puffing too. There were plenty of tourists about and Dowdie scorned them as they took pictures and flicked through guidebooks. We took refuge from the breeze inside the tower and sat on the dusty ground, our backs to the wall. The archway opened on a view of the Somerset landscape, the map of fields, roads, trees, rivers. It was like a fairy-tale, the window opening on a magic land. The air tasted clean and pure. I felt an expansion of my heart, my mind. A sense of opening, seeing oh-so-vividly for a moment how much an adventure my life could be. Beauty was everywhere and anything was possible. My heart seemed to burn.

The feeling lasted only a moment. I saw a girl staring at me. She was about eleven or twelve, standing with a couple, presumably her parents. The dad had a grizzly baby in a backpack, and the mum was fussing in her pocket for tissues. The girl looked at me again. I smiled and raised my hand in a tiny wave. Overwhelmed by shyness the girl smiled back, very briefly, before turning away and hurrying out of the tower.

On Sunday evening, back at home, I went to Johnny's house. I had sent him a text on the drive back saying I'd be round at seven.

I pushed my way through his back door as normal but pulled up short when I saw a woman sitting at the kitchen table, smoking a cigarette. She glanced up, and I opened my mouth to apologise for the intrusion. I couldn't quite find the words to say. The woman looked so much like Johnny. She was older than my mum – probably in her fifties – tall and lean, with long black hair carelessly pinned up.

The woman didn't seem perturbed by my appearance. She said: 'You must be Amber. He'll be back in a minute. He's just gone to the shop for some milk. I'm Marguerite, by the way. His mother.'

I was still struggling for something to say. I had no idea she would be here and after everything Johnny had said, I realised I had been expecting someone more obviously horrible. This was stupid, of course. The fact that she didn't look like a wicked witch didn't change the way she had treated her son.

Marguerite puffed on her cigarette, then smiled, looking utterly relaxed. She was simply dressed in expensive-looking jeans and a plain white T-shirt. She had beautiful skin, without a scrap of make-up, and no jewellery except for a simple wedding ring.

'Yes, I'm Amber,' I said, stupidly.

She looked at me. 'I'm glad he's found a friend at last. Impossible boy. He can't get on with anyone.'

I didn't reply so she continued: 'He says he doesn't want to go back to school. He'd rather retake his exams at the college here. I don't know what to do. His father's absolutely furious about his exam results – all the money he's spent on fees. It was rather stupid of him, don't you think, to fail like that?'

I shrugged, annoyed she should try and implicate me in any criticism of Johnny. Marguerite shook her head and stubbed out the cigarette.

'I don't know,' she continued. 'Maybe it would be a good thing. He was never happy at the school. I could move down here, work from home, and Toby could join us at weekends.'

I found my voice at last: 'Did you have a good holiday?' I

sounded hostile – more so than I had intended. Marguerite gave me a look.

'It was fine, thank you. Of course I would have been happier if Johnny had come too but he simply would not. He hardly ever returned my calls either.' She took out another cigarette but didn't light it.

'How do you manage, Amber? Is he civil with you? I suppose he must be, if you're his friend. He's at that age, I suppose. Nothing I do is right.' Something flickered across her face then; self-doubt, or regret. Then she looked up and gave me a strained smile.

'And what about you, Amber? Do you give your parents a hard time too?'

'Me? No. I mean, I don't think so. I don't know.' Then I thought about the events of the past few weeks, the whole horror.

'Yes,' I said. 'Yes, I do. Well, I did. I didn't mean to. It just – happened.'

It occurred to me then that although Johnny had told me the inarguably harrowing tale of his abandonment at the railway station, he had not told me about the times his mother baked his birthday cake, took him swimming, treated him generously or in any way went the extra mile for him. Maybe she never did any of these things and Johnny was right, she was eternally unloving and callous. But I didn't know, did I?

Marguerite and I stared at each other for a moment or two, and something close to amused understanding flashed between us. It was so brief that afterwards I doubted that it happened, because Johnny stepped through the back door and saw us together. Then the dynamic changed. Johnny and I were allies, Marguerite was Johnny's scourge, his unwelcome mother.

Johnny glanced at me. Then he said: 'Here's the milk.' He

plonked the plastic bottle on the table and with a gesture to me, slipped through the door and up the stairs to his room. I ran after him.

'She came down yesterday, the mother,' he said.

'It sounds like she's open to the idea of your staying in town and going to college.'

Johnny nodded. 'Daddy doesn't want to pay the fees any more if his layabout son isn't prepared to make the effort.'

I put my arm around him and pressed my face against his neck, inhaling his warm, clean, boyish scent. I hadn't got used to this yet, the contact between us. It still didn't seem ordinary. Johnny ran his hand over my hair.

'How was your weekend?' he said.

I grinned. 'It was absolutely brilliant.'

'You got on with Dowdie OK?'

'Yep.'

'I told you she'd be fine. So you can stop beating yourself up now?'

'I think so. And if you're staying too, then everything will be perfect.'

'Perfect?' he teased. '*Perfect?*'

'Well, it would be if I knew you were happy.'

Johnny drew away so he could look into my face.

'How about if I were just less miserable? Would that do you?'

'It would be a good start,' I said. Johnny could be at college within a fortnight if all went to plan. He'd retake eight GCSEs and begin a Photographic Art course. Already he was anticipating this would give another thousand students the opportunity to hate him.

'This isn't a public school. There'll be plenty of other emo fags at the college.' I tried to cheer him up – to help him cultivate a positive outlook.

'They'll think I'm posh,' he said. 'They won't like me, I'm telling you.'

Sometimes it was hard work being Johnny's friend, just as it was being Dowdie's. I had realised that the friends you love the most also make the greatest demands in return. A friendship like this wasn't static – it was like a fire you had constantly to tend and refuel.

There were times when you couldn't argue Johnny round. Whatever I said he contradicted. However much I encouraged, he found a way to be gloomy. Perhaps it had become another game. So I said, simply: 'Wait and see. I think it's going to be all right. At least – it will be better. And even if they hate you – which they won't – you'll still have one friend. You'll have me.'

Johnny laughed. Oh how I loved to hear him laugh. He slid his long arms around my waist and squeezed all the breath out of me.

The following morning I went back to school. It certainly wasn't easy. They'd all seen my pictures in the papers. Everyone stared. The teachers treated me with kid gloves. They were all sympathy and consideration, which made me very uneasy. When I got home, Mum was waiting for me. She had taken an afternoon off work to be there in case I was upset. Justin had gone to his childminder's after school, as usual, so it was just the two of us for a couple of hours.

'How was school?' She had a cup of hot chocolate waiting for me on the table, and a piece of cherry flapjack on a plate.

'Fine.'

'Any problems? Did the other kids say anything to you?'

'No. It was OK.' I couldn't quite bring myself to confide in her and share my feelings but that's not to say I wasn't glad she was at home.

'The first day is the worst. It'll be easier tomorrow. The novelty of seeing you will soon wear off,' she said.

I drank the hot chocolate. I was very happy to be at home, just then. If this whole adventure had taught me anything, it had made me realise how lucky I was to have parents who did the right thing. They were not as exotic or glamorous as James Renault, or Eliza, or even wealthy, cigarette-smoking Marguerite. But they were reliable, straightforward and honest. These are not mundane qualities – they are precious.

I sensed Mum had more to say, and she was nervous.

'Amber, what are your thoughts about this Amethyst child thing?' she said.

'What d'you mean?'

'Well, do you believe it? Do you think you are one?'

'I don't know.' It was the best answer I could give. I didn't know. I added: 'What do you think?' Perhaps she'd spent another couple of hours on the Internet this afternoon, catching up with the Amethyst forums and newsgroups.

She hesitated, then she said: 'I'm sorry Amber, I don't believe it. We all think our children are special – every parent does. And that's a very magical part of being a parent, seeing what's so beautiful and remarkable in a child and being able to treasure and nurture them. I suppose in a way this Amethyst thing is right because every generation has a new role and carries humanity into the future. But do I think you are more especially special than any other child? No, I don't.' She smiled and sighed at the same time. 'Does that disappoint you?'

I shook my head. 'Of course not, Mum. I think you're probably right. But I wish – I wish Dad would forgive me. He hasn't been the same. I know he loves me, but something's not right.'

Mum stared at me. Tears filled her eyes. 'It's not you, silly girl.

He's not angry with you. He can't forgive himself! He is so upset he didn't protect you. He can't stop kicking himself for trusting that man. And when he heard you telling the police about the guns and the explosion . . . My God, we nearly lost you, Amber. This was serious. Do you understand? And we weren't even there to help you. We left you alone and went on holiday abroad!'

'You didn't leave me alone. And it was my decision. I begged and begged you to let me stay. It wasn't your fault – or Dad's.'

'I know, I know. So does your dad. He knows it, but he doesn't feel it. He loves you so much, Amber. He thinks the sun shines for you. And he's still hurting that all this happened.'

'But it's not his fault. How can I stop him feeling bad?'

Mum slowly shook her head. She bit her lip. 'You'll just have to talk to him like you're talking to me now. You've hardly said a word to us since this all happened. You haven't spoken to me properly about what it was like and how you feel about it now. You told the police. Is it so hard for you to share it with your parents?'

I felt a stab of conscience. I hadn't meant to upset him, I just got the wrong end of the stick. I hurt my father, because I wouldn't go to him for help and comfort. Why was this so hard? Part of me didn't want to need him. But he still yearned to be needed.

'I'll try,' I said. 'I will try.'

Mum was right. After a few days at school the staring and whispering died down and other topics of gossip swept me from the top spot. Things had changed though. It's hard to say exactly why but presumably my involvement with the Community was part of it. Also, my relationship with Johnny had been noted by the school's emo crew. No one at my school knew him well yet but he had been seen, and according to the black-eyed girls in skinny jeans, Johnny was hot. This had added to my status and suddenly, strangely, it turned out I was cool after all. Was I pleased? More amused than pleased. Now the prize was in my hand I saw how little it meant. I was the same person. I still liked Walter and Lawrence of Arabia, but all of a sudden my liking these weird, old-fashioned things was quirky and cool. How random is that? I started getting invited to hang out with the emo crew in town on a Saturday. I went along once, though Johnny got fidgety and bored very soon and we ended up wandering off so he could take photos of a demolition instead. I think Johnny was getting tired of the emo thing now he was in danger of becoming part of a tribe. He'd started looking for a new way to rub people up the wrong way. He bought a musty old fur coat from a charity shop. Real fur, all mothy and tattered.

Two weeks have passed. It is October and today is Saturday, and I am walking along the riverbank with Johnny. The weather is oppressive. I am hot and sweaty. Climate change, I fancy. I am still anxious, you see. That hasn't changed. Some nights I still lie awake, my guts churning with fear because of global warming and world poverty and wars and environmental breakdown. Stupid of me? Or entirely sensible? Of course you would say – sensible.

Beside me Johnny is talking about a picture he's working on but my mind is only half following. I'm thinking about Throne. Before he died, James told me Throne would use me as a mouthpiece. I wonder if I have the power to channel a spirit. Does Throne speak through me, as he spoke through James?

Sometimes I think he does. Throne tells me I am not mad to be so worried. He says everyone is simply hypnotised into thinking all this will continue for ever when it is obvious everything is going to change and that we cannot carry on the way we are. I realise why James acted as he did in the face of this knowledge. James was afraid too, and he made himself ready in the best way he could.

I have long internal conversations with Throne. However, I have to admit that in my head he sounds very much like James.

'You're not even listening.'

'What? What did you say?' I rub the back of my sticky neck, and wish I'd tied my hair back. Johnny shakes his head and tuts. He talks about his pictures a lot, and in more technical detail than I need to know. It is his passion, though, and I want to encourage it. I am so keen to stave off his depression – to help him keep his future in sight.

'Sorry, I was miles off. Tell me again.'

He is happy to oblige and this time I pay attention, as far as I can. Halfway to the wood I flop down on the dry grass. Johnny sits beside me.

I ask him if he is ever afraid. He says no. He cannot understand why I tear myself up about the future of the world. What good does it do? It's a waste of time. I can't argue with him. Then he looks into my face and sees how real my feelings are. I wonder if Johnny is never afraid because he struggles constantly to find any real value in being alive. He takes my hand.

'What's the worst thing that could happen?' he says. I am taken aback. A storm of images fills my head. Animal testing, torture chambers, bomber planes, starving children, storms, wars, apocalypse. But I say, simply,

'Suffering and death.'

'Suffering and death.' Johnny repeats the words slowly. He picks a piece of grass and considers it. 'So we all suffer and die. What then?'

'Then – then nothing.'

'Nothing,' he says. 'The atoms of the body disperse. The waters rise and cover the face of the Earth. The stars shine. The universe unfolds. You see, nothing we do matters all that much.' Johnny looks up and smiles.

It is curiously comforting. Does that sound perverse? He is right, of course. In the end nothing matters that much. I realise the best thing I can do is to relish every moment of my strange little life and to make sure I stay wide awake. I have to keep asking questions. I have to do what I can to make things better.

I point to the river. 'You can dive in here. There's a deep pool in the riverbed.'

The water looks utterly delicious, cool and clear as glass. Underneath, the polished pebbles shine. Emerald weed ripples like a mermaid's hair.

'You're going to swim?' Johnny looks incredulous. I stand up, scan the path for passers-by, then take off my jeans, T-shirt and sandals. Of course I might get Weil's disease or I might spear my leg on a piece of junk. But probably I won't. At last I am prepared to take the risk.

I stand up straight, feeling the sun's heat on my bare skin. The sky arches over me. The surface of the river dimples and glistens. All the long hours I have waited by its side . . .

I take a breath and dive into the water.

CENTURY
SARAH SINGLETON

Mercy and her sister Charity live in a twilight world, going to bed just as the sun rises. Their house remains shrouded in perpetual winter, each day unfolding exactly the same as the last. Mercy has never questioned her widowed father about the way they live, until one day she awakes to find a snowdrop on her pillow: a first sign of spring – and a nod towards a new future.

A meeting with the mysterious Claudius unsettles Mercy and starts her on a winding path through the family's history, unearthing clues about her mother's death and their house frozen in time. But as each piece of the past slots into place, the world Mercy has known begins to unravel... Can she discover the truth without destroying her home, her father and all she has ever known?

ISBN: 978-1-41690-135-8   £5.99

HERETIC
SARAH SINGLETON

When Elizabeth finds a green-tinged creature in the woods she's amazed to discover that it's actually a girl of her own age. Isabella has spent the last 300 years deep in the faery world, hiding from persecutors who accused her of being the daughter of a witch.

But Elizabeth has her own persecutors to face. A Catholic priest is hiding with her family – an act of treason in 1585 – and the net is closing in. As they become friends, Elizabeth and Isabella must find a way to save the family from being torn apart . . .

"*Singleton's rich, painterly description is one of the great pleasures of the novel, as is her portrait of a seductive, perilous land . . . The clash between the mundane and magical has rarely been rendered so captivatingly sinister.*" – Amanda Craig, The Times

ISBN: 978-1-41690-403-8   £5.99

SACRIFICE
SARAH SINGLETON

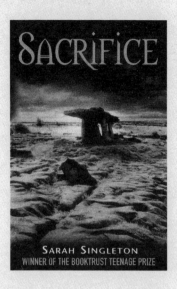

Jacinth, Miranda and Jack live in different lands, yet are all connected. Only by combining forces can they turn around the curse that has befallen their families for generations. Each is descended from a group of knights who wrested a revered relic from an African tribe long ago. Each has a duty to return the stolen lily which gave the knights amazing powers – powers that have warped and darkened over the centuries, leaving instability and death in their wake.

But a renegade ancestor is determined to retain the lily's power and influence – whatever the cost – and all three children are in terrible danger . . .

"Singleton has woven the threads of a traditional ghost story into a uniquely fresh pattern." – TES

ISBN: 978-1-41691-708-3   £6.99